THE

WIFE

BOOKS BY SHALINI BOLAND

The Secret Mother
The Child Next Door
The Millionaire's Wife
The Silent Sister
The Perfect Family
The Best Friend
The Girl from the Sea
The Marriage Betrayal
The Other Daughter
One of Us Is Lying

THE
WIFE

SHALINI BOLAND

Bookouture

Published by Bookouture in 2020

An imprint of Storyfire Ltd.
Carmelite House
50 Victoria Embankment
London EC4Y 0DZ

www.bookouture.com

ISBN: 978-1-78681-934-5
eBook ISBN: 978-1-78681-933-8

PROLOGUE

The skin beneath my fingers is warm and soft. Pliant. She's stopped yelling now, but I'm drowning in shock as she beats her fists against me. Kicks, scratches, tries to spit in my face. I can't let go. Can't let her ruin everything. Although I think it's already too late for that.

Her scent catches in the back of my throat. I grit my teeth. The world has suddenly and violently shrunk down to just me and her. Nothing else matters. Sweat beads on my forehead and under my arms. I should stop this. Release my grip. I should let her come for me again and take the consequences. But I can't. I daren't.

I have too much to lose.

CHAPTER ONE

THEN

The first thing I notice is the funny taste in my mouth – metallic and earthy. Blood. I run my tongue over my teeth and wince, realising I must have bitten my tongue. The second thing I notice is the worried face of my fiancé peering down at me.

'Toby,' I croak.

He crouches and takes my hand and I realise he's trembling. 'Are… are you okay? You really gave us a scare.' His face is whiter than bone, his neck red and mottled beneath a partially open shirt, his black tie pulled undone. 'We were so worried.'

'Where…?' I try to sit up, but my brain feels as though it's floating loose in my skull, so I give up and sink back down. It's then that I realise I'm lying on the floor, my head on a cushion. 'What happened?'

'Don't you remember?' he asks.

I try to think, but my mind is fuzzy. 'What's going on? Why do I feel weird?'

'You fainted, love.' Toby's mum Celia kneels by my side, one hand on my forehead, the other on my wrist. She looks different somehow. Maybe it's her hair – she's had it cut or styled or something. It looks straighter than usual, and browner. She must have had the grey coloured. 'Looks like you came down a real cropper.'

I now see that as well as Celia, Toby's dad Malcolm and his elder brother Nick are also in the room, staring down at me, deep worry etched across their brows. Nick and Malcolm are both wearing grey suits, which seems strange, and I notice how similar they look, with their square frames and brown eyes. Nick's hair not quite as grey as his dad's. Toby, on the other hand, is leaner, taller and more classically handsome, his hair a rich mahogany.

'You feel a little clammy, but your pulse is steady. I think you'll be okay.' Celia is a nurse, so if she says I'm okay, I guess I must be okay.

'I can't remember what happened.'

Celia looks up at her eldest son. 'Nick, can you get Zoe a glass of water?'

'Uh, sure.'

I notice Toby's right leg is quivering, and his hands are trembling. He's not the sort to get anxious, so his concern for me makes me love him even more. 'Toby, you're shaking!'

'I was so worried.' He swallows and leans in to kiss my forehead. 'If anything happened to you I don't know what I'd do.'

'I'm fine, silly. Just a bit dizzy, that's all. Tell him I'm okay, Celia.'

Toby glances at his mother and she gives him a comforting smile. 'Relax, Toby. Zoe's going to be just fine.' Celia sits back on her haunches. 'Well, this is an unusual wedding day.' She raises an eyebrow and squeezes my hand.

'Wedding day?' Only now do I remember. That explains Celia's hair, the suits, and – I peer down at myself – my lace wedding dress. 'Oh no! It's today! Did I wreck it? Is it too late?' This time I manage to sit up despite my woozy head. 'I can't believe I—'

'It's okay,' Toby interrupts. 'We've still got time. The ceremony isn't due to start for another' – he checks his watch – 'forty minutes.'

'What happened? You said I fainted, but I don't remember that at all. It's so hazy… I was getting ready and then…'

'Like Mum said, you hit the deck.' Toby shakes his head. 'Are you sure you can't remember anything about it? That's quite worrying, Zo.'

I frown and try to recall what happened, but my brain hurts. Little stabbing pains flit across my scalp, coming to rest above my eyes, where they throb and pulse like flickering lights. 'Last thing I remember, I was getting ready. Celia, you were here with Lou and Becky, helping me get into my dress. That's it. That's the very last thing I remember.'

Nick returns and hands me a glass of water.

'Small sips,' Celia instructs. 'We left you to go get our make-up done at the spa. Then Nick came in to borrow a phone charger. It's a good thing he was here, because that's when you fainted, and he called me. I told the other two to stay there – didn't want you getting crowded with too many people fussing. Looks like you hit the back of your head on the desk on your way down.'

I reach up to gingerly pat the back of my head and wince. Sure enough, I feel a pebble-like lump beneath my fingers.

'Do you feel nauseous at all?' Celia asks.

'A little. Not too much. I've got an evil headache though.'

My mother-in-law-to-be rummages in her handbag and pulls out a packet of paracetamol. 'Take a couple of these.'

I put the pills in my mouth one at a time, knocking each one back with a slug of water.

'Maybe we should get you checked out?' Malcolm runs a hand through his sparse grey hair. He turns to Toby. 'She looks decidedly peaky, son.'

'I know, but Mum said she'll be okay,' Toby replies uncertainly.

'I know what your mum said, but it can't hurt to—'

'Thanks, Malcolm,' I interrupt, 'but I don't want to miss my wedding because of a bump on the head. If I still feel bad, I'll go to the doctor's later.'

'Well, okay. But perhaps I should let Guy know. You might be unsteady on your feet as he walks you down the aisle.' Malcolm turns to leave.

Toby stands and puts a hand on his father's shoulder. 'Wait…'

'Toby's right. Don't tell my dad. He'll only worry.' I stagger to my feet and find to my dismay that I have to lean on a chair to steady myself. My legs are so shaky. What if I'm not strong enough to stand and say my vows? I think of all the people in the little chapel next to the hotel who have come to see us get married. All the weeks of planning. My utter joy and excitement at the thought of becoming Mrs Zoe Johnson. I can't not get married, no matter how shaky I feel. I let go of the chair and square my shoulders. 'Do you know what? Celia's right, I'm absolutely fine. Honestly, I already feel so much better. I think it must have been nerves that made me faint. Or maybe hunger. Thinking about it, I did skip breakfast.'

'Well, that'll be it,' Celia declares. 'Let me call room service and get you something sugary. A piece of cake maybe. In the meantime, you should sit down, love. Rest a while.'

'No, I'm fine, honestly. Lou and Becky will be back soon.' My bridesmaids must still be downstairs. As my sister couldn't be here, I asked my two best friends to step in. I went to school with Lou and I work at the salon with Becky.

Celia picks up the phone on the bedside table. 'I'll have the kitchen send tea and cake – enough for the three of you.'

'Four of us,' I amend. 'You should stay too.'

'No, I'll let you three have some time to yourselves. You don't want an oldie cramping your style.'

'Don't be daft. Of course I want you with us.'

'Okay, if you're sure.' She gives me a soft smile.

Celia is the closest I've got to a mum. My mother died when I was thirteen after a two-year struggle with cancer. And my younger sister Dina left home to go travelling when she hit sixteen. I've only spoken to her sporadically since then. Dad was devastated after Mum died. He never really got over it and was rarely there for me and Dina. Well, not emotionally anyway. He made sure we were fed and clothed, but he wouldn't talk about Mum, or about anything really. Our household was a sad place. I tried to fill the void Mum left as best I could, but I don't think I did a particularly good job. No wonder Dina got the hell out as soon as she could.

I stuck around in Shaftesbury, as I couldn't see myself living anywhere other than the small Dorset town where I grew up. But when I met Toby and his family, my world finally developed some colour. Some warmth. Ever since the two of us got together three years ago, his mum has treated me like the daughter she never had. We chat daily, meet for lunch, go on spa days, and tell one another pretty much everything. And Malcolm is a soft-hearted sweetie who would do anything for his wife. Don't get me wrong, I love my dad. It's just… difficult.

'I hope I haven't jinxed things.' I turn to Toby. 'It's supposed to be bad luck for us to see one another before the wedding.'

'You don't really believe that.' He gives me an indulgent smile.

'No, but I wanted to do things the right way. I didn't want any drama. And I wanted to wait until I reached the chapel to see you. Now I've ruined it.'

'You haven't ruined anything.' He puts his arms around me, and I lean into him. I'm only a couple of inches over five feet so my cheek rests comfortably against his chest. 'I know you wanted everything to be just so. It's what I love about you, Zoe. You love family. You love tradition.'

'Even though I fainted and now have a giant egg-shaped lump on my head?' I give him a wry look. 'That's not exactly traditional.'

'Zoe, it's all going to be perfect. You're perfect.'

My heart lifts at his words and for a moment my head clears, and the pain disappears. Until I remember… 'I'm not perfect,' I murmur. 'No one is.'

'Okay, well you're perfect for me.'

I inhale deeply and push out the knowledge that this isn't exactly true. I try to focus on the day ahead. To ignore the tiny bead of worry in my chest. Today is a day for fairy tales and happy ever afters. What's past is past. All that matters is that I'm about to become the person I've always wanted to be, with the man I love.

CHAPTER TWO

NOW

Serving platters are brought out and laid on the dining table by the waiting staff, who then give us a detailed account of the gourmet finger foods artfully arranged before us.

'I hope you're hungry,' I say, eying up the amazing selection. I thought the view of the forest through the mullioned windows was spectacular, but the sight of this food is just as incredible.

'I'm starving.' Madeline's eyes are wider than the plates. 'I actually skipped breakfast in preparation for this.'

Celia and I laugh at my sister-in-law's blissful expression.

The three of us are having a taster lunch at the five-star Regis Hotel where Toby and I got married. It's a beautifully restored country house just outside Shaftesbury, set on a hillside overlooking ancient woodland. The décor is laid-back luxury and it's a real treat being here for lunch.

It's coming up to Toby's and my ten-year wedding anniversary and we thought it would be lovely to have a party here to celebrate. It's quite extravagant, but Toby and Nick's landscaping business is doing really well these days, and he said he wanted to celebrate our life together. We laughed at the cheesiness of that line, but at the same time, it warmed me. Made me feel safe and loved. Celia and Madeline have been helping me organise the party, and today we're choosing the food.

'It's so nice to eat something that I haven't prepared myself.' Madeline runs a catering company and offered to do the food for our anniversary, but Toby and I thought it would be a bit mean if she had to work while everyone else was enjoying themselves. She has such a generous nature; we didn't want to take advantage.

'I can't believe we've been married ten years already.' I sigh. 'It only seems like a couple of years ago.'

'And what a wonderful ten years it's been, Zoe.' Celia pats my hand. 'I couldn't have asked for two more perfect daughters-in-law.'

Madeline and I share a smile. 'And we couldn't have asked for a more gorgeous mum-in-law,' I reply.

'Hear, hear,' Madeline agrees, raising her glass.

Madeline met my brother-in-law Nick the year after my wedding and married him the year after that. She and Nick are perfect for one another. She's been really good for him – we've all noticed his confidence and happiness grow since they've been together. And although she's nothing like my usual friends, who tend to be feisty, sharp-witted and sociable, Madeline is calm, loyal and kind, and we get on surprisingly well. I bring her out of her shell, and she always gives me good advice. The four of us have grown really close, and our kids adore each other. I feel extremely lucky to have the whole Johnson clan in my life. This party will be a celebration of that as much as anything.

'Okay, well I don't know where to start with all this food!' I sit back in my chair, feeling a little overwhelmed by everything.

'I'm going to go for the shrimp and avocado,' Madeline says, diving in. 'And these little Caprese bites look yummy.'

We load up our plates and start tucking in, oohing and aahing over each delicious morsel.

'Didn't you have your newspaper interview yesterday, Madeline?' Celia asks, dabbing at her lips with a napkin.

'Oh, yes!' I turn to my sister-in-law. 'I forgot to ask you about that. How was it?' She's been campaigning to stop developers building new houses on a patch of land next to the forest. Unfortunately, planning permission has already been granted, but the campaigners have requested an appeal and created a petition. If the development goes ahead it will really spoil the view from this hotel for a start, not to mention that the area in question is on a flood plain. You'd think with my husband also being a town councillor, he'd have been able to help, but he has no sway with the planning committee.

'I think it went okay,' Madeline replies. 'The journalist was really nice, and she seemed quite sympathetic. It should be in this week's edition, but she couldn't guarantee it.'

'Fingers crossed you get the appeal. Let me know if there's anything else I can do to help. More wine?' I hover the bottle above Madeline's glass.

She thinks for a moment. 'Why not. I can leave the car and we can share a taxi home, can't we?'

'Good idea.' I top up all our glasses. 'May as well enjoy ourselves.'

'How's work going?' Celia asks me.

'Yeah, it's pretty good. Crazily busy though. The salon's booked solid right up to Christmas Eve. We just have to hope no one goes off sick or we'll be stuffed.'

'Good thing I already made an appointment,' Madeline says, fake-wiping her brow.

'You never have to worry about that,' I reassure. 'I'll always make sure you're both taken care of.'

'It's good to have friends in high places,' Celia jokes.

'Talking of friends in high places,' I say. 'Cassie Barrington has an appointment at the salon next week.' Even saying her name makes my body tense up.

'*Barrington?*' Celia frowns. 'Any relation to Myra and Geoff Barrington?'

'She's their daughter,' I confirm.

'Cassie Barrington?' Madeline sits up straighter. 'The reality TV star? Is she really your friends' daughter, Celia?'

I turn to Celia. 'I didn't know you were friends with Myra and Geoff. Cassie used to be my best friend at school, but then she landed a spot on that TV show and now she lives in London.'

'Why did I never know about this?' Madeline looks intrigued.

'Because I've never talked about her.'

'Geoff Barrington was an old boyfriend of mine,' Celia says airily.

'Ooh, Celia.' I nudge her arm. 'Spill the gossip.'

She tuts. 'There is no gossip. We went out a few times, but I lost interest. Tell the truth, he was a bit of a bore.'

Madeline and I burst out laughing.

'What?!' Celia's cheeks are quite pink. 'He *was*. I much prefer my Malcolm.'

'Aww.' Madeline and I both coo over Celia's love for her husband.

'So, Zoe, are you going to be cutting Cassie Barrington's hair?' Madeline sounds impressed.

'Yes. But I'm not sure why she's coming to Waves. We don't keep in touch and she doesn't live round here anymore.'

'Maybe she's moving back to the area,' Madeline suggests.

'Maybe. I'm not looking forward to seeing her though. She's not exactly my favourite person in the world.'

'No? Why's that?' My sister-in-law leans forward. I love Madeline, but she definitely has a weakness for gossip. It's probably her only flaw. I should never have mentioned Cassie. News of her return will be all over town by tomorrow.

'Oh, it's nothing. We just drifted apart.' It was actually a lot more than just drifting apart. Back then, Cassie made it quite clear that our friendship wasn't high on her list of priorities.

'Maybe she wants to build bridges,' Celia says. 'She's probably quite a different person now to the one she used to be when you were children.'

'Maybe.' I shrug. But the thought of seeing Cassie Barrington again makes me anxious. Doubly so because it will be at my place of work, where I'll have to be professional and friendly. Apparently, when she made the appointment, she asked for me by name. I asked my boss Jennifer if Cassie could be given another stylist, but there was no one else available for that timeslot. I'm even toying with the idea of calling in sick that day, but I know when it comes to it I won't do that – I can't let my other clients down, or my boss.

I'm probably overreacting. Like Celia said, Cassie and I were friends a long time ago and we're both different people now. I'm not the pushover I used to be. I'm a working woman, the wife of a councillor, and the mother to two gorgeous children. I'm respected in the community, with lots of friends and a loving family. But I don't trust Cassie, and despite the self-assurance I've built up, the thought of seeing her again unsettles me.

Celia, Madeline and I agree to stop chatting for a while to make a note of our favourite canapés before the alcohol dulls our taste buds. With the savoury selections finally made, we order coffees and wait for the dessert trays to be brought out. I'm not used to eating so much at lunchtime, so I don't know how I'm going to be able to fit any more food in. Maybe I'll ask for a doggy bag and get Toby and the kids to help me choose the desserts.

Madeline drains the last drops of the second wine bottle into her glass. 'Ooh, Zoe, before I forget, are you still okay to have the girls next week while Nick and I are away?'

It takes me a moment to register that my sister-in-law is talking to me. I think I've had a bit too much to drink. 'Sorry, what? The girls? Yes, of course. Lucky you, having a birthday night away.'

'I can't wait. Beth's grumpy about it though – she wanted to come and stay with us in a posh hotel too.' Beth is Madeline's eldest daughter from her previous marriage, but she's only ever known Nick as a father. She was a toddler when Nick and

Madeline got together, and Nick adopted her as his own, as her biological father was out of the picture. She's always been a sweet child, but right now she's more like twelve going on eighteen, and Madeline's having a tough time with her wanting to grow up too fast.

My nine-year-old daughter Alice thinks her cousin Beth is absolutely wonderful. To be fair, Beth has always been great with Alice up until now, but I think she's going through a stage where she finds her younger cousin a bit babyish. I'll have to think of some activities that will interest them both.

'Don't worry, Mads, Toby and I will make sure she has a great time with us.'

'Thanks, Zoe. Beth might be tricky, but Freya will be a breeze. She can't wait.' My youngest niece is six, the same age as my son Jamie, and the two of them adore one another.

'Bet you and Nick are looking forward to it, too.'

'We really are. I hope he's going to be okay for it though. He's a little peaky at the moment.'

'Really?' Celia's head snaps up at the mention of one of her beloved sons being under the weather. 'What's the matter with him?'

'Sorry, Celia, didn't mean to worry you. He's fine. Just a little bit pale and he hasn't got a very good appetite at the moment. Nothing serious though.'

'Poor Nick,' I add. 'There are a few winter bugs going around. Fingers crossed he feels better for your trip.' Selfishly I worry that they'll be ill and won't be able to make it to the anniversary party.

'I'll bring him round some of my soup,' Celia offers. 'That'll perk him up.'

'Thank you.' Madeline gives her a grateful smile, although as she's a caterer, the one thing Nick is never short of is good food.

'So, how many RSVPs for the party have you had so far?' Celia asks me, changing the subject.

'Almost fifty yesses. I can't believe so many people are coming.' I feel a brief flutter of anxiety. 'You don't think it might all be too much, do you? The party I mean?'

'Too much?' Celia and Madeline give me a questioning look.

'Yes, I mean, do you think people will think it's over the top? Most couples do something for their silver or golden wedding anniversaries, but ten years… is it naff?'

'Don't be daft,' Celia says. 'Everyone loves a party. And your wedding was such a wonderful day, why wouldn't you want to recreate it?'

I think back to that day and try to remember it with happiness, but all I can truly recall is that before our wedding vows, I fainted. And when I came to, everything felt slightly… off. It's haunted me ever since. If I'm honest, I think I wanted to organise this anniversary party to exorcise the past. To give myself the wedding I never really had the first time around. Since then, I haven't quite been able to shake the feeling of sadness. Of longing for a missed milestone. I'd dreamed of an idyllic wedding day where every second would be a moment to cherish. A perfect day to start a perfect marriage with the perfect man. My heart hurts that I'll never have that memory. That it's spoiled.

'Are you okay, Zoe?' Madeline puts a hand on my arm. 'You look a bit down.'

'I'm fine.' I give her a bright smile. But coming back here and talking about my wedding day has begun to unsettle me. I'm getting the oddest feeling that there's something from that time I'm not quite remembering right.

As I'm picking at the edges of that buried memory, the waitress comes over with a tray of coffees and mini-desserts that look like pieces of art.

'Here we are, ladies. Hope you've got plenty of room for these.'

I give myself a shake and resolve to put away my anxieties for now. To enjoy the rest of the day. I think I'm just feeling overwhelmed and emotional, that's all. I need to focus on my family and on the fact that I'm celebrating a happy marriage. So what if my wedding day didn't go exactly to plan? Everything turned out great in the end, and that's what matters. And, anyway, this anniversary party will more than make up for it. I'm sure it will.

CHAPTER THREE

NOW

A Christmas music mix competes with the roar of the hairdryers and the raucous chatter of customers and staff. The atmosphere in the salon is one of excitement tinged with pre-holiday mania.

'I'm totally sick of Christmas already and we've still got three weeks to go.' Becky tosses her mane of red curls over her shoulder and rolls her eyes dramatically.

'Calm down, Scrooge,' I tease as we leave the salon floor and head to the small staffroom at the back to wolf down a quick sandwich in between clients. Becky's one of my best friends, although we're total opposites; we've worked at Waves together for over a decade. She lives with her long-term boyfriend Sam and neither of them want kids – they love their freedom too much and spend all their spare time going out to gigs and travelling the world. They're like a couple of perpetual teenagers. Sometimes I wonder how they can live like that, and other times I envy the pants off them.

She continues her tirade. 'The annoying songs we've all heard a thousand times before, the insane lights, the tacky decorations, it all gives me such a stress headache.' She puts her fingers to her forehead. 'I mean, I like Christmas as much as the next person, I really do, but why does it have to start so early every year? Jennifer had this place decked out in November. That's a whole month's worth of crazy. Of Slade and The Pogues, Band Aid and Chris flipping Rea.'

'You have to admit, she did a good job though.' Jennifer has really gone to town with the salon decorations this year, having decided on a tasteful rustic theme. There are twinkling white lights, wooden decorations, gingerbread stars, several wicker reindeer and a nine-foot tree in the window which has been liberally sprayed with fake frost.

'It's like working in Lapland,' Becky grumbles, taking her lunchbox out of the fridge. 'Which basically makes us elves. You watch, next year she'll issue us with pointy hats and stripy knee-high socks.'

'You're such a drama queen, Becky. I think your blood sugar might be low. Eat your sandwich.'

She gives me the middle finger before plonking herself down on the worn leather sofa. 'Sorry, just tired today. We were out late last night.'

My phone rings and I'm so hungry I want to ignore it, but it's my sister-in-law. 'Hang on a sec, Becky, I better take this.' I settle myself at the table on one of the wooden dining chairs. 'Hi, Madeline.'

'Hello, Zoe. Are you free to talk for a minute?' She sounds serious.

'Yeah, sure, I'm on my lunch break so fire away.' I gaze distractedly through the window at the tiny yard at the back of the salon. It's bare of any foliage at this time of year. Just a few dead-looking vines twisting up a trellis on the brick wall.

Madeline clears her throat. 'Okay, well it's just to say that we won't need you to have Beth and Freya this weekend after all.'

I sit up straighter, suddenly giving my full attention to the conversation. 'What happened? Did you cancel your London trip? Is everything okay? Nick didn't come down with that bug, did he?'

She hesitates. 'No, we're still going to London. Kim's going to have the girls for me instead.'

'*Kim?*' Kim is a good friend of Madeline's. Her daughter goes to school with my daughter, Alice. 'But I thought—'

'It's just with the party coming up, Nick and I thought you had enough on your plate.' Her words are clipped.

'No, not at all,' I try to reassure her. One of the juniors, Lily, comes into the staffroom and heads towards the kettle. I debate whether or not to go outside for more privacy, but I don't think I'll have time before my next client. Instead, I try to inject some lightness into my voice. 'Alice and Jamie are really looking forward to it, so there's really no need for Kim to have them. I was planning on doing makeovers with Beth and Alice, and baking with Freya and Jamie. It'll be fun.'

'Well, sorry about that, but I've arranged it with Kim now, so you don't need to worry.' Madeline sounds strangely defensive and formal, and I get a small knot in my stomach. An inkling that something odd might be going on.

Over on the sofa, despite my attempt at levity, Becky must sense my distress because she's mouthing if everything's all right. I shake my head in response and shrug.

'Madeline, is something wrong? Have I done something to—'

'Sorry, Zoe, I'm busy at work. Got to go.' The line goes dead. *What the hell?* I'm not having that. I call her back, my mind thick with confusion. I've never been good at confrontation, but I can't leave things as they are.

'Hello—'

'Madeline, is everything…'

'Sorry I can't come to the phone right now, but if you'd like to leave a message I'll get back to you.'

Damn! Voicemail. I wait for the beep and leave a quick message, keeping my voice low. 'Madeline, is everything okay? I get the feeling you might be annoyed about something. Maybe I'm imagining it, I don't know. Anyway, can you call me back, put my mind at rest? This is Zoe.'

I end the call and slump in my seat, staring at my phone screen, wondering if she will actually ring me back, or whether she'll ignore me. I don't buy her excuse that she had to go because she was too busy.

'What was all that about?' Becky asks. 'You okay?'

I stand and walk over to the sofa, sit down next to my friend, trying to think what I could possibly have done to upset my sister-in-law. In all the years we've known one another, we've never fallen out, and she's never used that distant, over-polite tone with me before either. Madeline has always been a person I can rely on to be there for me and I'd like to think that goes both ways.

'Zo?'

'Sorry, Becky. That was Madeline. She was changing some arrangements.'

'Arrangements? You mean the party?'

'No. I was supposed to be looking after my nieces this weekend while they're away, but now she's got someone else to do it.'

'Sounds like you dodged a bullet there,' she says through a mouthful of sandwich.

'No, not at all. I love my nieces. I was looking forward to having them over.'

She nudges me with her elbow. 'I was teasing.'

'Oh, yeah, sorry. I'm a bit distracted. It was weird. She sounded annoyed with me or something.'

'No one could ever be annoyed with you, Zoe, you're too… un-annoying.' Becky gives me a comforting wink. I give her a weak smile in return. 'You sure she wasn't just stressed, or busy? Sometimes it's hard to tell from a phone conversation. You might be worrying over nothing.'

I replay the conversation in my head. 'No. She was definitely pissed off.'

'Well then, you'll just have to speak to her about it.'

'I know. But you know how rubbish I am at stuff like that.'

'Put on your big-girl pants, Zoe.'

I stick out my tongue and sink back into the sofa, closing my eyes for a few seconds.

'Better eat your lunch if you're having any. Your two o'clock will be here soon.'

I sigh and pull a face. 'I've lost my appetite.'

'Okay, but don't expect me to pick you up off the floor when you faint from hunger at four o'clock.' She shoves the last piece of sandwich in her mouth and pops open a can of Fanta.

I wonder how I'm going to break the news to the kids. They've both been looking forward to having their cousins to stay. I decide that whatever's happened, it's obviously some misunderstanding that Madeline and I will be able to sort out. It's annoying that I can't fix it right now, because I know I'm going to brood about it all afternoon. But Becky's right – I'll speak to Madeline after work, sort it out and everything will go back to normal. At least, I hope it will.

I check my watch and see that Becky wasn't wrong. I've only got five minutes until my next appointment. I head to the fridge and take out the Ziploc bag with my cream cheese bagel. Becky nods approvingly as I take a bite and chew without tasting, my mind still on my sister-in-law.

CHAPTER FOUR

The seventeenth-century stone chapel is full to bursting with all our friends and family. It's mainly Toby's large extended family, but that's okay. They're about to become *my* family too. My normally straight dark hair has been curled and swept off my face, held back with the pearl comb that belonged to my mother. My ivory lace dress is fitted at the bodice, and flares out slightly at the hem, the whole ensemble studded through with seed pearls. I'm standing at the back of the chapel as though in a dream.

'You sure you're okay, Zo?' Becky gives me a worried glance as Lou straightens out my tulle wedding train.

It takes a few seconds to realise she's talking to me. It's sweltering in here. Forget the fact that it's December, and that outside it's threatening to snow. Here in the little chapel the walls are lined with piping-hot radiators, and the air is thick with body heat and CO_2. I can barely breathe. I should have considered the temperature of the venue beforehand. Should have made sure it was a little cooler inside. It's clear the congregation are finding it uncomfortable too, with top layers already discarded over laps and seat backs, and the order-of-service cards being used as makeshift fans.

I wipe the sweat from my top lip and forehead, wishing this dress weren't quite as tightly fitted. The bump on the back of my head is throbbing, my brain is fuzzy and there's the distinct possibility that I may throw up. 'I'm fine,' I whisper back. I decided not to tell anyone else about my fainting episode as I didn't want my big day to be overshadowed by everyone talking about it. Toby and his family agreed to keep quiet about it too.

'It's just' – Becky's forehead creases – 'you're quite pale. I mean, you look stunning, of course, but… you don't seem yourself.'

'She's getting married,' Lou hisses, smoothing her dark hair. 'It's a big day, of course she's not going to be herself. It's nerve-wracking. And you talking about it isn't likely to help.'

Becky glares at her. 'It doesn't hurt to ask. I'm just worried about my friend, that's all.'

'Um, she's my friend too.'

'Well, if she's such a good friend, you'd have noticed that she's paler than normal, don't you think?'

I probably should have considered the fact that despite being my two best friends, my bridesmaids aren't exactly the best of friends with one another, which is one of the main reasons I didn't ask them to stay over at the hotel with me last night. All they've done since they arrived this morning is bicker. I'm not sure why they're so antagonistic. They don't even know each other that well. I went to school with Lou Schiavone and I get the feeling she's a little jealous of my newer friendship with my work friend Becky Webb. But I shouldn't even be thinking about that right now. This is my wedding day. Not the time to be dealing with friend issues.

My sister Dina should have been here with me as well, but she said she left it too late to get a flight back from Thailand. So here I am with Becky and Lou as my bridesmaids.

Maybe it's just as well Dina couldn't make it. Especially as things were so shaky the last time I spoke to her. Although that's an understatement. My sister and I have a complicated relationship. One that I really don't want to dwell on right now.

My stomach flips as the wedding march starts up. I've been looking forward to this moment for months. I give a start as my dad takes my arm. My bridesmaids set aside their differences for the time being and pick up my train between them. I fight the urge to turn around and check if they're okay. But there's no need; I can sense the hostility bubbling away back there. I'll leave them to it.

Instead, I turn to my father. To my astonishment, his eyes are bright with unshed tears. 'You look beautiful, Zoe. Just like your mother.'

My breath catches and I exhale, feeling instantly tearful myself. 'Thanks, Dad.' He isn't given to fits of sentimentality, so his words and emotion mean a lot. I just wish I felt well enough to appreciate it. His face suddenly swims before mine and I have to take a deep breath to fight back a wave of dizziness and nausea. Please let me get through the next few hours without passing out again. Maybe I'm coming down with flu. Talk about bad timing.

I'm ready to walk down the aisle, but Dad holds me back a few seconds longer. 'I just have to ask, Zoe… are you absolutely sure you're ready? This is a big decision.' His words are blunt. A shock. His eyes search mine.

'What?' My brain clears for a moment and I glare at him, annoyed by the question. He's never expressed any doubts about my impending marriage before – never shown that much of an interest in my life at all, if I'm brutally honest, so why would he ask me this now, right when I'm about to say my vows? 'What do you mean, "am I sure"?'

'Never mind. It's nothing.' He flushes, clears his throat and stares ahead down the aisle.

If I felt stronger I'd challenge him further. But Dad and I don't talk much and I'm not about to start now, not with close to two hundred people staring our way. One of Dad's favourite sayings is, 'the best shortage is a shortage of words.'

'If you're happy, then so am I,' he continues, unconvincingly. 'You know, your mother would have been proud of you,' he adds.

I give an angry nod in response, not trusting myself to speak. Annoyed with him for invoking my mother. As if that makes his previous question okay.

Everyone keeps glancing back at us, waiting for us to make our walk down the aisle. The music is still playing, but we're not moving. I think Dad realises he's holding up the proceedings, so he takes the first step and I walk in time with him along the worn flagstones and past the wooden pews. Slowing my breathing. Swallowing down the nausea that keeps advancing in waves. I'm certain everyone can tell I'm not myself. I'm sure there are a few whispers going around. Or maybe I'm imagining it. I hope I look as beautiful as Dad says I do, and not as ill as I feel. This isn't how I imagined my walk down the aisle would be. I thought I would feel incredible, excited, blissful. At least I should be thankful that I fainted before the wedding and not during it. Although I don't want to jinx things. I grip my dad a little tighter and he pats my arm reassuringly.

White winter light seeps through the huge stained-glass window up above the altar, where four colourful saints watch our slow procession, as they've no doubt watched countless other brides before me. Most of the guests' faces are blurry, seeming to merge into one another as I pass by. But I manage to pick out a few familiar faces. I spot my glamorous colleagues from the salon where I work. I also see Cassie Barrington, with her boyfriend and parents. But Cassie isn't really my friend anymore – not since I realised that the only person Cassie cares about is Cassie. Unfortunately, I had to invite her and her family to the wedding as my dad is Cassie's godfather – not that this really means anything. It was just a role he and Mum were asked to fill, back when they were younger and friends with her parents.

I turn my thoughts thankfully away from Cassie as I spot Celia and Malcolm seated at the front, both of them looking as proud as anything. Toby's brother Nick gives me an encouraging smile from his place as best man next to the groom. And then of course there's Toby himself. The love of my life.

Dad hands me over to my husband-to-be and, for a moment, I feel like some kind of possession being traded away. Although I guess that's what brides used to be. I blink several times and give myself a little shake, attempting to banish these strange thoughts. I need to try to enjoy this. To soak up every second, rather than wishing it were all over and wanting to lie down in a darkened room.

Standing at the altar, Toby and I lock eyes and I can tell he's worried about me by the gentle concern there. He takes my hands and brings them to his lips. Kisses my fingers. This calms me and for a moment I try to imagine that it's just the two of us. That we're at home in our little terraced cottage at the foot of the hill with no one around to disturb us.

The vicar begins and I let myself sink into his words. Words that I've heard so many times before on TV shows and movies. Words that I've seen other friends recite. Words that my parents must have said to one another many years ago. That I'm now repeating and reciting myself. This is a defining moment in my life. Something I'll remember forever. Toby's hand trembles as he slides the ring onto my finger.

And just like that, the vicar pronounces us husband and wife.

From that moment on, the atmosphere changes to one of celebratory excitement. Of relief almost. Everyone claps and the small choir sings 'Can't Help Falling in Love'.

'Hello, Mrs Johnson!' Toby's expression is one of pure relief.

'Hello, Mr Johnson. I can't believe we're married!'

'I know. I thought you were going to faint again. Are you okay?'

'I'm fine.' Although the truth is I feel far from fine. I'm nauseous, and everything is still fuzzy, as though my ears need to pop. Even though I'm so happy that we're finally married I feel as if I missed it. As though I was elsewhere while it was all going on. I want to cry with the unfairness of it all. Why am I feeling like this today of all days? Why did I have to faint on my wedding day?

Toby and I sign the register as everyone else heads outside, no doubt eager to gulp down some cool air. Eventually, we follow them out too, but not before Celia drapes a white faux-fur shawl around my shoulders.

'It's freezing out there. Don't want you to catch a chill. Congratulations, you two. You make a beautiful couple.'

I'm grateful she doesn't ask how I'm feeling. Because then I'd have to lie and say I feel amazing. Like I'm walking on air. Instead of the strange unsettling disappointment that clouds my mind.

Our guests clap and cheer and throw silver and gold confetti as Toby and I step outside into the icy air. Celia wasn't wrong – it's bitterly cold out here. We don't linger. Instead, we all make our way along the paved pathway which leads to the hotel entrance. From the outside, it must look like a scene from a movie. Our route is wreathed with fairy lights and winter flowers – poinsettia, hellebores, holly berries and ivy. It should be a magical moment, but I don't appreciate any of it. My body is hot and cold, shivering and clammy. My mind is hazy, as though there's something I'm missing. I smile and laugh, and I hug and kiss my husband. But it all feels like an act. As if I'm going through the motions. What on earth is wrong with me?

CHAPTER FIVE

NOW

It's dark as I leave work bundled up in my hat and scarf, my breath making silver plumes in the cold night air. I walk quickly through the familiar streets until I reach the blue metal gates of my children's school. Alice and Jamie go to the after-school club three times a week, but thankfully they don't mind as they either get to socialise with their friends or catch up on their homework. The latter is great for me, because then I don't have the chore of supervising it at home, especially maths, which in Alice's year has already passed beyond my capabilities.

'Hi, Mrs Johnson.' Cheryl, the supervisor, greets me at the door after buzzing me in.

'Hello. Hope they've behaved themselves today.' I sign them out on the register and wave across the hall to each of my kids in turn. Jamie zooms over holding a still-wet painting, his brown hair and pale face splattered with green paint.

'Let's save this to take home tomorrow.' Cheryl takes the dripping artwork from my son as I help him out of his apron. 'Give it time to dry.'

I throw her a grateful look. 'Looks amazing, Jamie.'

'It's a Christmas tree. Like the one we're going to get.'

'I love it. What's your sister doing?'

'Talking.' He rolls his eyes and Cheryl and I laugh.

I look over and notice that Alice is indeed still chatting. Hope is among her gaggle of friends, and that reminds me that her mother Kim will be looking after my nieces this weekend instead of me. It also reminds me that I've yet to find out what's up with Madeline.

'Everything all right?' Cheryl asks.

I realise that my expression must have fallen. 'What? Oh, yeah, I just spaced out for a minute – long day. Jamie, fetch your sister, will you?'

He does as I ask, and returns with Alice, pulling her along with both hands.

'Hi, Mum.' Her blue eyes sparkle up at me. My daughter is a mini me – petite with black hair and blue eyes – our Welsh heritage, although we've only been to Wales a couple of times. My dad's from Swansea, but his parents died when Dina and I were really young, so I don't really remember them. There are no close relatives left in Wales since Aunty Caroline died so Dad never goes back, but I keep meaning to organise a trip.

'Hello, Mrs Lewis, Mr Choudhry.' I turn to see Cheryl opening the door to Kim Lewis and another parent I don't recognise.

'Right, get your coats.' I usher my children over to the pegs to collect their things before turning to Kim with a smile, but she isn't looking my way. Instead, her gaze is fixed on Hope at the other end of the hall. 'Hi, Kim.' I speak a little too loudly and it sounds forced.

She glances at me distractedly and manages a tight smile before heading over to her daughter. Now I'm really starting to get paranoid. First Madeline, and now Kim is acting like I'm persona non grata. What's going on? I glance down and notice the children by my side staring up at me.

'Can we go now, Mum?' Alice says. 'I'm starving. What are we having for tea?'

'Fish fingers.'

'Yes!' Jamie does a little victory dance at the thought of his favourite food, and the three of us head home.

On the way back, I can't stop checking my phone to see if there are any texts or voicemails from Madeline. Every time I look, there's nothing. The kids are chatty, and I feel bad for being so distant and distracted, fobbing them off with one-word answers as my mind scrolls through all the possible things I could have done to make Madeline and Kim act so coldly towards me. But I keep coming up empty. I love my sister-in-law and I really like Kim, so I would never knowingly do anything to upset either of them.

Perhaps I'm imagining the whole thing. Maybe Madeline was having an off day when she called me, and it came across as her being annoyed, when it was nothing of the sort. And maybe Kim was simply distracted just now. It's a stressful time of year with Christmas around the corner. Everyone tends to act a little bit crazy. Could that be it?

Or maybe *I'm* the one who's stressed and paranoid. After all, as well as working full-time and preparing everything for Christmas, I'm also organising an anniversary party. I must be mad.

'Mum, you're not listening.' Alice tugs at my hand.

'Sorry, Alice, what were you saying?' I resolve to give the children my full attention for the rest of the walk home.

Twenty minutes later, we reach the front door to our little cottage at the foot of the hill. For the first time, I notice that most of our neighbours have their decorations up. I haven't even thought about decorations yet, or a tree. I'll have to speak to Toby about us possibly picking one up this weekend. And I'd better get a move on with the gift shopping too. I resolve to make a list.

'We're home!' I call out as I push open the front door. The children tumble inside and call out to their father, who comes into the hall to greet us, arms wide to receive the kids who barrel into him like little rugby players. I lean over them to give him a kiss. 'You're home early.'

'I had a meeting at the town hall, but it finished sooner than I thought. Go put your feet up if you like – I can sort the kids out.' This is why I love my husband. He's always so thoughtful.

'No, I'm fine. They're hungry, I'll start making tea.'

'Mum, can I have something to eat?' Alice follows us into the kitchen.

'No, I'm just about to do the fish fingers.'

'Just something small. Pleeease.'

'You can each have a tangerine. Wash your hands first.'

The children wolf down their tangerines and then disappear up to their rooms to get changed.

I drop the tangerine peel into the bin and wash my hands. As I stand at the sink, Toby comes up and puts his arms around me, kissing my neck. I turn and kiss him back, properly. And run a hand down his cheek.

'Hey!' he jerks back. 'Wet hands.'

'Sorry.' I grin.

'No you're not.'

I put both my hands on his face. 'No, I'm not.' I giggle.

He shakes his head, smiling at my childishness. I take a clean tea towel from the drawer and pass it to him.

'Thanks.' He wipes his wet cheeks and puts the tea towel on the counter. 'How was your day?'

My good mood instantly evaporates when I remember what happened with Madeline. 'It was… weird. How was Nick today?' I turn on the grill and open the freezer door.

'Nick? Fine. Why?' Toby sits at the table, running his fingers absently over its scrubbed pine surface.

'So he didn't mention anything about their girls not coming over this weekend?'

'What do you mean?'

I try not to get short-tempered with my husband. He's obviously forgotten that Beth and Freya were supposed to be staying. 'You remember, Nick and Madeline are going to London for her birthday.'

'Oh, yes. That's *this* weekend?'

'Not anymore.' I explain the change in plans while cursing the fact we've run out of oven chips. I can't face peeling potatoes; I'll do pasta instead.

'To be honest, it'll be nice to have a weekend to ourselves,' Toby says, oblivious to my mood.

'Well, yes, but that's not the point. The point is that she's asked someone else to look after them, and she was funny with me on the phone. I've called her back and asked her to ring me, but she hasn't replied.'

'Maybe she's busy and she'll call later.'

'I know, I thought that. But then, when I picked up the kids, Kim Lewis came in and more or less blanked me.'

'Really? Are you sure?'

'I'm not a hundred per cent sure, but it's made me feel really crap and insecure. I don't know what I'm supposed to have done!' My voice cracks.

'Hey, hey, it'll be all right.' Toby stands and takes the packet of fish fingers out of my hand, laying it on the counter. He puts his arms around me and kisses my cheek. 'We'll sort this out, okay? I'm sure it's just a misunderstanding and everything will be back to normal before you know it. How about I call Nick now? Find out if he can shed some light?'

'Would you? Sorry, I feel like such a drama queen.'

'You're definitely not one of those.' Toby smiles. 'Just maybe overtired?'

I nod and try not to cry. I love my in-laws – if I've done anything to offend them I'll feel awful.

'Why don't you sit and relax while I call Nick?'

'I'd rather keep busy. I'll cook. Thanks for doing that.'

'Don't worry.' He unplugs his phone from the charger and leaves the kitchen. I hear his footsteps on the stairs and try to calm down. I hadn't planned on having a meltdown about this. I was going to try to speak to Madeline myself, but Toby was so sympathetic.

Honestly, it's sometimes worse when people are nice to you. Makes you feel so much more emotional. I put a pan of water on to boil and shove all six fish fingers under the grill. I wish I could hear what Toby's saying to Nick. I check my phone again, just in case I've missed a message from Madeline, but there's still nothing.

Thankfully, I don't have long to wait for my husband. Less than ten minutes later, he's bounding back down the stairs and into the kitchen. 'Well?'

'Don't look so worried. It's all absolutely fine.' Toby sits at the table and I come and join him.

'Really?' I allow myself a tentative moment of hope.

'Yep. Nick said that Madeline's mortified she upset you. She genuinely wanted to make life easier for us, and that's why she rearranged the sleepover. Nick said she's been so busy with work this afternoon that she didn't have time to check her messages.'

'And you believe him?'

Toby raises his eyebrows. 'Why wouldn't I?'

'Because she still hasn't replied to me. He might just be covering up the real reason.'

'What real reason? Honestly, Zo, I know my brother, and he was genuinely apologetic that you might have thought she was snubbing you.'

'Oh no, you didn't say those actual words, did you? That you thought she was snubbing me?'

'No, of course not, I'm paraphrasing. I just mean… there's nothing to worry about. Believe me.'

I hope Toby's right. But if he is, then that means I've blown up this situation out of all proportion. I feel hot with embarrassment. 'Nick and Madeline must think I'm a lunatic.'

Toby laughs. 'They love you and would never think that.'

'I hope not. I think I'll send her a quick WhatsApp just to smooth things over.'

'Okay, but there's no need.'

'I want to.' I take my phone out of my bag and compose a short message:

Hi, Madeline. Hope everything's okay. Do you fancy getting a quick drink later, or tomorrow? Xx

Toby sniffs. 'What's that smell?'

'I can't smell anyth—' And then I realise what it is. 'Shit! The fish fingers!' I rush over to the oven and pull out the grill pan, but it's too late. Six charred oblongs stare back at me from the wire tray. I'd scrape off the burned bits if I could, but they're too far gone to salvage anything.

'Here, let me.' Toby comes to take over, but I wave him away with a sigh.

'It's fine. I'll bin them. The kids will just have to have cheesy pasta instead.' I flick on the extractor fan while Toby opens the window to dissipate the smell of burning, letting the freezing December air into our toasty kitchen.

After a moment or two, I can see that Madeline has read my WhatsApp message. I wait anxiously for her reply, overcooking the pasta and accidentally scalding my hands with boiling water. I'm desperate for this uncomfortable situation to be resolved.

But I wait and I wait, and a reply doesn't come.

CHAPTER SIX

NOW

This morning at work was one of our busiest days so far. I've had back-to-back clients for five hours straight, with no time for so much as a sip of tea or coffee. It's probably a good thing, as at least it's stopped me brooding over the Madeline situation. Jennifer tells me my two thirty appointment has been cancelled so I now have an unexpected forty-five minute lunch break.

I have a sudden yearning to see my husband, so I call Toby to see if he's free to meet me in town. He's working locally so it would be great if he could get away. I could also find out if Nick's said anything more about Madeline. But when I call, Toby sounds stressed, like I've caught him at a bad time. 'Oh, Zoe, I'd love to, but Nick and I had our lunch ages ago. We're back working again now.'

'Are you still at the Coppice Street house?' He and Nick have been landscaping a driveway for a family who are new to the area.

'Yeah, it's going okay. They seem like nice people. Not too demanding, if you know what I mean. But we've got a lot to get through. They want it finished by the end of next week. Sorry I can't meet up.'

'No worries. I knew it would be a long shot. I'll see you later.'

'Okay, love you, Zo.'

'Love you too.'

I shrug on my coat and wink at Becky on my way out, who sticks out her tongue, envious of my unexpected break. I've decided to go for a walk; I could do with a change of scenery. Something to shake off this anxiety brewing in my gut. It's not just about Madeline, it's also about the upcoming anniversary party and all the old memories it's throwing up. As I leave the salon, stepping out into the wintry air, I remember how ill I felt on my wedding day. How unsettled and queasy. That strange fuzziness in my head. It's odd, but whenever I think about that time, the fuzziness returns. Like my head is stuffed with marshmallows. I hope this party isn't going to be a case of history repeating itself.

I leave the high street and turn onto Park Walk, an elegant walkway that runs alongside the ninth-century abbey wall. Bare-branched silver birches and sycamores sway alongside old-fashioned street lamps and an abundance of wooden benches are perfectly placed to take in the misty view of the Blackmore Vale. While it's busy in town, there are only a handful of people up here – joggers, dog walkers and a couple of families who look like tourists. During the summer months, it can get pretty crowded, so despite the freezing temperatures, I much prefer this time of year when there's space to breathe and I can stare uninterrupted out across the countryside.

My favourite bench is free, so I quickly head on over to claim it, running my fingers over the brass plaque before sitting down. It's situated almost at the far end of the walk, past the war memorial. The reason it's my favourite bench is that it's dedicated to my mother. I used to get annoyed if I came here and someone else was sitting on it. But now I've come to like the fact that strangers are looking out over the same view that Mum once enjoyed. That they'll read the inscription on the plaque and wonder about who she was, and what she was like. Getting Mum's bench inscribed was probably the last beautiful thing my dad ever did.

The other reason I love this bench is that during the winter, when there are no leaves on the trees, I can make out my house from here. It's easy to spot because its facade has been rendered and painted white, while all the other houses are grey stone. I can even see its splash-of-red front door. I like looking at it. Knowing that's the place where my family and I live. Where our children are being raised. Where we're creating shared memories.

I don't think I'll ever want to move house. Even though Toby keeps saying it's too small for the four of us now. That once the kids turn into teenagers we'll be bursting at the seams. I'm all for converting the loft – there's just enough room for a bedroom and en suite – but Toby's dragging his heels. He's hoping I'll change my mind about moving. Keeps pointing out bigger and better properties online. I make all the right appreciative noises, but I dread the day he pushes harder for us to actually leave.

I think it's because we've always been so happy there. Our little house reminds me of how my family home used to be before Mum died. Not the look and style of the place, but the atmosphere and feel. My childhood home was always full of warmth and laughter. A direct contrast to how things were afterwards. When Dad stopped talking and Dina grew distant. When I was the only one putting in any effort. Not that my effort seemed to make any difference.

Even before Dina left home, I could barely get two words out of her. I guess back then I was trying to take the place of our mum. I cooked and cleaned, sorted out school stuff, tried to be a shoulder to cry on. But instead of the two of us growing closer, Dina seemed to resent me. She thought I was interfering in her life. Told me to mind my own business and butt out. I was concerned that she was so secretive about everything. That she never confided in me or Dad. I should probably be grateful she didn't get into any trouble at school.

Maybe she was simply going through normal, grumpy teenage behaviour – something I missed out on as I was forced to grow up too quickly. But there weren't even any brief moments of bonding between us. No bright spots to see us through the erosion of our childhood relationship. I can't help think that if Mum hadn't died, the two of us would have been closer. We might have been friends. Instead, Dina treated me like an annoyance. Like someone she couldn't wait to get away from.

I take my tuna mayo sandwich from my bag, unwrap it and bite into it hungrily. I hadn't realised how starving I was. The air is chilly, and the seat is damp. Not exactly sitting-on-a-bench-on-a-hill weather, but I don't mind. I'll soon warm up after I get back to the salon. I try to concentrate on my lunch and not let past hurts and future worries creep in, but I'm not very successful. I wish I could be one of those people who live in the now. Who can meditate and remain calm. Do those people really exist though? Or are they just pretending to have all the answers to life?

Before leaving for work this morning, I told Toby that Madeline still hadn't replied to my WhatsApp message. He tried to convince me that Madeline's fine with me. The thing is, I really don't think he and Nick are attuned to these kinds of situations. It's like being back at school when some alpha girl would be passive-aggressively bitchy to me, and most of the boys would be oblivious and think I was being oversensitive. It's a subtle thing, but it's a real thing. And while Madeline isn't being bitchy, she's definitely avoiding me for some reason. Meanwhile Toby thinks I've got no reason to worry.

The only other person I could possibly speak to about this is Celia. But then I'd be putting her in an awkward situation where she'd be caught in between her two daughters-in-law. Oh, this is so frustrating. I desperately want Toby to be right, and for it to be a simple misunderstanding. But I'm not holding my breath.

As I'm chewing over my dilemma – and my sandwich – something catches my eye at the base of the hill... It looks as if someone's coming out of my house! It can't be Toby, because he said he's working. But who else would it be? An intruder? I get to my feet and hurry to the steps which lead down the hill to my street, fumbling in my bag to call the police. I stop dead when I get close enough to see that it *is* Toby, and he's with someone. A woman.

I flatten myself against a tree, barely able to breathe. And then I realise that I recognise the woman. It's *Madeline*. I don't know whether to be relieved or not. They're standing on the pavement; their heads close together. I didn't think those two had the kind of relationship where they talked to one another alone. Unless… maybe he's been speaking to her on my behalf? Trying to work out why she's been standoffish with me. If that's the case, then why didn't he tell me? Instead, he lied and said he was working. Why would he have done that? They lean in towards one another but I'm too far away to tell if they're giving one another a peck on the cheek or… or something more.

I realise a piece of undigested sandwich is lodged in my gullet and I have to cough to clear it. I thrust a shaking hand into my bag and pull out my water bottle, gulping down the icy liquid until my throat feels a little clearer.

I stay where I am, watching the two of them part ways. My husband heads to his work van and Madeline to her dark-green catering van parked further down the road. Should I call Toby? Have it out with him? Ask him why he and Madeline met in our house while no one else was there? But what if he lies and gives me some bullshit answer? He's already lied to me once today. *Shit.* I check my watch. I'm due back in work. I'm already cutting it fine – my next appointment is in ten minutes.

I end up having to jog to the salon, arriving back hot and sweaty, my heart pumping from the exertion, but also from anxiety. How am I meant to work with so many questions swimming around my head?

All afternoon, as I chat to my clients, I find myself having to fake interest in their conversations. Normally I enjoy hearing about their loves and lives, as if I'm catching up with old friends. Not today though. Instead, I spend the remaining hours feeling sick to my stomach. This time it isn't just Madeline I'm worried about – it's Madeline and my *husband*. Is this the reason she's been *off* with me? Are she and Toby… But I can't even *think* it. Then why was she secretly meeting him?

The word *betrayal* keeps popping into my head. But never in a million years could I think Toby is the type of man to cheat. He's loyal and kind. He has strong family morals. Toby has always been an incredible husband – attentive, loving, considerate, fun. We've rarely had a cross word. Of course we have the odd disagreement like any married couple, but on the whole, it's been a pretty perfect ten years of marriage. Which is one of the main reasons we're having this party – to celebrate that fact.

Toby loves me. He wouldn't jeopardise what we have. It's part of why I love him so much. The absolute trust I have in our relationship. No, I'll give him the benefit of the doubt. Perhaps he really was intervening with Madeline on my behalf. Asking her if anything's wrong. But, honestly, that doesn't sound like the type of thing Toby would do – not without running it past me first. I'll just have to hope he brings it up when I get home. Best case scenario is he says, 'Oh, hey, guess what, I spoke to Madeline today and she explained why she was acting so funny.'

Finally, the day is over and I'm able to leave work. But I still have to pick up the children from after-school club. Somehow, I manage to get through all that without breaking down and calling Toby to ask him outright. This is a conversation that will be best handled face to face. And I need to be calm, because there could be a perfectly innocent explanation.

Back home, there's no sign of my husband's van, and the house is dark. All my nervous energy suddenly dissipates, and I'm overwhelmed with exhaustion, my shoulders sagging.

'Come on, you two, in you go.' I usher Jamie and Alice inside and turn on the hall light. The house is warm, but it feels somehow strange to me. I keep thinking about Toby and Madeline being in here today. I wonder which room they went into. 'Hang up your coats. Jamie, don't leave your shoes in the middle of the hallway!'

'I was going to move them, Mummy, but I'm doing my coat first.'

Guilt tugs at my chest. I shouldn't take out my worries on my children. 'Sorry, Jamie, you're being really helpful.' My phone pings, but I ignore it for the moment.

'Am I being helpful too?' Alice asks. 'Shall I help make dinner?'

'That would be very nice.' I pull the children in close for a hug, kissing the tops of their heads. Their hair smells of shampoo and cold air. 'Guess what?'

'What?' They both reply.

I release them from our hug and root about in my bag, pulling out a couple of items. 'I bought more fish fingers and chips!' I wave the packs in the air.

'Yay!' Alice cries.

'Don't burn them this time, Mummy,' Jamie adds.

'I'll try not to.' I give him my most serious look and we all burst out laughing. 'Right, go wash your hands and get changed. I'll start cooking tea.'

'And I'm helping,' Alice says.

'Me too.' Jamie doesn't want to be left out.

'After you've got changed.'

They run up the stairs and I try to hold onto their enthusiasm as I go through to the kitchen. I turn on the grill and nervously check my phone. There's a message from Toby, saying he's going to be a bit late home. *Probably because he had an extended lunch break*, I think bitterly. But immediately I shake myself free from that line of thinking. No point getting worked up before I even know what their meet-up was all about.

This time, with the help of my children, I manage not to burn their fish fingers, and they enjoy supper at the kitchen table while regaling me with stories of their day. My husband still hasn't appeared. It's not like him to be this late unless he's on council business. As a landscape gardener, it's more practical for him to start early and finish before it gets dark which, at this time of year, is around four thirty. It's now almost six thirty.

I let the children watch half an hour of TV before we go upstairs, where I help them get ready for bed, followed by a story in Alice's room. I'm just coming to the end of the chapter when I hear a key in the door, followed by the sound of my husband walking into the hallway. My heart thuds, and I realise I'm nervous.

'Daddy!' The kids jump out of bed and race out of the bedroom and down the stairs. I don't even bother trying to call them back. They'll want to jump all over their father for a good five minutes. Instead, I tidy round my daughter's room, putting away clothes and other bits and pieces. After a while, I hear the clomp of their footsteps coming upstairs. Toby pokes his head around the door.

'There you are. What are you doing up here?'

'Hi, just having a tidy up.' I can't even look him in the eye. 'You're late back.'

'I know, sorry. Nick wanted to have a drink after work.'

'Oh? Anything the matter?'

'The matter?' he repeats. 'No, just a drink to unwind. It's been a long day.'

Jamie and Alice have climbed back into her bed. 'Can you finish the story, Mum?' Alice asks.

'I'll do it.' Toby comes and sits on the bed while the kids snuggle up to him. Normally I'd stay too, but I need a few moments to compose myself. Work out how I'm going to handle this. We're usually so in sync with one another, so open and honest. It feels alien to be suspicious of my husband. He's my partner in everything. He's never kept secrets from me before. Never lied.

I head to the bathroom, where I stare critically at myself in the mirror. My face is pale and there are bluish smudges beneath my eyes. My skin isn't too bad – a little dry around the eyes, and there are more lines there than I'd like. Not too bad for a working thirty-seven-year-old with two kids. My hair is shiny and sleek, but it has to be because it's my job. I can't go to work with bad hair. I'm not any worse looking than Madeline, am I?

I don't even know why I'm going down this rabbit hole. I can't believe I'm thinking these things. There could be any number of reasons why Toby and my sister-in-law met up today. So why did he lie to me? And why is Madeline not returning my calls or messages? Something's up, and I need to find out what.

CHAPTER SEVEN

The rain lashes against the plate-glass windows as pedestrians are buffeted along the pavement, their clothes and hair frenziedly whipping around them. Inside, as I sweep the floor of the salon, the sound of the vile weather is drowned out by the whine of hairdryers and the thump of music.

I've had my Saturday job at Waves Salon for almost a year now, and it's been great to earn my own money and have respite from studying. Especially now that it's just me and Dad at home. Although it may as well just be me with all the conversation I get out of my father. I'm also trying to recover from the fact that my younger sister Dina has just gone off travelling. She only gave us one week's notice that she was leaving, and Dad didn't even seem that bothered about it. Just told her to stay out of trouble.

I can't say I'm surprised that she left. She was always going on about how she couldn't wait to get out of Shaftesbury. But it's still a shock. Her leaving makes me feel like I've failed somehow. Like I've let her down. Like I've let Mum down. Like I didn't do enough to keep our family together. I guess it's kind of a slap in the face.

I could never imagine going off and leaving my home town. I love it here. I'm in the final year of A-levels at sixth form college, but my plan is to train as a hairdresser once I've finished. My boss,

Jennifer, has agreed to take me on here full-time and I'm looking forward to it. Put it this way – I have no clue what else I'd do if I weren't doing this.

One of our stylists, Debbie, beckons me over to wash her client's hair, a smart-looking brunette woman who I vaguely recognise from college, although she isn't one of my lecturers. The woman smiles and I lead her over to the basins at the rear of the salon. She puts her handbag on the floor by her feet and sits down in one of the leather chairs.

'You go to the college, don't you?' she asks as I drape a towel over her shoulders.

'Yes, I'm doing my A-levels.'

'My name's Sally Bennet. I run the marketing department there.' She leans back over the basin.

'I thought I'd seen you around. Is that comfortable for you?'

'Yep, fine thanks.'

I switch on the shower head and let the water run for a moment before testing the temperature.

'What A-levels are you doing?' she asks.

'English, Art and History.' She's obviously a talker. Some customers just want to relax while they're having their hair washed. But other customers, like this lady, love to chat. Jennifer says we have to take our lead from them, and only talk if that's what they want. I start soaking her hair. 'Does that feel okay? Not too hot?'

'No, you're fine. You'd never believe it was May, would you? It's horrible out there.'

'I know. I'm not looking forward to walking home later.'

'I read a piece about the salon in the local paper last week, written by one of the staff here I think. Do you know who that was?'

'Oh, yes, that was me.'

'Really?' She pauses. 'Well it was very professionally written.'

'Thank you.' It's a good thing she can't see my face, because I can feel my cheeks turning pink.

'Did you have any help writing it?' she asks.

'Jennifer – she's the owner –gave me a few bullet points to include. She knows I'm doing an English A-level and that I enjoy writing, so she let me do it.'

'So the article was all your own work?'

'Uh, yes.' I turn off the water and reach behind for a bottle of coconut shampoo.

'Impressive. The piece in the paper said you also organised a fundraiser recently.'

'Yes, just after Christmas. The salon was a sponsor. It was in aid of the local cancer hospice.' I squirt a couple of blobs of shampoo onto her wet hair and start massaging it into a lather.

'That's a great cause. How much did you raise in the end?'

'Just over three and a half thousand.' I can still hardly believe we raised that much.

'Wow, that's fantastic.' Sally sounds genuinely impressed.

'My mum died of cancer five years ago and I wanted to do something as a kind of memorial. It wasn't just me though. My friend Cassie helped, and a few others.'

'But you organised it, yes?'

'Well, yes, it was my idea, but I had a lot of help.'

'Of course. It takes a lot of work to put on those kinds of events.'

I start rinsing the shampoo from her hair. The smell of coconut always reminds me of summer – Mum used to wear a sun lotion that smelled similar.

'How old are you, if you don't mind me asking?'

'Eighteen.'

'Ah, so you're in your second year. How's the studying going?'

I shrug. 'Okay. It's all a bit intense though.'

'Do you know what you want to do afterwards?'

'Yes, I'm going to train to be a hairdresser. Jennifer's going to take me on full-time once my A-levels are over.' I get a warm feeling as I tell her my future plans. I'm so glad I'm not like a lot of my friends, who have no idea what they want to do next.

'Oh.' Sally sounds surprised. 'I thought you might have applied to uni.'

'That was the original plan, but I've realised that I don't want to study anymore. I want to start earning, get my own place. And I enjoy working at Waves. I think I'd like being a hairdresser.'

'That's great.'

I spend the next couple of minutes towel-drying her hair, applying conditioner, and massaging her head. She's quiet for a while and I let my mind wander, thinking about the long summer holidays ahead and whether I'll have saved enough money to go away with my friends.

'That feels great.' Sally interrupts my daydream. 'If you're half as good at cutting hair as you are giving head massages, you'll be a top hairstylist.'

'Thank you. Everyone loves having their head massaged. I think it's because our scalps are usually so neglected.' I start rinsing the conditioner from her hair.

'Actually... I've just had a thought.'

'Oh? Do you want me to get Debbie?'

'No, it's not about my hair. Like I said earlier, I run the marketing department at the college.'

'Sounds like an interesting job.' I'm unsure as to where she's going with her conversation.

'The thing is, my department's just created a new role for a trainee PR officer. Only we haven't had many decent applicants.'

'Oh. That's a shame.'

'Does it sound like something that might interest you?'

'Interest me? Sorry, I'm not sure what you mean.' She must think I'm such a dork.

'Would you be interested in applying for the job of trainee PR officer?' she explains.

'Um… I don't know. What's a PR officer?'

'Oh, sorry, PR stands for public relations. Making sure the public has a good perception of the college. Generating positive publicity. That kind of thing.'

'Oh, right,' I reply, as though I know what she means.

'After hearing about the success of your charity event, and reading your brilliantly written article, it's occurred to me that you might be the perfect candidate for the position.'

'What? Me?' I realise I've sprayed water over the top part of her face. 'Oh, sorry, let me wipe your forehead.'

She blinks as water runs into her eye. I get the corner of the towel and dab her face, apologising and praying Jennifer isn't looking over this way.

'Don't worry, I'm fine,' Sally says generously. 'We'd train you up and tell you exactly what was expected. But the idea is that you would eventually be a self-starter, creating opportunities and networking locally to raise the profile of the college. Does that sound good to you?'

It sounds absolutely terrifying. But also strangely exciting, and so grown-up. It would be an impressive thing to do. 'I… I don't even know what to say.' I turn off the water for a moment, my brain whirring. 'I'm flattered that you think I could do it.'

'Zoe, I think you'd do a great job. And I'd be there to help you. Like I said, it's a position for a trainee, so you wouldn't be expected to know everything. But I see potential in you to learn the role. We'd also pay for you to study one day a week at the college. The salary would be modest for the first year but could possibly rise quite sharply.'

I try to imagine what it would be like to get the job. It feels so daunting. Working full-time at Waves would be the safe option. The comfortable option. I know it so well. I know the people. I enjoy it. Taking this PR job would be scary, and I might not like it. I wrap Sally's hair in a towel, and she sits up and turns around to look at me.

'Oh bless you.' She raises an eyebrow. 'You look just a little bit terrified! It's a lot to take in, I know. But the deadline for applications is next Wednesday, so let us know if you're interested by then. Preferably beforehand.'

'Wow. Thank you.' The more I think about it, the more interested I become. This could be a once-in-a-lifetime opportunity. And if it didn't work out or I hated it, I'm sure I could retrain as a hairdresser.

'What do you think?' she presses. 'No, actually, that's not fair of me, putting you on the spot like that. Think about it, okay?' She bends to retrieve her handbag from the floor.

'I think I might be interested.' I inhale and give her a cautious smile.

Sally echoes my smile. 'I knew you would be! Great!' She reaches into her bag and pulls out a bunch of forms, taking the top one and handing it to me. 'Here's an application form. But you can also apply via our website if you prefer. Remember, the deadline is Wednesday. Interviews will be held in two weeks' time, and the job start date is September.'

'Thank you.' I take the form, fold it in two and stuff it into the back pocket of my jeans. I have the feeling that this is one of those life-changing times. One of those events where I'll look back in ten years and say this was the moment that launched my career, my life.

My heart beats faster as I consider the opportunity before me.

CHAPTER EIGHT

NOW

'Come on, you two. Out you get!' I chivvy the kids along. Why do they always take so long getting out of the car? I prefer walking to school, but in typical Monday-morning style we overslept this morning, so had no choice other than to drive if we wanted to avoid being late. Plus, I wanted to get to the playground at a reasonable time so that I could catch Madeline. But with the time it took to scrape the ice off the windscreen and then the nightmare parking, we may as well have walked.

Once Alice and Jamie are on the pavement with their backpacks over their shoulders, I slam the door to my blue Vauxhall Corsa and click the lock. I'm still no closer to finding out why Madeline's avoiding me. And I didn't have the courage to ask Toby what she was doing with him in our house last week. I gave him every opportunity to tell me about it. I said what a shame it was that he and I couldn't meet for lunch that day, but he just compounded his lie by apologising for being so busy at work. There's definitely something going on, but I'm not in the right frame of mind to deal with it. I feel so wobbly at the moment. Fragile.

The kids and I hurry along the icy roads to school. It looks like the gates opened ages ago. Most of the parents have dropped off their kids and are leaving already.

'Hi, Zoe!' I turn to see a couple of the mums, Ellen and Liz, with their three kids and adorable chocolate lab.

'Boots!' Alice runs to give him a hug.

'Come on, Alice, you're going to be late.' But I can't resist stroking Boots either.

'Hi, Ellen, Liz. You okay?'

'Usual Monday morning madness.' Liz raises a perfectly plucked eyebrow.

'Same here.' I smile.

Jamie and Alice head into the playground with their friends and we watch until they're all safely inside the building.

'We've gotta run,' Liz says with a wave, 'work calls.'

'But let's catch up with a cuppa soon,' Ellen adds.

'Definitely. And hopefully Georgina can make it next time.' As my friends stride away down the pavement with Boots tugging on his lead, I half scan the streets around for any sign of Madeline, but I must have missed her. I was going to play it casual and ask about her weekend away. Act like I wasn't hurt at her treatment of me. But if she's not here, I can't do any of that. I'm destined to spend another day wondering and brooding.

Wearily, I turn away from the gates and head back to the car, more slowly this time. Monday's my day off, so I don't have to rush to the salon. Up ahead, a familiar looking vehicle comes down the road – a dark-green delivery van. *Madeline's* dark-green delivery van. As she approaches, I catch her eye, smile and wave. She purses her lips, gives a small nod and keeps going. Okay, so I didn't imagine that. She snubbed me, which means she definitely has some kind of issue. I clench my fists and stride back to the car.

This is ridiculous. I'm not going to spend the whole day stewing about my stroppy sister-in-law. I'm going to drive round to her house right now and ask her what's going on. If I'm supposed to have done something wrong, the least she can do is allow me to defend myself. I get into my car and do a clumsy five-point turn, earning dirty looks from a couple of impatient drivers. Eventually, the car's facing the right way and I head towards my sister-in-law's house, trying in vain to compose myself. But my right hand is shaking and the rest of me is all tensed up.

It takes longer than usual to reach their house, which is on the other side of town. The traffic always seems worse on a Monday morning. Nick and Madeline's home is a large, square, detached Georgian property. I guess you'd describe it as imposing. Toby mentions it a lot when he's trying to persuade me that we should move. I agree that it's a gorgeous house, but I still prefer our cosy cottage. I pull up on the road outside, take a breath and exit the car.

Madeline's van is parked in the drive, but there's no sign of her. I assume she must have gone in already. I walk up the path and pull on the ornate metal doorbell. As it chimes, I try to get my head straight and think about what I'm going to say. But my brain is mush. I'll just have to wing it.

After waiting for thirty seconds or so, I tug on the bell once more. The chime sounds again. Perhaps she's upstairs, or in the loo. I wait for two further minutes and ring again, trying to peer through the semi-opaque front door. But I can't see any movement in the hallway beyond. I knock on the glass and ring one more time before turning around and heading back to my car. I wonder if she's in there, hiding from me.

My first instinct is to call Toby and tell him how she blanked me. But knowing how the two of them met behind my back, I'm reluctant to talk to him about her. I get the feeling he'll stick up for her no matter what I say. And then something else occurs to me. What if Toby didn't ask Nick about her like he said he did? What if Toby already knew why Madeline is acting strangely around me? The memory of their parting kiss flashes into my mind, even though I was too far away to be absolutely sure that it wasn't anything more than a peck on the cheek. But here I am, speculating again. I need to stop this.

As I slide into my car, I suddenly know what I need to do to get some perspective on this. I need to speak to Celia. I was hesitant before because I didn't want to put her in the middle of anything. I didn't think it was fair. But now I feel as if I have no choice. Not if I don't want to drive myself mad. And I trust Celia to be fair-minded. She loves her son, but she also loves me and the kids. And she won't want anything to break us apart. Above all else, she's family oriented.

I remember Malcolm telling me about an incident back when Toby and Nick were children. Toby's teacher had told him to stop crying in class, that he was acting like a baby. But when he got home from school, it turned out that Toby wasn't being overdramatic at all; he was suffering with appendicitis and in terrible pain. Well, Celia marched into the school the next day and gave Toby's teacher an absolute earful about it, reducing the poor woman to tears. Celia is the same with Alice and Jamie – won't hear a word said against them. I love her for that fierce protectiveness. Her family really are the centre of her universe.

I glance back at Nick and Madeline's house before starting up the engine, half expecting to see my sister-in-law watching me from one of the windows. But as far as I can see, they're blank, save for their white cat Minnie sitting on one of the upstairs sills, licking her paws. The house is still. I put the car into first gear, pull away noisily from the kerb and make my way down the quiet street. I hope Celia's home. She works different shifts at the hospital, so it's pot luck whether she'll be there or not. Although she's cut back on her hours this year, so I'm really hoping she'll be in.

Celia and Malcolm only live a few streets away from Nick and Madeline. A couple of years ago, my parents-in-law moved from their large 1930s house to a smaller modern bungalow. At first, Nick and Toby were horrified by the move. They couldn't believe their mother and father were selling their beloved family home. But Celia insisted that the bungalow was far more practical. Their old house had too many maintenance issues, and although Malcolm is really handy, she didn't want him spending his days with a toolkit in hand, or up a ladder fixing the roof and gutters.

I turn left and wait while a woman in gym gear and a high ponytail jogs across the road, pushing a souped-up baby buggy. The woman waves her thanks and I continue down the road, still hardly able to believe that Madeline wouldn't open her door to me.

On the opposite side of the road I notice a couple walking towards me, hand in hand. He's tall and dark-haired with a beard, bundled up in a scarf and thick navy parka. She's small, wearing a stylish red wool coat and black gloves; her hair is long, dark and wavy. She looks so familiar that I almost don't register it. But then it dawns on me – she's the spitting image of my sister! Same height, same face, same way of walking. *It's her.* The hair's a little longer and it's wavy instead of straight, but it's been so long since I last saw her. 'Dina!' I cry, despite the fact that my window is up and she won't be able to hear me.

There's an almighty bang and I realise with a sinking sensation that I've rear-ended the car in front – a newish looking Lexus. I hadn't even noticed there was a car there; I obviously wasn't concentrating. I turn back to where the couple were walking a second ago and catch sight of a flash of red disappearing around the corner of a side street. If that really was Dina, I can't let her disappear. I have to go after her!

I fling open my door at exactly the same time as the guy in the Lexus exits his car.

'I'm sorry,' I say, barely concentrating on him. 'I'll be back in a minute!' I take off down the street after the couple.

'Hey! Where d'you think you're going?!' A hand grips the shoulder of my coat and yanks me backwards.

I half turn and try in vain to shake him off. The man's face is red and he's wearing a look of outrage.

'Let go of me!' I cry. 'I have to… I said I'll be back in a second! I just… I saw someone who I think might be my sister—'

'You're not going anywhere until I've got your details! You can't just run off from the scene of an accident.' The man is tall and broad shouldered, well groomed, wearing a suit. 'This car is brand new! How the hell did you get a licence? You weren't even looking at the road. I saw you in my mirror, staring over there at the pavement like an idiot.'

'Honestly, I'm sorry,' I repeat, shaking myself free of his grip and taking a step away from him in the direction of where the couple disappeared. 'Look, please just let me quickly go and see if that's my sister. She's literally just gone down that road. *Please*. Would you mind?'

'*Would I mind?*' he says incredulously. 'Yes, I would mind. You need to give me your details.'

'I'll only be a minute and then I'll come straight back, I promise.' If the man didn't look like he'd tackle me to the ground, I'd run after them and deal with the consequences of the crash later.

'If you do a runner, I'm calling the police. I just don't bloody believe this. I wasn't even supposed to come through Shaftesbury, but there was flooding, so the satnav brought me this way. This is all I need!'

I feel like crying, but I can't add a police enquiry to everything else going wrong in my life. 'I wasn't going to run off, I just need to… oh never mind. Can we do this quickly then?' I resign myself to the fact that I'm going to have to stay here and deal with this.

He rolls his eyes and mutters under his breath, shepherding me back down the street.

Before moving our cars to the side of the road, he takes photos of both vehicles from all angles. Then we spend a good few minutes exchanging numbers and insurance details. And all the while I'm cursing myself for not getting away from him in time to see if that really was my sister.

Finally, the man calms down somewhat and apologises. 'I'm sorry for shouting at you and grabbing your coat. It's just, it's a brand new car.' He looks genuinely miserable and I end up feeling sorry for the trouble I've caused him. Finally, he gets back into his Lexus and I don't waste any more time. I dash across the road and head down the side street – a narrow residential road with a lot of parked cars – but, unsurprisingly, all this time later I can't see the couple anywhere.

They could have gone into one of the properties or got into a car and driven away. Why did I have to crash into that stupid car? I'm such an idiot. I spend the next twenty minutes walking up and down the side street, peering down connecting roads and into people's windows, trying not to look suspicious. The last thing I need is for someone to call the police, thinking I'm casing the area. It feels like I'm wasting my time anyway. They're obviously long gone. I berate myself for not concentrating on the road. But it really shocked me to see Dina's face again after so many years.

Of course, I only saw her from a distance, so I know the chance of it actually being her is slim. After all, I haven't heard from my little sister in ten years.

Not since she went missing.

CHAPTER NINE

When I finally reach Celia's bungalow, I'm properly shaking, and it's got nothing to do with Madeline's weird new attitude towards me. Did I really just see Dina walking along that road? Or am I losing the plot? I barely even register the fact that the front of my Corsa is all banged up. Things are so out of kilter at the moment that my car accident feels like barely more than a blip. Everything has been overshadowed by that possible sighting of my sister.

But if she's really back, then why hasn't she been in contact? And who was the guy she was with? I guess I should call Dad. Then again, I don't want to get his hopes up.

Outside, the sky is so dark and heavy with rain it feels like dusk, not nine in the morning. Celia's red Smart car is parked in the drive and her kitchen light is on. I see her at the window washing up, her head bowed over the sink. As I head towards the front door she glances up and waves, her face lighting up at the sight of me. Good. At least she's not blanking me too.

I don't bother knocking. Celia is at the door in seconds, wiping her wet hands on a green and white checked apron that's tied over her jeans and grey wool jumper. 'Hello, love, this is a nice surprise. Haven't seen you for a few days.'

'Hi, Celia.' I step into the hallway with its familiar smell of freesias and Pledge furniture polish. 'Sorry I've been AWOL; things have been crazy recently.'

'You staying for a coffee?'

'I'd love one.'

'Come through.'

I follow Celia into the kitchen, catching wafts of her perfume, White Linen by Estee Lauder, as she walks, her neat grey-brown waves bobbing. Passing all the framed family photos on the wall, I catch sight of a familiar one taken on our wedding day. Toby and I are both smiling at the camera as though it's the happiest day of our lives. So why does my stomach clench at the memory?

I quickly shift my gaze to one of Toby and Nick as teenagers pulling goofy faces, envying them their closeness. How did Dina and I grow so far apart? Sometimes I wish I could go back in time to see whether I could have done things any differently. To work harder at our relationship. I only have one sister, but I may as well be an only child for all the contact we have now. If she really has come back, maybe it's not too late to rectify things. Although, once again, it will be me doing all the running because I doubt very much that Dina's come back to make up.

'You coming?' Celia calls from the kitchen.

I gladly move away from the wall of photographs.

Celia's kitchen is homely but smart, with oak cabinets and white granite worktops. More framed photos of the family adorn the wall next to the fridge, but I don't let my gaze settle on them. Instead, I sit down at the round oak table while my mother-in-law potters about the kitchen making us both a drink.

'Are you okay?' she asks, her back to me as she spoons coffee into the machine. 'You look a bit frazzled, if you don't mind my saying.'

'I am frazzled. I just drove into the back of someone.'

'What?!' Celia turns around and marches over to sit next to me. 'Why didn't you say anything? Are you hurt at all? Whiplash?'

'No, I'm fine. I think I'm just in shock.'

'I'm sure you are!'

'Not because of the crash though.'

'What do you mean? What's happened?'

'I think I just saw my sister.' Saying the words out loud to Celia brings up all the turbulence of her disappearance. I bite my lip to contain my emotions.

'Your sister?'

I nod.

'But… she's been missing for years.'

'She has.' I haven't let myself dwell on her disappearance too much over the past decade. Instead, I tried to get on with my life as best I could. Throwing myself into my work and family life. But today has brought up all the old feelings and resentments – my anger with Dad for not trying harder to search for her. The fact that it was all left to me. My fury with Dina that she thought so little of Dad and me to not even bother to keep in touch. My outrage at how she behaved the last time we spoke. And the unnamed fear that maybe something bad happened, preventing her from getting back in touch with us.

If she really is back in Shaftesbury again, I'll have to confront all my simmering emotions. I won't have a choice, and the thought terrifies me.

'Are you all right?' Celia jogs me out of my spiralling thoughts. 'Do you want to tell me what happened?'

I hesitate and then let out a sigh. 'It might be nothing. But as I was driving over to yours, I saw this striking couple walking down the street. They caught my eye. And the woman… she was petite. Wearing a red coat. She had this long dark hair and her face was…' I break off, unable to continue for the moment.

'She looked like your sister?'

I nod. 'The spitting image.'

'Oh, love.' Celia comes and puts an arm around me, giving me a brief, comforting squeeze before sitting back down. 'Did you stop the car? Speak to her?'

'That's the thing.' I clasp my hands behind my head and push out a breath. 'I wasn't concentrating on the road, and that's when I drove into the car in front. The driver was livid; it was a brand new car.'

'Oh you poor thing.' She gets up again. 'Let me finish making us that coffee. I'll put some sugar in yours.'

'So by the time I'd exchanged details with the other driver, my sister had gone. I'm so annoyed with myself for not going straight after her.'

'Did she see you?'

'No, at least I don't think so. Although the crash was quite loud, so I suppose she might have looked over. But even if they did see the crash, they didn't stick around. As soon as I could get away, I scoured the roads nearby, but there was no sign of her or the man she was with.' I let out a frustrated growl. 'Why did I have to go into the back of that car?'

'No good worrying about that now. What's done is done. Have you told Toby yet?'

'No, I came straight here. I think I should call the police, tell them there's been a possible sighting of my sister.'

'Good idea. But, Zoe…'

'What?'

'Try not to get your hopes up too much. I remember what it was like back when she went missing. I don't want you going through that stress again.' She brings our drinks over to the table.

'Thanks, Celia.'

'Do you want to give the police a ring now, while I'm with you?'

'I could, but I think I'd rather go to the station in person. I think they might take it more seriously if they talk to me face to face.'

'Shall I come with you?'

'I don't want to put you out. I think I'll just have this coffee and then pop down there.'

'It's okay, I'm not working until this afternoon. I'll come along with you. Unless you want to be on your own? Don't want to be a pushy mother-in-law!'

'Don't be daft. That's the last thing you are.'

'Good, that's settled then.'

We finish our drinks in record time and Celia peers out the window. 'Looks like it's going to pour down any minute; we should take the car. Shall I drive? You probably still feel shaky after your prang.'

'Are you sure?'

'Wouldn't have offered otherwise.' She pats my arm. 'Come on.' I follow her into the hall, where she pulls on a pair of tan leather ankle boots and grabs her raincoat off the bannister.

We slide into her car just as the first heavy spots of rain begin to splat onto the windscreen. 'Thanks for doing this, Celia.'

'It's no problem at all, love. How are the plans for the party going?'

My shoulders drop. 'Slow. There's so much still to organise and not much time to do it. Especially now that…' I tail off.

'What? What is it?'

I find myself explaining about how Madeline has been acting strange around me – cancelling my nieces coming over at the weekend and snubbing me. I was planning to tell Celia about Toby meeting up with Madeline in our house, but when it comes to it, I can't quite find the words. At the end of the day, Celia's his mother. And part of me feels ashamed that this has happened, even though I know it's totally irrational to feel that way. Also, if there does turn out to be an innocent explanation, then it will look like I don't trust my husband.

'Are you sure you're not reading more into this than there actually is?' Celia glances over at me as she pulls out of the driveway. 'You do seem quite tense lately, Zoe. Which is absolutely not surprising given the stress of Christmas and work and the party. But maybe it's like Madeline said and she was only thinking of you – taking some of the pressure off so that you could have a clear weekend.'

'But if that's the case, then why hasn't she been returning my calls?'

'Maybe she hasn't had the opportunity. You know it's her busiest time of the year at the moment. She was looking forward to her birthday trip away, but at the same time she was worrying because of having to delegate. And you know how hands-on she likes to be. I told her I'd love to help out more with Beth and Freya, but I've too many shifts at the hospital this month. I think I might cut down on my hours next year so I can lend more of a hand with my grandchildren.'

'That would be lovely, Celia. You should definitely take things easier.' I'm surprised and a little hurt that Madeline hasn't confided any of her worries to me. We normally talk to one another about these types of things. But now it seems Madeline is growing closer to Celia, talking to her rather than me.

I try to bat away an unwelcome tinge of jealousy. I'd always thought of Celia as being closer to me than Madeline. Perhaps my mother-in-law is growing weary of me. I immediately dismiss that thought as my overtiredness talking.

'I feel for Madeline, I really do, but she's definitely avoiding me.' I hate how petulant I sound.

Celia doesn't reply and I'm worried she might be upset with me for going on about Madeline. I realise it was a bad idea to talk about my sister-in-law with Celia. She isn't one for gossip or bad-mouthing people. Maybe she thinks I'm being out of order. I need to rectify my mistake.

'Sorry, Celia. I'm sure you're right. I think I'm just rattled after seeing Dina. Ignore me.' I exhale, trying to get rid of all the negative thoughts swilling around my brain.

'Look,' Celia glances across at me again. 'I'm going to tell you something that might shed some light on why Madeline may have been a bit off lately.' She turns on the wipers as rain continues to splatter the windscreen. 'I probably shouldn't say anything, but I'm sure you can be discreet.'

'Of course.' I'm more than a little intrigued.

'Madeline and Nick are going through a few difficulties in their relationship at the moment.'

'Oh.' That's the last thing I expected. 'Poor Madeline... and Nick, of course.'

'I don't know the ins and outs of it – I didn't ask – but Nick confided that they're going through a rough patch. That's why he took her away for her birthday – so they could have some time on their own to fix things.'

'Well that sounds hopeful. But...' I tail off.

'But what?'

'It's just... if that's the case, why would Madeline be sniffy with me? It's awful that they're going through a rocky patch, but why take it out on me? Why not confide in me instead? I thought we were close.'

'You are. But Madeline can be insecure and, given her circumstances, I think she might be a little jealous of your marriage, what with the anniversary party and everything. Give her some time. She'll be fine.'

I guess that makes sense, but instead of putting my mind at ease, Celia has set it racing again. Could Madeline's so-called jealousy have driven her to do something awful, like try to get closer to Toby? Or am I letting my imagination run away with me?

'She was fine with me at our taster lunch last week.'

'Yes, you're right, she was,' Celia muses. 'Well, I'm sure whatever the problem is, it won't last. You girls will make it up. After all, you're family. And Madeline's very fond of you, no matter how she might be acting at the moment.'

I wish I could ask Celia to have a word with her, but that doesn't seem fair. Maybe she will anyway, without me having to ask. 'Thanks. I hope you're right.'

'Of course I am,' she replies jokily. 'You know, maybe this isn't anything to do with you at all. Maybe she's just worried about the appeal to stop the redevelopment. I know she's been worrying a lot about it recently.'

'Maybe.' But I sense that Madeline's problem has nothing to do with the appeal. It's something more. Something personal. I suppose I should be relieved that Celia doesn't know why Madeline's been acting strangely. It means my mother-in-law isn't involved in whatever's going on.

'Here we are.' Celia flicks on the indicator. It's only taken a few minutes to drive to the police station. I stare out of the windscreen in dismay. It's bucketing down outside. Grey sheets of water sluice the exterior of Celia's Smart car, running in rivulets down the icy pavement. 'I hope that lot doesn't freeze later,' she comments, eyeing the weather through narrowed eyes while she swings expertly into a narrow parking space outside the station.

'I think this space is for police cars only. The visitor car park is over there.' I point to a large empty lot a few yards away.

'Yes, but it's pouring, Zoe. We'll get drenched if we park so far away. We won't be long. It'll be fine, come on.'

I feel guilty for dragging her out in this vile weather with me. 'You really don't have to come in. Why don't you wait in the car, stay dry?'

'I don't mind coming to give you some moral support. Make sure they take you seriously. Don't want them fobbing you off like last time.'

We make a run for it, dashing up the ramp and into the drab brick building.

The reception area is empty, and a uniformed officer comes to the front desk to greet us. She looks about my age.

'Celia!' The officer smiles at my mother-in-law. 'How are you?'

'I'm fine thanks, Mandy. How's your little one doing? Her arm healing up okay?'

'Should be out of plaster by Christmas, fingers crossed.'

Celia turns to me. 'Mandy's daughter broke her arm a few weeks ago. I was one of the nurses on duty when it happened.'

'Sorry to hear that,' I offer.

'Could've been worse,' Mandy replies. 'Polly and her friends were daring each other to jump off the shed roof – little monkeys. I'm lucky she didn't break her neck.'

'Mandy,' Celia says, 'I've left my car parked out the front. Is that okay? We won't be too long.'

'It's fine. Sounds like it's hammering down out there. Anyway, how can I help?'

'This is my daughter-in-law Zoe, née Williams. I don't know if you remember, but ten years ago her sister Dina went missing.'

She thinks for a moment. 'Oh, yeah – Dina Williams. Last seen overseas? I didn't have much involvement I'm afraid, but I was sorry to hear about that.' She gives me a sympathetic smile.

'Anyway,' Celia continues, 'this morning, Zoe thinks she saw her walking down…' Celia turns to me. 'Where was it you saw her?'

'Not far. Just over at Bimport, past the ambulance station.'

Mandy nods. 'Okay, hang on, let me get the sarge.'

A few minutes later, she returns with a police officer who I'd guess is in his early thirties. He has fair hair that's flecked with grey and he's vaguely familiar. 'Mrs Johnson, hello.'

'Hello,' Celia and I both reply.

He turns to me. 'Not sure if you remember me. I'm Sergeant Alfie Graham.'

The name rings a bell, and then it comes to me. 'I spoke to you back when my sister first went missing.' I remember thinking he looked too young to be a policeman. Now he looks more than capable. 'How's your colleague, Sergeant McCormack? Give her my best wishes.'

'She retired five years ago. Happily tending her smallholding in Wiltshire.'

'Sounds nice,' I reply.

'I'm sorry we weren't able to help find your sister.'

'Well, that's why we've come to see you,' Celia says.

'Mandy told me. You think you might have seen her in Shaftesbury today?'

'That's right.'

'Okay, well we'll have a drive around, see if we can spot her. It's a shame about the weather though. Chances of her being out in this are pretty slim. I'll get a copy of her photo off the Missing Persons Register. We'll also run a few checks to see if there's any record of her moving back to the area. But that might take a while.'

We follow him into his office, and I spend the next few minutes describing how she looked this morning – her clothing and hair, and also the man she was with. And that's it. That's all we can do for now. Celia and I get up to leave.

It hurts to think that my sister may be back in town but hasn't contacted me. Okay, so we weren't exactly close, and we didn't part on the best of terms, but that was all years ago. I'd have thought she would at least have wanted to speak to Dad, if not to me. I just have to hope that the police have better luck locating her than I did. And if they do, I pray that Dina isn't in the same vindictive mood as when we last spoke.

CHAPTER TEN

I'm twenty minutes early for my appointment so I sit in the busy waiting room, pick up a gossip magazine and start leafing through it absent-mindedly. It's two years out of date and I haven't heard of a single person in it, so I give up and replace it on the end table, deciding to stare out the window instead. A flock of sparrows lands on the frost-tipped hedge, hopping from leaf to leaf. They stay for a good long while until, as one, they rise up and move on to their next destination. Did they just decide to move on, or did something startle them?

Yesterday, Toby and I returned from a two-week honeymoon in Lanzarote. Our hotel was set right on the beach and the weather was glorious. The complete opposite to a freezing Dorset winter. But, despite the weather, it feels good to be back in Shaftesbury. I'm looking forward to spending the rest of my life here with Toby. That is if I can shake this damned fuzzy headache I've had ever since we got married.

The wedding reception flashed by in a blur. Toby was a dream husband, staying by my side and making sure I was happy. Celia and Malcom were the perfect in-laws, dealing with everything at the venue and checking that I was okay after my fainting episode. I danced with Toby and with my friends. I managed to avoid my ex-friend Cassie, apart from a fake hug. And thankfully my bridesmaids didn't kill one another. Even so, I was relieved when the day was over, and Toby and I could finally be alone in our hotel room. My headache had reached epic proportions by that time, but I took some more painkillers, and I lied, telling Toby I was fine. No sense in ruining both our days.

The pain has eased to a dull throb since then, but it's still there in the background, overlaying everything, along with a faint sense that the world is out of kilter. It's the reason I'm at the doctor's today. I thought I'd better get myself checked out. Especially as I haven't told anyone that I'm still suffering with it. Like our wedding day, I didn't want to ruin our honeymoon, so I powered through, pretending everything was okay, dosing myself up with headache pills and staying out of the direct sun as much as possible. But it can't go on like this. I'm beginning to worry that it might be something serious.

Finally, my name flashes up on the screen. They've still got me registered as Miss Zoe Williams. I'll have to change that at reception after my appointment. I head down the corridor to Dr Philips' room. She's been my GP since I was a child and I dread the day when she says she's going to retire. She's always got so much time for me. I never feel rushed or squeezed in like many of my friends say they feel with their doctors.

'Hi, Zoe.' Dr Philips gives me a warm smile that makes me feel a little tearful. What's wrong with me? 'Congratulations on your marriage. I bumped into your dad in town last week; he told me you and Toby were on your honeymoon.'

I take a seat. 'Thanks. We just got back from Lanzarote yesterday.'

'You've got a lovely tan, so I take it the weather was good?'

'Amazing, thanks.'

'Wonderful. So, how can I help?'

'I've got this headache; it started on my wedding day, actually. I fainted. Fell and hit my head on a desk and I've had a headache and felt sick and dizzy ever since.'

Dr Philips frowns as she types into her computer. 'How long ago was this?'

'Just over two weeks.'

'Did you get it checked out at the time?'

'No. It was right before the wedding ceremony and I really didn't want to make a fuss. Not with a chapel full of people and a reception booked and paid for.'

'Hmm, yes, I understand. That's bad timing. But you should have got it looked at straight after.'

'My mother-in-law's a nurse and she gave me the once over. Said I was good to go.'

'Oh, yes, Celia Johnson. She works up at the hospital, doesn't she? Okay. Are you taking any pain medication?'

'I'm alternating paracetamol and ibuprofen.'

'Is it having any effect?'

'Not really.'

Dr Philips nods and continues typing. 'Loss of appetite?'

'Yeah, but not all the time. Sometimes I'm starving.'

She opens a drawer and takes out a clear pot which she hands to me. 'Can you go to the loo and pee into that?'

'What, now?'

'Yes, just quickly for me, and come straight back.'

I nip down the corridor to the ladies loo and hurry back with the sample, nervous about what she might be checking for. Dr Philips takes the pot from me, unscrews the lid, and dips a stick into it.

'Have a seat,' she says, gesturing to the chair. I sit down as she walks back over towards me, frowning at the little stick. Finally she looks back up at me, her eyes wide. 'Well, it seems like double congratulations are in order.'

My stomach gives a little somersault as understanding sets in. 'You mean...?'

'Yes. You, my dear, are pregnant.'

I exhale. 'I wasn't expecting that. Not at all.' In fact it was the absolute last thing I was expecting. I thought she might say 'concussion' or 'brain tumour' or something equally scary. But this… this is scary in a different way.

Dr Philips smiles. 'We can work out how many months you are. Oh, and you'll have to stop taking that pain medication. We'll do a blood test while you're here too.'

I blink several times and try to work out how I feel about the news. At least it explains the reason for my exhaustion and also why I fainted on my wedding day. 'So… this is why I've been feeling so strange.'

'It would seem so. But let me know if that headache doesn't go away within the next couple of weeks. And make sure you drink lots of water.'

Dr Philips asks a few more questions and carries out a couple more tests, determining that I'm almost two months' pregnant. I'm in quite a daze as I leave the surgery. I wonder how Toby's going to feel about becoming a father. He's always said he wants a family, but we were going to wait at least a couple of years before trying. He and Nick work with their dad in the family landscape gardening company and they're busy expanding it at the moment, trying to make it more profitable. It used to be just Malcolm on his own doing driveways and gardens, but Celia suggested that their boys should get involved and make it more of a family business. I'm not sure either of them were that keen to start with, but now they both love it and Toby says it's got potential to be really successful.

Toby has also started campaigning to become a local councillor. Starting a family could help with that dream. At least I'm hoping he'll see it that way.

Outside, the light dips into dusk. I walk quickly through the bustling streets, the Christmas lights and street lamps casting a festive glow over our little town. I place a hand over my stomach and consider the new life growing there. I realise I'm excited to tell Toby. To tell everyone! I wonder what Dad will say. Whether he'll show any emotion over becoming a grandfather. Or if he'll take it in his stride like he seems to do with everything.

What about my sister? I should probably tell her she's going to be an aunt. Maybe it will heal things between us. Although probably not. I think events might have gone too far for that. I sigh and shove my hands into my coat pockets. Thinking about Dina has put a dampener on my news.

I turn off the main road onto Gold Hill and negotiate my way carefully down the slippery cobbled road, its cottages huddled together against the chilly December evening, their lighted windows casting an orange glow across the cobblestones.

Our little house is one of the terraced cottages at the bottom of the hill. It's a work in progress that we're gradually doing up, but if we're going to have a baby in seven months' time, we'll have to get busy on the second bedroom.

Toby's pickup truck is parked outside, and the lights are on in the house. I take a deep breath and stride up to the front door, put my key in the lock and turn it. As I walk inside, I call out to my husband.

'Hi, Zo, I'm in the kitchen!' he replies.

I normally hang my coat on the hook, but today I don't bother, instead walking straight through to the cosy room at the back of the house, the oil-fired range doing a good job of keeping things warm. Toby's face lights up as I walk in. He's sitting at the small, square kitchen table but gets to his feet, cups my face in his hands and kisses me. 'I missed you.'

'Me too,' I reply.

'Wish we were back in Lanzarote.' He gives me a wistful look and pulls me down onto his lap.

'I know. It feels like a century ago. How was work?'

'Cold.' He laughs. 'It was good to see Dad and Nick again. Oh, Mum and Dad have invited us over for dinner tomorrow night.'

'Cool, what time?'

'Seven-ish.'

I get to my feet.

'Hey, come back here,' Toby says, trying to pull me down onto his lap again. But I resist as I want to see his face when I break the news.

'It's actually good we're going to see your parents tomorrow.'

'Oh yeah?' Toby raises an eyebrow. 'Why's that?'

'Because we might have some news for them.'

'News?'

I put a hand on my stomach, but he's not getting the hint. 'I went to get a check-up at the doctor's after work today.'

'Everything okay?' His face pales. 'You're not still dizzy are you? After the wedding and everything?'

'Well, yes I am, but there's a reason for that.'

'Oh no. Zoe, tell me everything's okay.' He stands and runs a hand through his short, dark hair.

'Everything's okay, but… I'm pregnant. We're having a baby.' My belly is fluttering with nerves.

'What?!'

My heart drops. Isn't he pleased?

'That's… that's fantastic news.' A smile slowly suffuses his features.

I exhale. 'Really? You're happy? I know it wasn't what we—'

'I'm over the moon, Zo.' He kisses me and places a hand on my belly. 'I can't believe there's a baby in there.'

'I'm so glad you're happy about it.'

'Of course I am. It's brilliant news. But it's so hard to take in. A baby…'

'It's mad, isn't it. I can't believe it either.'

'Mum and Dad will be ecstatic. And Nick. He'll be an uncle!'

'I wonder what my dad will think?'

'He'll be happy, surely?'

'And Dina… I'll have to give her a call. Tell her she's going to be an aunty. Although she's seven hours ahead over there so I'll have to leave it until tomorrow morning. I wonder if she'll come back to the UK after it's born. I hope she does. I want her to be part of our lives.' I realise that I mean it. It's time we put the past behind us and moved on. If she's willing to.

'So when's our little nipper due?'

'Beginning of July.'

'Amazing.' Toby sits back down heavily, his eyes still wide, his breathing deep and slow.

'Actually, I think I'm going to text Dina now. She's a night owl so she might still be up. If not, she'll see my message first thing tomorrow morning.'

'Okay, while you're doing that, I'll go upstairs for a shower and then when I come down we should do something to celebrate. Go out for dinner, or a drink – oh no, you can't drink now, can you?'

'I don't feel like it anyway. All I fancy doing is curling up on the sofa with a cuppa and some good telly – if that's okay?'

'All right, we'll do that then. I'll order in a takeaway.' He shakes his head. 'Still can't believe we're going to be parents! It doesn't seem real.'

'Tell me about it.'

As Toby bounds up the stairs, I draw my phone out of my bag. Before I can change my mind, I tap out a text to my sister. If she wants to ignore it, that's her choice. But at least she won't be able to accuse me of keeping her in the dark.

Hey, Dina, guess what? You're going to be an aunty!

There's no reply, but that doesn't necessarily mean anything. It's almost 1 a.m. in Thailand, so she's probably asleep. Or more likely out partying. I'm sure she'll reply tomorrow.

I lay my phone on the table, shrug off my coat and put the kettle on. Although I realise I'm not in the mood for tea or coffee. My taste buds must be out of whack. Instead, I pour myself a glass of water. My phone pings. Nervously, I check the screen and see that she's replied.

Congrats

It's not exactly the gushing response I was hoping for, but at least she replied. I need to keep the conversation going.

Thanks. Think you'll be able to make it back for a visit?

The baby's due in July. Dad would love to see you too.

She responds a moment later:

Not sure

From her short replies, I can tell she's still cross. But I'm the one who should be angry, not her. If I can forgive her, surely she could be a little more enthusiastic.

I can pay for your flight home if that helps.

Okay, thanks. I'll think about it.

Wow, she couldn't be any less excited if she tried. I should never have messaged her. I knew it might be a mistake, but I stupidly thought that me being pregnant might make her realise how important family is. No such luck. I'm getting the feeling that she doesn't ever want to come back home. The only way I'll ever get to see her again is to fly over to Thailand and turn up unannounced on her doorstep.

I should give her up as a lost cause. But she's my little sister. I sip my water and try not to let this stress me out. Dina has always been dismissive, hurtful even. This is nothing new, so why do I let her upset me? I put my phone away and try to ignore the prickling tears behind my eyes. Today should be a happy day. I'm not going to let my sister spoil it. Although the rocks in my chest let me know it's already too late for that.

CHAPTER ELEVEN

NOW

After my trip to the police station with Celia, I spend the rest of the day cleaning the house, running errands and speaking to my insurance company about the accident. I'm now going to lose my no-claims bonus and the insurance premium will probably go up, but there's nothing I can do about it – the accident was my fault. Aside from the car, my head is buzzing with everything else. I keep replaying the moment I saw Dina today – that is, if it actually was her. Perhaps I've got it wrong. Sergeant Graham never called me, so they obviously had no luck spotting my sister. Maybe their record checks will yield some information in the next few days.

Normally, if any unusual situation occurs in my life, the first person I would tell would be Toby. I'd have rung him at work, and he'd have made me feel better about it. Today, I didn't tell him any of it – not about the crash, not about seeing Dina, and not about going to the police station. I guess I'm still suspicious and angry with him since his lie. I don't feel the same trust I did only a few days ago.

The children don't go to after-school club on Mondays, so I'm picking them up at regular school-finishing time today, which is lovely as we get to spend extra time together. Often they'll want to invite friends over to play, but I'm thinking that today when we get home, we can make some decorations for the tree. As I walk the short distance from the house to school, I'm thankful the rain has finally eased to a less aggressive steady drizzle. However, the pavement is icy in patches, and I feel like a baby giraffe as I pick my way carefully along, steadying myself against walls and lamp posts.

I'm dreading running into Madeline or Kim in the playground. Their daughters usually go to after-school club on Mondays, so hopefully I won't see either of them. But if I do, I'm not sure whether I should try to initiate conversation and risk being ignored, or simply keep my head down and pretend I haven't seen them. The way I'm feeling right now, I'd prefer the latter option, but I still need to speak to Madeline about the party preparations. She's supposed to be collecting the cake from the bakery, and the balloons and decorations from the party store on Friday, but I'm not sure if she's still on board with it all. I messaged her again to ask if she'd rather I did it, but she didn't reply. And unless she gives me the receipts, I won't be able to pick them up. All I need is a yes or no from her. Surely that's not too much to ask.

Jamie comes out of his classroom first, happy to see me and chattering about his day. But when Alice comes out, her face is pulled down into a scowl, which is strange.

'Hello, everything okay?' I ask, pulling her into a hug and kissing the top of her head. 'Let's walk quickly, get home where it's nice and cosy.' I take each of their hands and we start walking. I keep my head bowed, avoiding eye contact with the other parents. But I needn't have worried – the weather is so dreadful that everyone just wants to leave and get back to their warm, dry homes.

'Mum, today was really bad.' I look down at my daughter and see that she's trying not to cry.

'Alice, what happened?'

'I don't want to talk about it now because I might get upset and people will see and then everyone will call me a cry baby.'

It looks like my daughter's day was on a par with mine. 'Okay, let's get home. We'll stride quickly. Careful though; it's icy.'

Once we're inside and the children are settled in the kitchen with a drink and a snack, I ask my daughter to explain why she's so upset.

'Don't worry, Alice,' Jamie says, trying to sound grown-up, 'I'll look after you.'

'You're a very good brother.' I kiss his round cheek and wish Toby was here to see how cute our son is being. But then I remember that I'm not exactly happy with my husband at the moment.

'Hope didn't invite me to her birthday party.' Alice kicks repeatedly at the table leg until I reach down and place a hand on her knee to stop her. I have a horrible feeling that this exclusion is something to do with the reason Madeline and Kim are ignoring me.

'They're going to see *Peter Pan* at the theatre, and everyone was talking about it today and planning what outfits they're going to wear. And I felt really left out because I'm not going. So I just had to sit there while they talked about it, and it was horrible.' My daughter's face is red, and she looks like she's about to burst into tears at any moment.

'Oh, Alice.' I give her a hug as my anger rises. It's one thing for my friends and family to take issue with me, but to penalise my daughter is downright cruel. 'Who else has been invited? Is it everyone from your class?'

'No. There's eight girls going, including Hope. But it's our whole group of friends!'

Jamie gets out of his seat and gives his big sister a cuddle. He's being such a sweetie.

'Did you say anything about it to Hope?' I ask.

'I did ask her if I could go, but her mum said that she was only allowed eight people because otherwise it would be too expensive. But I'm one of her best friends. And even Cassidy and Ella are going and I'm much better friends with Hope than they are!'

'Tell you what,' I say, getting to my feet, 'why don't I book us tickets to see *Peter Pan*? And then at least you'll be able to talk to them about it afterwards.'

'Can I come too?' Jamie asks, his eyes wide.

'Course you can!' I bop him on the nose with my finger and he giggles.

Alice shakes her head. 'Thanks, Mum, but it'll look really lame if I go with you instead of them.'

I sigh, privately agreeing with her. I know this isn't the end of the world – children can be cruel sometimes. But in this case, I really believe that this exclusion is coming from the mother rather than the daughter. I can't even call Kim up to ask why, as that would make me look like an overprotective parent.

Kim and her husband Thomas have RSVPed to come to our anniversary party, so it's a bit rich that they've chosen to exclude Alice from Hope's birthday outing. That is, if they even still plan on coming to our party. The way Kim's been acting lately, I wouldn't be at all surprised if they don't show up.

There's nothing I can do about it. I can't exactly force Hope to invite Alice. I decide instead to try to distract my daughter from her disappointment.

'Hey, you know the Christmas decorations at the salon?' I walk over to the cupboard and pull out a few items, bringing them over to the kitchen table.

'You mean the reindeer and the tree?!' Jamie cries, his eyes suddenly alight with joy.

'Yes, and the gingerbread decorations,' I add. Alice isn't being drawn in by our enthusiasm yet. 'Well, how about we make some decorations of our own? We could surprise Daddy with some gingerbread stars and Christmas tree biscuits. Look, I got some cookie cutters so we can make different Christmas shapes. And we can ice them too!'

Jamie picks through the various metal cutters, choosing his favourites. Alice grudgingly selects an angel-shape cutter, and we all get busy, our minds temporarily taken away from our anxieties. And while Alice isn't exactly bursting with festive spirit, at least she isn't as sad as she was earlier.

As we combine the gingerbread ingredients, sifting, mixing, beating and kneading, my mind keeps returning to Madeline and Kim. I'm not sure what to do for the best. Instead of feeling excited for the party this weekend, I'm beginning to wish I'd never suggested having it in the first place. Everything feels as though it's coming apart. My husband is distant, my sister-in-law is avoiding me, my dad is in his own little world. And to top it all off, my sister might be back in Shaftesbury after ten years but wants nothing to do with me. The only person who seems to have my back these days is Celia. But even she isn't taking sides. Which is probably a good thing. She's one of those people who never bad-mouths others and always tries to see the good in them. I wish I could be more like that.

'Okay, you two, we need to wrap the dough and put it in the fridge for fifteen minutes.' I take a roll of cling film out of the drawer just as my phone starts ringing. Normally, I'd ignore it while I'm in the middle of doing something with the children, but it's not showing a number on the screen so it might be the police. 'I'm just going to take this, won't be a minute.'

'Okay,' Alice replies, still absorbed in kneading the dough.

I leave the kitchen and answer the call, making my way into the living room. 'Hello?'

As soon as I speak, the line goes dead, just a dial tone humming at me down the line. I wonder if I might have inadvertently pressed a button and cut them off. Hopefully they'll ring back.

'Mum!' Alice calls from the kitchen. 'Are you coming?'

'In a minute!' I decide to ring Sergeant Graham, just in case it was him with some vital information about my sister.

'Shall we put the dough in the fridge?'

'Wrap it in cling film first!'

I should go back in there and supervise, but instead, I put a call through to the station. The duty officer answers straight away and tells me that there's no news yet, and that it wasn't them who called me. I thank him and end the call.

I should probably dismiss it as a cold call, or wrong number. But a tiny part of me can't help wondering if it might have been Dina wanting to get in touch. Maybe she heard my voice at the end of the line and chickened out. It's frustrating, and only serves to add to my anxiety. At least I'm mildly comforted by the thought that if she called once, perhaps she'll call again. Although I can't help feeling nervous about what she might want, given how we left things last time. I can only hope that she's grown up since then and changed her ways. After all, we were still teenagers when she first left Shaftesbury, our relationship awkward and immature. Even as adults, our sibling issues remain stuck in the past. Perhaps if we were able to reunite properly, face to face, things would be different. We could break the cycle. It would be amazing if we could reconnect in a good way and put the past behind us. But with a shrinking heart, I realise that's probably wishful thinking.

CHAPTER TWELVE

NOW

As the key turns in the lock, I experience a small beat of dread in my chest.

Toby's home.

Normally I look forward to his return from work. But things have been hideously awkward ever since Friday. I managed to avoid talking to him too much at the weekend, concentrating instead on the children. And I pretended to have a headache for most of Sunday. But this can't go on. I need to confront my husband about his tryst – or whatever it was – with Madeline at our house last week.

As Toby walks through the front door, Alice and Jamie shoot into the hall to welcome him, brandishing their freshly made Christmas decorations and basking in his feigned surprise that he can't believe the children made such wonderful gingerbread biscuits; surely fairies must have delivered them to the house on unicorns. Either that, or they must have bought them at a very posh and expensive shop.

Despite my ambivalence towards Toby at the moment, we both go through the regular evening routine of supper and bath time for the kids, followed by a bedtime story and then fielding Jamie's multiple trips downstairs for water, or not being able to sleep, and just general delaying tactics. Alice is still upset about Hope's party, but I try to take her mind off the disappointment by getting her to read a book before falling asleep. Hopefully it's working. I want to go up and check on her, but I'll leave it a while longer.

Toby's almost finished grilling the fish and boiling the potatoes, so I step in to blanch some green beans and broccoli. He tells me about his day, and I tell him about my hellish morning. To which he nods but stays silent. He doesn't even ask any questions.

'You don't seem very surprised,' I add. 'Or concerned.'

'Mum already told me,' he says in a blank voice, turning off the grill. 'Why didn't you call me at work?'

'I didn't want to worry you. I'm absolutely fine so—'

'Not the point.' Toby moves past me, his whole body rigid. He takes a bottle of white wine from the fridge. 'Zoe, I was shocked when Mum told me about everything that happened. I was really worried about you.'

Not worried enough to call, I think. But I hold my tongue.

'How do you think it felt having Mum tell me all about your traumatic morning? It was so awkward and upsetting. I could tell she was surprised you hadn't told me. I'm grateful she didn't pry – thankfully she's not like that – but I really want to know why you told *her* and not *me*.'

I didn't anticipate Celia calling him up. I guess I should have, but I was too busy worrying about everything else.

He sighs. 'Are you okay at least? Were you hurt at all in the accident? And are you absolutely sure it was really Dina?'

'I'm fine.' I sound distant, my voice monotone and almost offhand. 'The car's not in such good shape. And no, I'm not a hundred per cent that it was Dina, but if it wasn't her, then it was her double.'

'And the police didn't come up with anything after you left?'

'No. Nothing.'

'Have I done something wrong, Zoe?' He frowns. 'Are you pissed off at me? That's a stupid question – of course you are. It's obvious.'

I don't know how to reply. My guts are twisting at the thought of asking him about Madeline. What if they were having a perfectly innocent meeting and I now accuse him of something awful? Or, even worse, what if it *wasn't* perfectly innocent? I'm not prepared for this conversation. My skin feels hot and my mouth is dry as sandpaper.

'So?' Toby says, pouring us both a large glass of wine. 'Are you going to tell me what's wrong? Or are you going to keep avoiding and ignoring me forever?'

I'm just about to dismiss his concerns, when I stop myself. There's no point in lying about my worries. I've never been very good at hiding my feelings, and these past few days have been no exception. I take my glass of wine and knock back a couple of large gulps.

'I saw you. Last week.'

'Saw me?' Toby looks confused, but there's a faint flush of red on his neck.

'Last Friday I called you at work to see if you were free to meet for lunch, but you said you'd already had your lunch with Nick.' I'm staring hard at him to see his reaction, but he's waiting for me to continue without giving much away. He takes a sip of wine. I notice the potatoes are still boiling and I realise the vegetables are already green mush. 'So I went and sat on my mum's bench at Park Walk. At this time of year you get a clear view of our house from there.'

'And?'

'You were there. With Madeline. I saw you leave together.'

His face turns red to match his neck and, for a moment, he looks like he's going to deny it. Instead he shakes his head and looks cross. 'So?'

'What do you mean, "so"?'

'I was talking to her about the thing.'

I throw up my hands, annoyed with his defensive tone. 'What thing?'

'You know, the *thing*. The thing you were telling me last week, about her being weird with you and cancelling the girls coming over to stay.'

'And you needed to meet at our house to talk about that? You had to lie to me about it?' This conversation is going down a route that I didn't want it to go down. But I can't help the fact that my emotions are getting away from me. I've had a really stressful few days, and the one person I thought I could trust is feeding me some cock and bull story that makes absolutely no sense.

'I didn't lie.' He frowns. 'I just didn't think it was important. It slipped my mind, okay?'

'And you think I'm going to believe that?' I put my wine glass down on the table to stop myself from breaking it, either by squeezing too hard or hurling it at my husband's head.

'Zoe, what is this? Why are you picking a fight over nothing?'

'Okay, so if it's nothing, what did she say?'

'What do you mean?' Toby shifts from one foot to another before draining his wine glass. It's obvious he's stalling for time so he can think of a suitably believable answer. How is this happening? This is Toby, the love of my life, acting like a cheating husband. It can't be true.

'I mean, what reason did Madeline give for being so rude and cold towards me; for not letting the girls stay? She must have told you.'

'It's what Nick already told me. She said that she was trying to be thoughtful. She said what with you working full-time and organising the party, the last thing you needed was a couple of kids to stay.'

'Okay, so if that's the case, why has she been avoiding me?'

'I don't know. I didn't ask her about that.'

'Sorry, Toby, but that doesn't sound right to me. Why would you need to go all the way home at lunchtime to have a two-minute conversation that you already had with Nick?'

'Oh, for goodness sake, Zo!' My husband shakes his head. 'I'm sorry but I can't keep this up any more.' My heart plummets as I wonder if this is the moment where he breaks up with me. But strangely, he gives me a sheepish grin. 'You're far too suspicious and you're ruining the surprise.'

'*What?* What surprise? What are you talking about?'

'Well if I tell you that, it won't be a surprise, will it?'

'Toby!'

'Please don't spoil it. It's our ten-year anniversary and I wanted to do something nice for us.'

'You mean all this strangeness is because of an anniversary surprise?' I'm finding it hard to switch from sick fear that my marriage might be over, to relief that my husband might have been planning something nice. 'Is that why Madeline's been avoiding me?'

'Look, if I'd known that it would cause all this upset, I'd never have arranged any of it. I'm so sorry, Zoe. Madeline's been helping me to plan an extra anniversary treat. If I'd realised you'd seen us on Friday, I would've come clean straight away. The last thing I meant to do was cause you any worry!' He gives me a tentative smile. 'I mean, me and *Madeline*, really?'

My heart is still racing with stress and I still can't quite let my guard down. Not yet. 'What about this weekend? Why didn't she want me to have Freya and Beth?'

'Because I asked her if she'd mind if they didn't come over. I wanted you to have a break. You've been working so hard, and this party seems to have added a layer of worry to everything.'

'It's not the party, it's the thought that you were lying to me and keeping secrets.'

'But—'

I hold my hands up. 'It's okay, I can kind of understand why, now, but you can see why I was so distant this weekend.'

'Yes, of course, it must have been— Oh, shit, the potatoes!' He reaches over and turns off the hob, staring into the pan.

'Don't worry. We can mash them,' I offer.

Suddenly we're both laughing, and he takes me in his arms and gives me a hug which turns into a kiss, which quickly grows deeper. He takes my hand and leads me upstairs. I check on the children, who by some miracle are both asleep, and Toby and I fall into bed. We haven't had sex this spontaneously for months.

Somehow, against all the odds, everything seems to have turned out right once again.

Afterwards, when we're back downstairs having another glass of wine and trying to salvage the ruins of our dinner, I push away the tiny voice that wonders if Toby was being entirely truthful.

CHAPTER THIRTEEN

EIGHTEEN YEARS AGO

I stand on the wooden porch, knocking on the door impatiently, hoping and praying that my best friend Cassie is home. She doesn't have a Saturday job, so she'll either be revising or she'll have gone shopping in Salisbury. I can't wait to tell her my news.

At last, she pulls open the door, dressed in leggings and a baggy sweatshirt, her blonde curls pulled into a messy bun on top of her head. 'Zoe!' she squeals. 'I didn't know you were coming over.' She flings her arms around me and we hug, even though we only saw one another yesterday. 'I'm so happy to see you – French revision is doing my head in. Quick, let's go upstairs before they come out of the kitchen and start trying to be sociable.'

I giggle. Cassie's parents are lovely, and they always show such an interest in me and my life, but Cass hates it when they start talking to her friends. I think she's embarrassed by them. If you ask me, she's lucky. I'd rather have enthusiastic parents like that than disinterested ones like my dad. Not that I don't want my dad. It's just… it's complicated. I follow Cassie up to her bedroom where she closes the door and bounces onto her king-size bed.

The floor is littered with books, clothes and make-up. I pick my way through the debris, slip off my shoes, and sit cross-legged on the bed next to her. 'Revision not going so well?'

'Ugh, kill me now. Can we please fast-forward to July when all our exams are over, and we have nothing but weeks of chilling out in the sunshine?'

'Yes, please. I can't wait.'

'Why aren't you at Waves?' She always does a little wave with both hands when she says it. 'I thought you were working today.'

'I was. I've finished – it's almost six o'clock.'

'Is it? I thought it was about four. I've been swallowed up by revision all afternoon. Don't know why I'm bothering because I don't even need A-levels. It's not like I'm going to university or anything, even though Dad's now trying to bribe me to go.'

Cassie's parents have said they'll give her cash if she does well in her A-levels. They're giving her a thousand pounds for every A grade she gets, and then she's on a sliding scale for lower grades. It's the only reason she's bothering to study. Now it seems they're trying the same tactic to get her to go to uni. I doubt it will work though – she's got her heart set on heading to London and 'making it big'. If anyone else had told me this was their plan, I'd have been sceptical, but if you knew Cassie Barrington, you'd instantly realise that she has the X factor. That certain something that draws people in. She's magnetic, and I have no doubt she'll achieve what she sets out to do. She always does.

'Anyway, Cass, listen, I've got some news.' I lean forward, excited to tell her about the strange ending to my day.

'Ooh, is it about Lou Schiavone and Matthew Dern? I heard they started going out, but he's only just broken up with Katy.'

'I didn't know that. Tell me all about it, but not right now because I need to tell you what happened today.'

She pouts at being distracted from the gossip on our friends, but I give her a fake glare, so she nods at me to carry on.

'Okay, so this woman from the college came into the salon today, her name was Sally something or other, and—'

'From the college? Our college?'

I nod. 'Anyway, she runs the marketing department there and she said she was impressed with the cancer fundraiser I organised.'

'Cool.'

'I know, right. And then she said she loved the piece I wrote in the local paper for the salon.'

'What piece?'

'Oh, yeah, I wrote something for Jennifer. It was an article to go with an advert for Waves. But that's not the important thing. The important thing is that she's asked me to come for an interview for a job!'

'A job? What, you mean at the college?'

'Yep. It's a trainee PR job – that's public relations.'

'I know what PR is.' Cassie rolls her eyes.

'Oh, okay, sorry. It's just that I didn't know what it was at first.'

Cassie laughs and gives my shoulder a light shove. 'So she asked you to go for an interview for a job and you don't even know what it means? Honestly, you're hilarious, Zo. She must've thought you were a right muppet.'

'I did feel a bit dorky, but she was so nice and said she thought I'd be good at it.'

'Did you tell her you're planning to work at Waves?'

'I did. But the job she was talking about seems so amazing. It's all about creating publicity for the college and building up its profile. It could be a really exciting career.'

'So does she actually want to give you the job then?'

'No, I have to go to the interview. But she seems to think I've got a really good chance of getting it, what with the success of the charity fundraiser and everything.'

Cassie nods thoughtfully. 'Yeah, we did make a really good job of that, didn't we?'

'So what do you think?' I really want my friend's seal of approval. 'I'm so tempted to go for it. All I have to do is fill in the form she gave me or apply online.'

'If you think you could cope with it, then I'd say give it a go. I mean, if it doesn't work out, it's not the end of the world.' She frowns. 'Although… what about Waves? Wouldn't you be letting them down? Didn't you already agree to work for them? It might not look very professional to change your mind.'

'I know.' I twiddle a strand of hair. 'Ugh, why are decisions so stressful?'

'Maybe because it's not something you're sure about. I mean, if you were passionate about it, it would be a no-brainer. You'd go for it. Like when Jennifer offered you the position at the salon, you jumped at the chance.'

'Yes, but that was because there was no alternative. It was pretty much my first and only option.' I start chewing the strand of hair.

'True.' Cassie looks thoughtful. 'Well I guess it can't hurt to go for the interview. If they offer you the job and you change your mind, you can always turn it down.'

'Exactly!' I feel a sudden relief. 'I'll just take it one step at a time.'

'In fact' – Cassie gives me a grin – 'you know what might be fun?'

'What?'

'If I apply for it too. If you don't mind, that is. I mean, I've probably got no chance, but I'd love to give it a go. After all, I did help organise that fundraiser, so I guess I'd be just as qualified.' She leans back against the headboard and closes her eyes for a few seconds. 'Oh, this is so exciting – our very first job interviews! We can prep for it together!'

I'm shocked by Cassie's suggestion that she should apply too. The charity event was my idea and hard work; Cassie just helped on the night. But I don't want to come across as mean-spirited. What kind of a friend would I be if I stood in her way?

'Yeah, of course you should apply too.' I try to sound more enthusiastic than I feel. 'But I thought you wanted to go to London and become a famous superstar?'

'Yeah, well, that's the plan, but it would be a lot easier to do that if I got some PR experience. It would give me loads more credibility. I could get the job here and then find a PR job in London. Meet some influential people who could help with my career. It's actually quite perfect. Anyway, I thought you wanted to be a hairdresser. That's your dream, isn't it? And you'd be so good at it. You're such a creative person, Zo.' She squeezes my arm.

I suddenly realise that my short-lived dream of a new and exciting career in PR might be over before it's begun. I doubt whether I'm good enough to get this job when people like Cassie will also be applying. Of course, I'll still go for it and give it my best shot, but – realistically – what chance do I really have of landing it? While Cassie's face is radiant with excitement, my earlier optimism is crumbling by the second, my stomach knotting up with doubt. I hadn't realised how much I wanted the job until now.

CHAPTER FOURTEEN

NOW

'Oh my goodness, Zoe, it's so lovely to see you! It's been far too long!' Cassie Barrington sweeps into the salon, her curly blonde tresses cascading over the shoulders of her pale-pink faux-fur coat. Everyone's head swivels in our – or should I say *her* – direction. She's always had that effect on people. Jennifer in particular is thrilled about Cassie's hair appointment at Waves, and I don't blame her. The salon is crazily busy in the run up to Christmas, but thanks to Cassie's visit, Jennifer will now be able to create some great publicity in the slower months of January and February.

'Hi, Cassie, how are you?' I force out a smile, sure she must sense my insincerity.

'Oh, you know, same old. But, more importantly, how are *you*? I can't believe I'm here, back in our lovely little town!' She dimples, leaning in to kiss my cheek, and I'm obliged to reciprocate, catching a waft of something expensive and seductive. Noticing at the same time that her skin is smoother than my nine-year-old daughter's. The last time I had a proper conversation with Cassie was back when we were at college together. Of course, she also came to my wedding, but we barely spoke that day, or if we did, I don't remember. She doesn't look as if she's aged at all since then. In fact, she looks younger, if that's possible. Fresher. Sleeker.

Our receptionist Mia takes Cassie's coat and helps her into a gown. It's obvious Mia's starstruck by the way she's gawking. Cassie thanks her graciously with a flash of perfectly white teeth, that somehow manage to not be *too* white.

'Come and sit down.' I lead her over to a chair by the window, as per Jennifer's instructions earlier – *The more people who see her in here the better*, my boss had said. 'Would you like a drink? Tea, coffee or a glass of Prosecco?'

'Do you have any Perrier?'

'No, but we've got Hildon. Still or sparkling?'

'Sparkling please.'

I send Lily, one of our juniors, to fetch her drink while I swallow my nerves and face Cassie in the mirror. I'm braced for a lightly mocking smile or some faintly passive-aggressive comment, but her demeanour is open, her smile genuine.

Cassie became semi-famous after she starred in a reality TV show back when she'd just turned twenty. Now she's an occasional TV presenter who also writes a regular column in a magazine, as well as appearing on various panel shows.

She leans back in her chair. 'I can't believe we lost touch for so many years, Zo. But seeing you here again feels like it was just last week that we used to hang out at each other's houses. I really miss that.' Her voice seems to catch with emotion, but I can't imagine how she could be that choked up to see me. Not after how she more or less ditched me as a friend after she got what she wanted.

The emotions are all so fresh in my mind – how she treated me back then: so casually, as though my own life was secondary to hers. How *I* was always the one who had to stand aside to make way for *her* life.

Of course, as I half expected, Cassie was offered that wonderful PR job at the college. She didn't exactly steal it from me, but it was pretty damn close. Looking back, I guess if I'd really wanted a career in PR, I could have pursued it more aggressively. I could have looked for another position and I could have turned down the job at Waves. But I was young, with no idea about how to go about finding another opportunity like that. And Dad wasn't focused on helping me with my education or career – he just let me get on with whatever it was I was doing at the time.

When I discovered that Cassie had got the job, my initial reaction was extreme disappointment and disbelief, followed by a strange sort of relief that I could carry on with my existing plan to work for Jennifer. And, as it turns out, I love my hairdressing career. It's fulfilling and creative and I'm bloody good at it.

But that's not the point. The point is that my then best friend shafted me. She manoeuvred her way into a fantastic opportunity at my expense. Cassie got the job, but only stayed for a year until she had enough experience to land a PR job in London, leaving the college without a backward glance. Then she used her PR contacts to get a place on a reality TV series.

A couple of years afterwards, I ran into Sally Bennett from the college and she confided that she wished she'd given *me* the job instead. But her boss had been won over by Cassie's apparent confidence. Sally told me that after an initial month of enthusiasm (which coincidentally was the same length as the trial period) Cassie had been terrible at her job – lazy, constantly late, and always taking sick days. After she quit, there had been no more appetite or money to develop a PR department, because Cassie had driven the job into the ground.

With Cassie here sitting in front of me, I try to put all that out of my head, but it's not easy. 'So how did you end up coming back to Shaftesbury for a haircut? I thought you'd have a posh London hairdresser.'

'Well, I did, but annoyingly he's gone off travelling for a year with his girlfriend – how dare he, right?' She gives a short laugh to let me know she's joking. 'I'm back here to visit the parents so I thought I'd make an appointment for old times' sake – and catch up with you, of course.' Lily returns with Cassie's sparkling water and sets the bottle and glass on the little shelf in front of the mirror. Cassie thanks her and then refocuses her attention on her flawless reflection.

'So what are we doing with these locks today?' I take a section of her hair in my hands and examine the ends. 'It's in amazing condition and the colour looks great. So… a trim?'

'Well…' She tilts her head and gives me a mysterious smile. 'I was thinking of something a little more drastic.'

'Oh?'

'Like a pixie cut.'

'Very funny.' I look at her luscious long blonde waves and think there's no way on earth she can be serious.

'I'm not joking. All this hair is driving me mad. Plus I need to shake up my image, get people talking about me again, you know?'

Actually, I don't know, but I guess that's the nature of her work. She has to constantly stay in the forefront of people's minds to maintain her profile. 'I see what you're saying, but a pixie cut is pretty extreme. There are so many other styles that would look incredible on you and still make people sit up and take notice.'

She gives a little pout. 'But why do half measures when we can go all out?'

Normally, I love having the opportunity to do hair makeovers. It's fun and rare to get people brave enough to go for total restyles. But in this instance, I'm suddenly and inexplicably nervous. This is my ex-best friend, plus she's a celebrity. What if I screw it up? Although I've never screwed up a cut before – well, not since I was a junior anyway. 'It's absolutely your call,' I say carefully. 'I just want to make sure you've given it enough thought.'

'Oh, believe me, I've been thinking about it for ages.'

'Everything okay?' Jennifer has wandered over to check up on us. 'Cassie, can I get you anything else besides the water?'

Cassie gives my boss one of her megawatt smiles. 'We're all good, thanks. I love the rustic Christmassy vibe in here, it's so cute.'

'Thank you.' Jennifer almost looks flustered, which is a first.

'Cassie wants to have a pixie cut.' I decide it can't hurt to have another opinion.

'Really?' She stares at Cassie critically for a moment. 'With that bone structure I think it would be a knockout!'

Cassie beams. 'I'm so pleased you approve. Zoe here is being a bit of a wet weekend about it.'

'Erm, excuse *me*!' I fake an outraged tone.

'Well, you are! Come on, be excited. You'll cut my hair fabulously and then everyone will talk about it, and I can tell them what an incredible hairdresser you are. It's a win-win situation.'

I inhale as Jennifer gives me a meaningful stare and mouths at me to do it.

I finally let myself be excited about this. Cassie does have the perfect face for ultra-short hair. If anyone can carry it off, she can. She spends the next few minutes showing me photos on her phone of the type of cut she's got in mind, and we finally settle on a definitive style. I ask her if she'd like to donate her hair to charity. She absolutely loves that idea and takes a selfie, which she posts on Instagram to her two hundred and sixty thousand followers with the caption: *Watch. This. Space.*

I feel a little queasy at the thought of all those people witnessing my hair skills. But then I put it out of my mind. 'Okay, because you're donating it, I'll plait it first, all right?'

'Okay, but aren't you going to wash it first?' she asks with a frown.

I raise my eyebrows. 'No point in washing all that hair when you're only going to have a fraction of it left.' I comb it through, plait it and tie it off with bands before reaching for my scissors. I realise everyone in the salon is now watching us. A couple of customers have their phones out and are videoing the event. Cassie winks at them in the mirror. But up close I can see her swallow in anticipation. 'Ready?' I ask.

She nods, and her fists clench in her lap. For once, Cassie Barrington is unable to speak. She blows out a breath as I start to cut.

Once it's done, everybody cheers. Cassie moves her head back and forth, trying to get used to the missing weight. 'Okay?' I ask.

'Yeah. It feels so weird. My neck's cold.'

'You'd better invest in some warm scarves then; there's lots more to come off yet!' I send her to the rear of the salon to get her remaining hair washed and when she returns, she's back to her excited self again. I settle her in her seat and start combing and snipping.

'I just realised, it must be coming up to your ten-year wedding anniversary,' she says, eying me in the mirror, occasionally glancing at what my scissors are doing.

'It's on Friday actually.' I try not to think about the fact that my planning of it has almost ground to a halt. Madeline still hasn't got back to me about the cake and the decorations and she was also going to help me with the room layout. I still haven't put together a playlist, and I need to try on my dress and fit in time for Becky to do my hair. And aside from all that, my trust in my husband is still at an all-time low, despite the fact that on the surface we've kissed and made up.

'This Friday? Nice.' Cassie pauses and reaches for her glass. 'Are you doing anything special for it? Ten years is a big deal.'

As she sips her water, I reluctantly tell her about the upcoming party, praying she doesn't ask for an invitation. If she comes, I just know I'll spend the whole evening being annoyed that she's there. Plus, everyone will be gawking at her and she'll end up being the centre of attention as per usual. I realise my thoughts are mean-spirited and uncharitable, but I can't help them.

'Ooh, a party at the Regis. Sounds like a laugh. Is all the old gang going to be there?'

'Not really,' I reply, trying desperately to think of a way to change the subject. But my mind is coming up empty.

'What about Lou Schiavone? And Danny and Will?'

'Oh, well, yes. They're coming.'

'I haven't seen them in ages.'

'But that's about it in terms of school friends. I don't think you'd know anyone else there. It's mainly Toby's friends and family.'

'Oh, that doesn't matter. Lou, Danny and Will were always good for a laugh.'

I try to summon up the willpower to resist. But it's no good. I scream inwardly as I say the words, 'You know, you're very welcome to come, if you're still here by then.' *Please say no. Please say no.*

'Oh, you're so sweet, but my boyfriend's down too so I couldn't very well leave him with Mum and Dad while I go off to a party.'

'Oh that's a shame,' I reply, hoping that puts an end to it.

'Unless he could come too?'

My heart drops down to my shoes. 'Um, yes, numbers are a bit tight, but I guess that would be okay.'

'You're sure?'

'I wouldn't have offered otherwise.' Although she made it impossible for me not to offer without being rude.

She claps her hands excitedly. 'You'll love Lyle – he's so hilarious. Honestly, he's the life and soul of the party. I can't wait to show him the Regis – he's American and goes nuts over old buildings. It's going to be so fun. I picked the best time to come home for a visit, didn't I?' She sighs. 'I still can't believe you're married and a mum and everything. Our lives are so different. You're a proper grown-up.'

'Did you never meet anyone you wanted to settle down with?'

'No way.' She grins. 'I've had a few marriage proposals in my time, but I can't be doing with all that drudge and domesticity. I'm a career girl and I love my social life too much to give it up.'

'It's just…' I tail off.

'Just what?'

'Well, I remember when we were younger, talking about how we wanted our wedding days to be, and you always talked about having the biggest, flashiest wedding day ever.'

Cassie snorts. 'Yes, I did, didn't I? I think I just liked the idea of a party where I was the centre of attention.'

I catch her eye in the mirror and we laugh.

'Did you enjoy your wedding day?' Cassie tilts her head and gives me an odd look.

I straighten her up again and start snipping at her fringe. 'If I'm honest, the whole thing went by in a bit of a blur.'

'Yeah, you did look a bit spaced out.'

'Thanks a lot!'

'No, I just meant—'

'It's fine, you're right. I found out later that I was pregnant at the time. Which explains why I felt so out of it. I actually fainted before the ceremony.'

'You didn't!' Cassie's mouth drops open.

'Yeah, I fell and hit my head on a desk. I must have got light-headed or something.'

'What bad luck – fainting on your wedding day! I thought your weird mood might have been something to do with your sister not showing up.'

'My sister?'

'Yeah. She was a little troublemaker, that one.'

Cassie's mention of Dina makes me uncomfortable and I stop cutting for a moment. 'Why do you say that? I mean, I know she wasn't the most sociable girl in the world, not after Mum died, but she wasn't *that* bad.' I'm defending my sister, even though I know what Cassie's saying is true. I just don't like anyone else criticising her.

'Forget it.' Cassie waves away my question with a flick of her wrist.

'No, you must have a reason. What did she do?'

'Nothing. It was just a vibe she gave off.'

'Anyway, I think she might be back in town.' I start cutting again.

Cassie looks up sharply and I almost stab her in the eye with my scissors. 'Watch it!'

I lean down to check whether I've drawn blood. Thankfully she appears unharmed. 'Are you okay?'

'I'm fine. You need to be more careful with those scissors, Zoe.'

'Sorry, but you did flinch.'

'I don't think I did.'

'Okay, well, sorry.'

'That's all right, no harm done.' She pats the spot above her eye where the scissors caught her.

My heart is hammering, and I wipe a smear of sweat from my top lip. That was a near miss. But she definitely flinched.

'What makes you say Dina's back?' Cassie asks before taking a few sips of water.

'I thought I saw her in town the other day. It was just a glimpse, but I'm pretty sure it was her.'

'Hmm, I doubt that.' She shifts in her seat.

I try not to let Cassie's words unnerve me. She always loved to stir up trouble and it seems she hasn't changed. I should know by now not to take too much notice, but she's got me thinking about Dina and about her absence on my wedding day. About how my memories of everything back then are so hazy.

'What would *you* know about where Dina is?' I flash Cassie a smile to let her know I'm not accusing her of anything.

She shrugs. 'Nothing. Just… why would she bother coming back here when she's off travelling the world?'

'Same reason as you're here,' I reply. 'Because it's her home.'

Finally, I finish the cut, blow-dry the remaining damp sections and apply some product. I have to admit that it really does look amazing on her. Almost everyone at the salon comes over to admire how gorgeous she looks. But, strangely, Cassie has gone quiet.

I spin her chair around and give her a handheld mirror so she can see the back of her head in the main mirror. 'You look really stunning, Cassie. What do you think?'

She pats the back of her head and pulls a few strands at the front. 'It really is short.'

'It is,' I agree. 'But it suits you. You'll definitely cause a stir. Are you going to post an "after" picture on Instagram?'

Cassie checks her phone. 'Sorry, Zoe, but I'm going to have to go.'

'Oh, okay. Is everything all right?'

'Yeah, fine. Just running a bit late.' She stands and hands me back the mirror, while trying to extricate herself from her gown. 'I've got to meet Lyle.'

Cassie hastily pays, without leaving a tip, and almost dashes out of the salon. I can't help feeling worried by her sudden departure, but Jennifer is reassuring, telling me that I'm worrying over nothing. 'You did a great job, Zo. She looks just like a blonde Audrey Hepburn – stop stressing. This will be such good publicity for the salon. I hope she does an Instagram post soon. Did you remind her to tag us?'

'No, I forgot. I'm sure she will, but if she doesn't I'll message her.'

'Brilliant. Well done, Zoe. I'm buzzing.'

But despite Jennifer's optimism, I'm more than a little uneasy. I don't know how my life has suddenly become so confused and complicated. Lately, it seems as if the whole world is behaving oddly. I can't seem to get a straight answer out of anyone. And after Cassie's strange comments about Dina, my instincts are telling me that something there is definitely off.

CHAPTER FIFTEEN

NOW

'We've run out of Cheerios.' Alice waves the empty box at me.

I slosh boiling water over the teabag in my mug. 'Who put the empty box back in the cupboard?'

'It wasn't me,' she replies, outraged that I would dare suggest such a thing. She looks pointedly at her brother.

'*I* didn't.' Jamie's eyes are wide.

'Must have been the fairies then.' I give my children a stern look.

'What about Daddy?' Jamie points at his father accusingly.

'Don't look at me.' Toby raises his hands in the air. 'I think it must have been the Cheerio Monster.'

The three of them laugh and giggle at the kitchen table, while I continue multitasking, making the children's packed lunches, emptying the tumble dryer and trying to eat a hasty breakfast of tea and Ryvita.

'Right, you two, go upstairs and bring your school things down.'

No one responds.

'Alice, Jamie! Get your school stuff!'

'We're playing monsters with Daddy,' Jamie says, followed by a roar.

'*Now.* Or we'll be late.'

'Do as your mother says.' Toby ruffles Jamie's hair and they reluctantly slope off upstairs.

I instantly feel guilty for shouting at them, especially as Alice has been quite gloomy about being left out of Hope's party. I shouldn't begrudge them a bit of fun with their dad. Even if it means they'll be a bit late for school.

'Everything all right?' Toby looks up at me. 'You seem a bit…'

'Cranky. I know. Sorry.' I get back to folding laundry, noticing Alice's sport's top is still a bit damp. I stick it on the radiator.

'Anything I can help with?' He tilts his head, and I wish I could let go of all my anxiety and be as relaxed as him.

'Just worried about the Cassie thing.' I leave the laundry for a moment and bring my tea over to the table, plonking myself opposite my husband. I'm not usually the type of person to wallow and feel sorry for myself, but I've been doing a lot of that lately. I need to snap out of it.

'You mean her haircut?' Toby asks.

'Yeah, the dreaded haircut.' I shake my head and suck in air through my teeth. I haven't mentioned the odd conversation I had with her about Dina. After a night's sleep, I'm not sure there was anything in it, other than my own paranoia. 'She was so quiet after I finished the cut. Which was strange after her being so enthusiastic at the start. I shouldn't let it bother me. The style really suited her, so I don't know why she rushed out like that.'

'Maybe it was nothing to do with the cut. It could have been any number of reasons. You shouldn't worry. I'm sure it's fine. And even if it isn't, so what? She asked for the haircut. If she doesn't like it, that's not your fault.'

'You're right.' I give a relieved sigh as the children clatter back into the kitchen with their bags. 'Thanks for keeping me sane.' I lean over the table and give him a kiss.

'Any time.' He grins. 'Right, better go. I'm late as it is.'

I go through the usual routine of checking Alice and Jamie have everything they need for the day, doling out their lunchboxes and water and making sure they haven't got any outstanding school letters for me to sign. Finally, shoes and coats are bundled on and we're ready to go.

We leave the house, hunched against the cold wind and spitting rain, and walk the short distance to school. I have another anxious drop-off, trying to avoid running into Madeline or Kim at the school gates. Luckily, as we approach the building, the sleety rain grows heavier, so I keep my hood up and my head bent low, making my escape as soon as the kids have run inside. Maybe I should face them. After all, Toby is adamant that Madeline doesn't have a problem with me. But I don't have the mental energy right now. I wonder what sort of anniversary party I'm going to have with close friends and family ignoring me. I think I'd be tempted to cancel if it wasn't two days away.

For the rest of the morning, work keeps me busy and stops me dwelling on my mounting worries. Instead, I focus on the haircuts, and on my clients' chatter, hearing about their loves, lives and holiday plans.

'Do you want me to blow-dry it straight or wavy today?'

My current client is Jess, a twenty-something medical student home from university for the holidays.

'Straight please. I can never get it as smooth as you do, so I'm going to take advantage of your skills.' Jess has thick brown hair that tends to go frizzy. She's a sweet girl; I've been cutting her hair since she was a kid.

'Straight it is.' I pick up my comb and unhook the hairdryer.

Jess sighs. 'But looking at that weather, I'm not sure if there's any point.' We simultaneously turn to look through the plate-glass window at the relentless rain. 'I'm supposed to be going to a party tonight.'

'You can borrow a brolly if you like.'

'Thanks, I've got one, but it won't make much difference – that rain is flying sideways. Never mind.'

I'm about to say something sympathetic, but as I'm looking out at the rain, a woman stops and stares into the salon window.

She's standing beneath a black umbrella and wearing a raincoat with the hood pulled up. I catch her eye and I freeze, my breath stopping in my throat. It's Dina!

I barely have time to blink before she's moved on, out of my view. This time, I don't hesitate. I drop the hairdryer, and mumble a half-formed, 'Sorry,' to Jess, and race outside.

The freezing air shocks me for a moment, takes my breath and makes me shiver. I'm wearing black jeans, ballet pumps and a black chiffon top, and I'm soaked within seconds. But I ignore my discomfort, frantically glancing left and right in the hope that this time I'll find her. The high street isn't busy, but there's no one around who looks vaguely like the woman I just locked eyes with. Maybe she went into a shop. How will I find her? I head up the road a little way, opening shop doors and glancing in, before moving on.

My teeth chatter as icy rain slides down my face. People are openly staring at me – the mad woman wearing inappropriate clothing in a freezing rain storm.

'You'll catch your death, dear.' An elderly lady puts a hand on my arm as her umbrella strains against the wind. 'Are you all right?'

'I'm okay. I'm trying to find my sister. Have you seen anyone who looks a bit like me? She's got an umbrella and her hood's up.' I realise I sound slightly manic and that these last two points apply to ninety-nine per cent of the people out today.

The woman shakes her head. 'Sorry, no. You need a coat, dear. You're shivering.'

'I'll be fine.' But even as I say the words, I know what I'm doing is ridiculous. At this rate, I'll make myself ill, and it's clear that even if that was Dina, I'm not going to find her like this. Meanwhile, poor Jess is back in the salon still waiting for her blow-dry, and I'm not sure how I'm going to explain the soggy state I'm in.

The woman shakes her head and moves on down the road, occasionally glancing back at me. I'm still looking up and down the street in the hope of spotting Dina when my gaze lands on Jennifer, who's leaning out of the salon doorway beckoning me back inside, her blonde hair being tugged from perfection by the gusting wind. I give one last cursory glance around me before jogging back down the road, heavy with disappointment. I can't believe I let my sister elude me for a second time.

'I'm so sorry.' As I reach the shop porchway, I shiver out an apology to my boss.

'What on earth are you doing out here?' she cries with a worried frown. 'You're soaked through. You're gonna get ill. And you just left your client sitting there. If there's a problem or emergency, you should have told me!'

'Honestly, I'm really sorry, Jen. I'll finish her blow-dry now.'

'Er, I don't think so, babe. Have you seen yourself? You need a set of dry clothes. I've asked Lily to take over for you – it'll be good practice for her. Told your lady that you're not feeling very well. You can go round the back, and I'll let you in that way. Here…' She hands me a thick parka and an umbrella.

'I can't put this on, I'll get it wet.'

'Don't worry, it's been in lost property for a month.'

'Okay, thanks.' I pull it on, luxuriating in its thickness. I take the umbrella and make my way quickly around the block, battling the wind and rain, until I reach the salon's back entrance. Jennifer has already unbolted the gate, and I close it behind me before hurrying across the bare yard towards the warmth of the staffroom.

Jennifer opens the door as I approach and stands back to let me in. 'God, Zoe, look at the state of you. You're absolutely drenched. Here.' She hands me two large black towels and a bundle of clothes. 'Not sure if they'll fit you, but at least they're dry.'

'Thank you,' I reply sheepishly.

My boss rolls her eyes. 'Get changed, and I'll be back in a sec so you can tell me what all that was about.'

She returns to the salon and leaves me alone. I strip off all my wet clothes and let them fall in a dripping puddle onto the floor by my feet. I wrap one towel around my body and the other around my head. Then I examine the bundle of dry clothes – black jeans, a salon T-shirt and a salon sweatshirt – the uniform the juniors wear. After I'm reasonably dry, I pull on the clothes. The fit isn't too bad except for the jeans, which are way too long, but they're fine after I roll them up a few times.

Jennifer comes back into the staffroom as I'm gathering up my wet things from the floor and stuffing them into a plastic carrier bag.

'Well?' She raises an eyebrow. Jennifer is a lovely employer, but she can be quite scary when she's cross.

I tell her about having twice seen a woman who I think might be my sister.

'Wow.' Jennifer motions to me to sit down at the table as she does the same. 'That's…'

'I know, right. But still, I shouldn't have gone running out of the salon like that without any explanation. I just wasn't thinking.'

'It's fine, I understand. Is there anything I can do to help? Did you call the police?'

'I will. Look, don't worry.' I blow on my freezing fingers, then shove my hands between my thighs to try to warm them up.

Jennifer frowns. 'I'm sorry you didn't find your sister. I know how traumatic it was for you back then.'

'That's okay, it's not your fault. I'm sorry it interfered with my work.'

'Do you really think it was her?' Jennifer's being polite. I'm sure she thinks I was seeing things, and I suppose I can't blame her.

'Honestly, it looked just like her. And she was staring at me through the window. Why would anyone else do that?'

'Maybe you should get back out there and keep looking.' Her jaw tightens and I can tell this is the last thing she wants me to do, not with a salon full of clients.

'There's no point. If Dina wants to talk to me, she knows where I am. She's obviously run off because she doesn't want to be found.'

I'm talking as though it was definitely my sister out there, but I know there's a chance that it wasn't. That I saw what I wanted to see. Maybe because it's coming up to ten years since we last had contact. I don't know. After so long, I think it's about time we made up. But even if I wanted to, I'm not sure Dina would feel the same way. If it really *was* her, then what on earth is she up to? Why would she return to Shaftesbury but not make contact with me or our father? What does she want?

I refocus on my boss. 'You should get back to the salon; it was pretty manic out there when I left.'

She waves away my concern. 'They'll be fine for a while without me. Anyway, I've put Becky in charge. She won't take any shit.'

'Good call. There's an hour until my next client, unless you need me to do anything else?'

'No. Look at you, you're shivering. Stay here, have a hot drink and get warm.'

'Thanks, Jen.'

She gives me a brief nod before heading back into the salon.

I sigh, berating myself for running out on my client like that. The last thing I need is for my boss to be pissed off with me. I'm used to being in her good books. It doesn't feel right to let her down. I get to my feet, turn on the kettle and take a mug from the cupboard, trying to decide whether I'm in the mood for tea or coffee. Finally, I take one of Becky's hot chocolate sachets, promising myself I'll replace it later.

I'm just pouring hot water over the chocolate powder and stirring it in when Jennifer comes striding back into the staffroom.

'Oh, hey, Jen, do you want a drink?'

'What the hell is this?' She waves her phone at me, her eyes blazing.

I put down the kettle, unnerved by her attitude. 'Sorry, what's *what?*'

She stands in front of me and thrusts her phone into my hand. 'I don't frigging believe it! Look at this! Just *look!*'

CHAPTER SIXTEEN

THEN

Diagonal sleet comes at the windscreen, blurring the icy roads. I take the car at a crawl along the narrow country lanes, ignoring the frustrated driver behind me who's right on my tail, flashing his lights. Ever since I got pregnant, I've become far more cautious. I'm not about to risk my unborn child's life for a time-saving of two minutes. Mr Angry will just have to wait.

I'm finally on my way to Dad's place to tell him the news. I've been putting it off for weeks, in the wake of Dina's lukewarm response. Mainly because I don't want Dad's lack of enthusiasm to further rain on my parade. It's a stark contrast to Toby's family's response – they couldn't have been any more overjoyed if they'd tried. Ever since we told them we were expecting, they've been calling round and checking I'm okay, buying little gifts and generally being unbelievably supportive.

The other reason I've delayed coming to see him is because his comment at the wedding annoyed me – asking if I was sure about getting married. If Dad had bothered to be more involved in my life he would know that of course I was sure. But I shouldn't work myself up. It's bad for the baby and it won't make for a particularly pleasant visit if I'm in a mood before I even step through the door.

I reach the end of the country lane and pull onto the road where Dad lives. It's only ten minutes outside town – the same house where Dina and I grew up. A modest 1930s property on a main road but set quite far back and screened from the pavement by tall evergreens. Dad has let the bushes grow far too tall. They now block all light from the rooms at the front of the house. I've told him he should get them cut back, but he doesn't do anything about it.

Mum used to be the one with green fingers, and I have vivid memories of the four of us spending weekends outside, planting, trimming and weeding. That was back when he used to laugh. My father has since let the gardening slide. In the summer, the vast back garden would be a jungle if I didn't badger Dad into getting the lawnmower out every once in a while. I used to do it myself before I left home.

I turn into Dad's driveway and Mr Angry zooms past with his hand down on the horn. It makes me jump, and I almost crash into the gatepost. Some people are utter arseholes. I realise I'm shaking and there's a fluttering in my belly. Is that…? Could that be the baby? Or perhaps it's just anxiety caused by that idiot. *If he's upset my baby, I'll…* I sigh, relax my shoulders and give a wry smile, placing a hand over my stomach. I'm already so protective. I need to calm down and forget about that guy. He's not important.

I park the car next to Dad's ancient blue Ford Mondeo and hunch myself against the icy rain as I hurry up to the front door. I still have a key, so I use it and call out to let him know I'm here. Dad comes out of the kitchen into the hall. 'Hi, love. It's coming down out there.'

I wipe the rain off my face.

'Nice to see you with some colour in your cheeks. You were very pale at the wedding.'

'Hi, Dad.' I lean in for a brief hug and a peck on his cheek. 'We had good weather on our honeymoon.'

'Oh yeah? That's good. Had a good trip, did you?'

'Yes, thanks. You should have come to Celia and Malcolm's for Christmas. Everyone missed you. How was Wales?'

'Oh, you know, the usual.'

'And Aunty Caroline?'

'Fine. She sends her love. Want a cup of tea? Kettle's on.' He turns and heads back into the kitchen.

'Just a glass of water please.'

He glances back. 'No tea? What's wrong with you?'

The kitchen is a mess, with papers and bits of old machinery covering the worktops and table. Empty mugs and dirty plates plug the gaps. Dad has always been fairly messy but living on his own has made him so much worse. I raise an eyebrow.

'Don't start,' he mutters. 'I'll have a tidy round in a day or two once I've got this bike engine running.' Dad's only passion in life – since Mum – is motorbikes. He's always tinkering with bits of old engine. Mum never used to let any of it inside the house, and he respected her wishes, for a long time even after she died. But lately, he's let all that go.

'Want me to help clear up?' I offer. 'I could do the dishes and tidy away some of this…' I gesture to the sink area.

'No, I'm in the middle of something.' He tuts. 'Stop fussing, Zoe.'

'What is it you're doing? Actually, don't worry. Shall we sit in the lounge?'

'What's wrong with in here?' He points to an empty seat.

I take off my coat and sit down, knowing better than to object. I swear Dad doesn't use any of the other downstairs rooms apart from the kitchen and the loo. He has a little TV above the breakfast bar that he watches, even in the evenings, despite the fact that I bought him a flat-screen TV for the lounge last Christmas. And the dining room is completely redundant. I don't think anyone has set foot in there for over a year.

Mum used to love it when we all sat in the dining room for Sunday lunch. She would make an occasion of it, with all the best china and glasses. And she loved having Christmas dinner in there too. Every year we would decorate the room with tinsel and table decorations, play seasonal music and light a cheerful fire in the hearth. A couple of years after she died, I tried to recreate a similar Christmas day for the three of us. But Dina was disappointed that Dad had forgotten to get us any presents, so she spent the whole day in her bedroom refusing to come out even when I begged her to join us for lunch. If only she had been a bit more willing to try. To meet me halfway… but it's no good wishing. Not now anyway.

Dad walks over to the sink. 'Water, you say?'

I nod and he pours me a glass before making himself a cup of tea.

'I've got some news.'

'Oh yeah?' He spoons sugar into his mug and turns around, stirring his tea.

'How would you like to be a grandad?'

He glances up sharply. 'You're…?'

'Yep. Due in July.'

'Oh, Zoe.' He puts his mug on the counter and nods, his eyes softening. 'Congratulations, love.'

'Thanks.'

'You feeling all right?'

'A bit tired, but I'm okay.'

'Your mum had terrible sickness with Dina. Not so much with you.'

'I haven't had much. Just a bit at the beginning. On my wedding day actually.'

'Good, glad you're feeling okay. Thought it was a bit strange you not having a cuppa.'

'I've gone right off caffeine.'

'So, July?'

'That's right.'

He nods and picks up his mug. Blows on his tea before taking a sip. I'd thought he might at least have given me a hug or something. But old habits die hard. Dad never has been one for displays of affection.

'Have you heard from Dina lately?' I ask.

'Not for a while, no. Still in Thailand I take it?'

'That's the thing, Dad. We texted before Christmas, but I haven't heard anything since. I tried her mobile yesterday but the number's out of service.' I'm hoping my sister didn't change her number on purpose, just to worry me, or to cut off contact. I wouldn't put it past her. 'Have you got another number for her?'

Dad gets up and reaches for a pad on the counter. 'Here. This is the only one I've got.' He passes it across the table, and I see the familiar digits written in Dad's scrawl.

'That's the same number she gave me. The one that doesn't work anymore.'

My father turns and picks up the ancient house phone from the counter. He painstakingly presses the buttons and waits. Seconds later he replaces the receiver with a frown. 'Hmm, you're right, but I'm sure she'll call once she gets a new phone.'

'I hope so. It's not great to think of her over there with no way for us to get in touch.'

'Hang on.' My father opens a kitchen drawer and roots through a multitude of junk before pulling out a scrap of grey cardboard that looks as though it was torn from a cereal carton. He hands it to me. 'That's the hostel where she's staying.'

I examine the address on the card, written in dad's handwriting. 'Have you got a phone number for the place?'

He shrugs and shakes his head while I try to bring Google up on my phone before remembering that Dad doesn't have broadband or any type of mobile signal here.

'Okay, well at least it's something to go on. I'll go home and see if I can find a number for the hostel.' I stand and gather up my wet coat and bag from the back of the chair next to me.

'You're not staying longer? I could make us a sandwich. I think I've got some ham in the fridge.'

I'm not sure if I want to stay for lunch. Usually we run out of things to talk about after five minutes. I look up at my dad's expectant expression. At his baggy jogging bottoms and old navy fisherman's jumper. At his two-day-old chin stubble and his bloodshot eyes. He's only in his early fifties, but somehow looks much older. 'I can stay if you like?'

He grimaces and slurps his tea. Maybe he sensed my hesitation. 'Don't worry. Second thoughts, you get off and find that number for your sister. I've got this engine to sort out.'

'I can keep you company while you work.'

'I work best when I'm on my own.'

'Fine.' I shrug on my coat and slip the piece of cardboard into my bag. 'I'll give you a ring if I—'

'Yes, yes. See you soon, Zoe.'

He follows me into the hall, almost impatiently, and I wonder if he'll mention my pregnancy again. But he doesn't. Just ushers me out of the house like I'm an unwelcome distraction. It's always like this with Dad. We almost connect, and then it all falls apart before we get anywhere. You'd think I'd learn not to be disappointed each time it happens.

I let the rain soak me as I head back to my car. Dad closes the front door before I'm even inside the vehicle, dripping all over the seat and steering wheel. Anger sweeps over me and I can't wait to leave. I tell myself I'm not even going to bother trying to find a number for the hostel. But I know that's a lie. Dina might be the last person I want to speak to, but she's still my baby sister. I need to know that she's okay. If not for me, at least for Dad.

I'm back home a little over ten minutes later, sitting in my warm, clean and tidy kitchen, feeling a little calmer. A quick Google search on my laptop yields a basic website for the Thai hostel. There's a contact page with a map, address, email address and phone number. I call the number and, after interminable ringing, it's eventually answered by a guy with an Australian accent.

'Hello, can I help?'

'Hi, is that the Lazy Days hostel?'

'It is. Do you want to make a booking?' He sounds rushed, irritated. Like I've interrupted him. His impatience makes me stutter.

'Uh, no. No thanks. I, uh… Do you have someone staying there called Dina Williams? She's my sister and I can't get through on—'

'You mean Dee?'

'Short, with long brown hair, blue eyes.'

'Yeah. English chick. Worked here last year. Bolshy.'

That sounds like Dina. 'I didn't realise she worked there. Is she around? Can I talk to her? Tell her it's Zoe.'

'Like I said, she worked here last year, but she's not here anymore.'

'Oh. Well, do you know where she went? Do you have a forwarding address or number?'

'All I know is she said she was heading home to the UK.'

'Really? The UK?' He must be mistaken. 'Do you know when that was? Was it before Christmas?'

'Way before that. Can't remember exactly, but it was months ago.'

Months ago? That doesn't sound right. 'Would anyone else there have an address for her? It's just… her phone isn't working, and I haven't been able to get in touch.'

'No, none of us knew any more than what she told us.'

'Can you ask around? See if she mentioned a place to anyone else?'

His sigh travels down the phone line.

'Please.'

'Let me have your number. I'll ask, but I doubt anyone knows. No offence but she wasn't exactly the most likable person.'

'Oh, right.' Back home, Dina always had a chip on her shoulder. She was never easy to get on with. But I somehow assumed that after she went off travelling, she'd managed to find some peace. That she was off having fun. I'm a little sad to discover she hadn't been liked. At least not by these guys. Sure, her messages to me are never particularly long. And they're mainly in response to me checking to see if she's okay. But I always imagined she was having a good time – making friends, having amazing experiences, maybe even finding love or romance. To hear this guy speak so badly of her makes me feel a bit sad, and defensive on her behalf.

'Sorry,' the man sounds apologetic. 'You're her sister, I shouldn't have said that.'

'I know she might not be the most outgoing person in the world but, like you said, she is my sister, so I'd like to know that she's okay.'

'Yeah, of course. I'll ask around. I'm Matt, by the way. What's your number?'

I give him my details and hang up, not holding out much hope that he'll call me back. I wonder if it's true that she came back to the UK last year. Or maybe it's just what she told him. If they weren't friends, then it's quite probable she lied about coming home. When I last spoke to Dina before the wedding, she was apologetic about not being able to fly back, so I'm sure she was still in Thailand. But what if she was lying to me? What if she's in England and she doesn't want me to know?

CHAPTER SEVENTEEN

NOW

I take the phone from Jennifer and look down at the screen. It's Cassie's regular online magazine column. My heart plummets as I read the headline:

When Hairdressers Attack

Below are side-by-side colour photos of Cassie Barrington – one of her looking happy and glamorous with her long golden locks. The other of her wearing a crumpled sweatshirt and no make-up, looking glum with her new short haircut that's completely messed up and un-styled. My whole body fills with reluctant understanding and dread as I start to read:

It's everyone's worst nightmare, and this week it happened to me. Not so much a bad hair day, as a catastrophic one. It happened when I was back visiting my cosy little hometown of Shaftesbury in Dorset, super-excited to catch up with my school pals and visit all my childhood haunts. I love living in London, but I've been yearning for a bit of simplicity, not to mention my dad's home-cooked meals (he's a far better cook than my mother – sorry, Mum, but you know it's true). I've been eating out locally, shopping in cute country boutiques, and I thought while I'm here, I'd visit one of the hairdressing salons – support local businesses, and all that jazz.

I was a little nervous to place my trust in someone else's scissors, as my own stylist has been cutting my hair for years. You know how it is when you find a good one – you never let them go, you'd follow them to the ends of the earth! Anyway, this particular local salon has a great rating online and I've known some of the staff for years, which is part of the reason why I decided to go there in the first place – I knew it would be good for their business to have a customer like me, someone who's in the public eye.

What I wasn't expecting was that their jealousy of my success would lead to the situation in which I now find myself. That is, without my trademark mane of hair that I've had since I was a teen. I'm not ashamed to say that I'm crying as I type this.

Although I'm still freezing from my earlier soaking, I feel myself break out into a horrified sweat. I daren't look up at Jennifer, but I feel her distressed gaze boring into me. At this point I'm not sure if I want to continue reading. But of course I have no choice but to keep going.

It's probably my own fault for being so naive and trusting. The stylist they assigned me obviously wanted to make a name for herself by doing something bold and creative. She intimated that it would be good for my image to get a pixie cut, that people would love it, that I had "just the right bone structure to carry it off". It was clear she thought my current style was out of date and I needed something "fresh and exciting".

I can't let the salon carry all of the blame as I stupidly let myself be talked into the makeover. But I'm writing this week's column to serve as a warning to my readers against those hairdressers who think they know best and want to impose their thoughtless creative ideas onto poor unsuspecting customers. The whole thing has left me with a bad taste in my mouth and the feeling that I was taken advantage of. Not to mention the fact that it cost me a pretty penny too.

But never fear, you know me, I don't stay glum for long. I'm sure next week's column will be cheerier. Perhaps I'll do a piece on wig shops. What do you think?

As always, love and peace,
Cassie x

I read it through twice before lifting my gaze to face Jennifer, who looks furiously close to tears, her eyes bright, her mouth pulled into a thin line. The piece is basically a hatchet job on an unnamed Shaftesbury salon, but everyone locally will know she's referring to Waves. *The absolute nerve of the woman.* I feel physically sick as I hand Jennifer's phone back to her.

'I'll call her,' I offer. Although the thought of speaking to Cassie right now has me feeling even sicker.

'It won't do any good.' Jennifer looks down at her phone again before switching it off in disgust. 'It's out there now. I'd be surprised if we get any new bookings after that.'

'Everyone who knows us will know it's all lies. The magazine can print a retraction. An apology. You could sue or, even better, contact a rival magazine. I bet they'd love to do a piece on your side of the story.'

Jennifer gives a bitter laugh and shakes her head. 'That will only give her more oxygen. I'd rather just ignore it and let the whole thing die down.'

'What a bitch. You know that it never happened like that. I was against the pixie cut from the start.'

'I know you were, Zoe. But she's your friend. You've known her for years, haven't you?' I'm starting to get an inkling that Jennifer might hold me partially responsible for what's happened.

'Cassie used to be my friend a long time ago, until she shafted me when we were at college.' I never told Jennifer how Cassie ruined our friendship to further her career – mainly because it would have involved me potentially turning down my apprentice-ship at the salon.

'So you knew what she was like?' Jennifer's eyes narrow.

'Yes, which is why, when I saw her in the appointment book, I asked if someone else could take her as a client. Although I had no idea she'd pull something as vile as this.'

Jennifer purses her lips, thinking for a moment. 'Do you think this was all just some scheme to get back at you?'

'I honestly don't know. But I've never done a single bad thing to her, if that's what you're thinking. If anything, I should be the one to be upset with her, not the other way around.'

Jennifer throws her hands up in the air and gets to her feet. 'You know what, I'm not interested in your childhood vendetta. All I know is that I've spent years building up a business, and now it's being trashed by your ridiculous squabble.'

I take a breath, shocked by Jennifer's outburst. And yet, I can't blame her. I'd be upset if it was my business being bad-mouthed with no cause. 'I'm so sorry.'

'Well it's a bit late for that.'

'At least the piece doesn't mention Waves by name. There are over half a dozen salons in the area. No one will even know which one it is.'

'Oh come on, you don't believe that any more than I do. Half the town saw Cassie bloody Barrington in here.'

Only because you insisted I put her by the window, I think to myself. My shoulders slump and in my head I curse Cassie. Why does she always have it in for me?

'Anyway, I'd better get back out there.' Jennifer walks towards the salon, her back rigid.

'I'm so sorry, Jen.'

She shrugs without turning around and I feel like absolute crap. I try to work out whether this was my fault or not. Should I have warned Jennifer not to let Cassie into the salon? *No.* No one could have predicted that she'd do something like this. The woman is a menace.

I follow Jennifer back out into the salon, head to the reception desk and type Cassie's name into the client database. Her details come up on screen and I compare her phone number to the old one of hers I have in my phone. It's the same number so I return to the staffroom and bang out a text:

Cassie, that's not what happened, and you know it.

Unsurprisingly, she doesn't respond.

I'm still holding my phone when it rings, making me jump. I have a fleeting hope that maybe it's her. But, no. It's Celia. I think about ignoring it as I don't feel up to chatting right now. But maybe what I need is a friendly voice, so I take a breath and hit reply.

'Hi, Celia. How are you?'

'Sweetheart, I just saw Cassie's dreadful magazine article.'

'News travels quickly.' I sound more upbeat than I feel.

'I know. Pauline from Neighbourhood Watch emailed it to me. I think she took a small amount of pleasure in asking if my daughter-in-law worked for a local salon, when she knows full well you do.'

'Great. That means everyone will have seen it by this evening.'

'Are you all right, love?'

'Not really.' My voice wobbles.

'I thought you might need cheering up, so I'm sitting up the road in Angelique's Café and I've ordered us two vegetable soups and some crusty bread rolls. Can you make it? Or are you too busy?'

Bless my mother-in-law. I check my watch and see that I have forty minutes until my next appointment. 'Celia, I'll be there in five minutes.'

'Wonderful. I'm at the back by the newspaper rack.'

I shrug on the wet parka I was wearing earlier, pull on my boots, grab my umbrella and slip out the back way. Maybe Jennifer will have calmed down by the time I return.

Angelique's is buzzing with the lunch crowd, but I see Celia waving me over as soon as I walk through the door. I pick my way through the tables, nodding to various friends and acquaintances as I go, conscious of my bedraggled hair and second-hand clothing, and even more conscious that they might have read Cassie's piece and realise she was referring to me.

My mother-in-law stands and greets me with a big hug that almost has me collapsing into tears. But I remember where I am and manage to hold myself together.

'Your hair's wet. Didn't you use your umbrella?'

'It's a long story.' I hang my coat on the back of my chair just as the waitress comes over with our lunch. I didn't think I was hungry, but as I get a waft of garlicky soup, I can't wait to dig in. 'Can you believe that article she wrote?'

'Some people are just nasty. There's nothing you can do about it. Let's eat.'

I lean back in my chair for a moment and let my mother-in-law's words soak in. Surprisingly, they make me feel a lot better. Instead of being anxious about the article, I should just accept that there's nothing I can do about it and move on. I've apologised to Jennifer, and if she thinks about what happened, she'll know it's not my fault.

'You just need to keep your chin up, Zoe. That Cassie Barrington's a talentless z-lister who has to lie to get a pay cheque. You should pity her.'

'Celia, I honestly don't know what I'd do without you.'

'You'd come to the same conclusion on your own. Now let's enjoy our lunch and forget about she who shall not be named.'

'Deal,' I reply, tearing off a piece of bread roll and dunking it in my soup.

'That's not the only bizarre thing to happen today. I saw Dina again.'

'Really?' Celia doesn't sound altogether convinced, so I tell her what happened earlier in the salon. She listens carefully, waiting until I've finished before replying. 'Your nerves must be shot to pieces. It's a good thing you've got your party coming up to take your mind off all this.'

'Only it's not exactly taking my mind off it. It's throwing up all these strange memories.'

'Oh?'

'You know, of how Dina couldn't make the wedding, and then when she went missing.'

'Well, it seems to me that you're letting yourself worry about things outside your control. If Dina's here in Shaftesbury and she doesn't want to contact you, then you have to respect that.'

'But she's my sister.'

'I know, love. But you still can't control what she does. Likewise with Cassie – you can't stop her behaving like a little bitch.'

I raise my eyebrows, rarely having heard Celia swear before.

'You need to put both of them out of your head and move forward with your life. Forget the past. No good comes of dwelling on it.'

'I suppose you're right.'

'No suppose about it.' She lays down her soup spoon for a moment and reaches into her handbag. 'Before I forget, here are the latest flyers from Madeline about the redevelopment appeal. Can you put some in the salon, and stick one in the window?'

'Sure.' I take the bundle from her and slip them into my bag. 'I'll ask Becky to ask Jennifer – I don't think I'm in the position to ask for any favours at the moment.'

Celia nods and gets back to her soup. 'Needs a little more salt.'

I look around, but there's none on the table. 'I'll get some.' I stand and head to the counter just as my phone rings. There's no number displayed, and I briefly wonder if it might be Cassie ringing me before dismissing that idea as preposterous. I doubt I'll hear from her for at least another ten years. If I'm lucky, that is.

'Hello?'

There's no reply.

'Hello?'

My pulse begins to pound, and the noises of the café seem to fade away.

'Dina, is that you?'

Whoever it is hangs up and the sounds of the café return – laughter, chatter, the clink of cutlery against china.

'Excuse me.' I look up to see a member of staff waiting to get past me. I apologise and move out of the way, remembering that I was heading to the counter to get salt for Celia. Now all I can think about is whether that was my sister on the other end of the line. And if it was, why won't she say anything? What does she want?

CHAPTER EIGHTEEN

NOW

With the children in bed, Toby and I are in the living room deciding what to watch on TV. I'm in the mood to watch something light-hearted, whereas Toby's trying to persuade me to watch some dark political thriller that I don't currently feel my brain can cope with.

I've told him about Cassie's horrible magazine piece and about the phone call, but I played both incidents down as I couldn't face rehashing them again. I'm fed up with all the uncertainty over my sister and the drama with Cassie. I've decided to concentrate on looking forward to our party and trying to forget all my anxieties. I need to focus on the good things in my life. Ten years of a happy marriage and two beautiful children is an incredible thing to celebrate. If my sister wants to get in touch, she will. And, like Celia said, if Cassie wants to be a bitch, then that's her problem.

I glance down at my phone to see a missed call from my dad. I click on his voicemail message.

'Hello, Zoe. Just checking in to see how you're doing. Haven't heard from you in a while.'

As Toby is still scrolling through the Netflix menu, I give my dad a call.

'Hi, Dad, got your message.'

'You okay? You sound a bit... down.'

'I'm okay, just tired.'

'You sure that's all it is?'

'Yeah, of course.' It's not like Dad to be overly concerned. 'Are you still coming to the party on Friday? I know parties aren't really your thing, so you don't have to come if you don't want to, but it would be good to see you there.'

'Of course I'll be there. I can sit in the bar and read the paper.'

I give a wry laugh. 'Perfect.'

'All right. Got to go. My dinner's ready and the microwave's beeping at me.'

'Okay, Dad. See you Friday.' I end the call and feel a pang of something. A longing for more simple childhood days. For the times when we used to have family trips out to the beach, and picnics in the park. When Dad would bring home fish and chips after work and Mum would call him her hero. For the times when I never questioned the love and security I felt at home with my parents. I just assumed it would carry on forever. Until it didn't.

Toby's still focused on the TV. 'Everything all right?' he asks distractedly.

'Yeah, fine. Just gave Dad a quick call.'

'He okay?'

'Yeah.' I sigh and lean back into the sofa. 'So? What are we watching? Did you find any comedies?'

Toby points the remote at the television and clicks it off. 'No.'

'I really don't want to watch anything depressing.'

'Me neither. I think we should forget the TV and go out.' He looks at me, waiting for an answer.

'*Out?*' This is unexpected. 'But dinner's in the oven.'

'So? We'll save it for tomorrow.'

'What about the kids? We can't just abandon them.'

'I'll ask Mum to come over. She's always offering to babysit, and we never take her up on it.'

In my head I run through all the reasons why we shouldn't go out tonight. The main one is blindingly obvious. 'We're bound to run into people who've heard about Cassie-gate. It'll be so embarrassing.'

'Who cares what people have heard? We know it's all a pack of lies, and anyone who matters will know that too.'

'I don't think I can face it.' I shrink down into the sofa.

'Zoe, this isn't like you. Look, the party's on Friday so you'll see everyone there anyway. May as well go out now and get used to it. But I really don't think you need to worry – people are more interested in their own lives than in ours.'

I know he's probably right. I wonder at how our lifestyle has changed so much over the years. When we were younger there was never any hesitation about whether or not we should go out, no matter what the drama – and there was always something or other going on. 'Where would you want to go?' I ask.

'I don't know… doesn't matter… the Cross Keys?'

'The pub down the road? Hardly seems worth it.'

'It's a change of scenery, Zo, and the food's great. Come on. You need cheering up.'

'Is it that obvious?'

'Yes, it is. It's our anniversary on Friday; we should be excited about life, not miserable.' He gets to his feet and holds out his hand. 'Come on, where's the Zoe I know and love? The one who's always up for a laugh?'

I wonder where she is too. After a moment, I take his hand and let him haul me up off the sofa. I give him a small smile, a bubble of nervousness building in my chest. 'You're right. Let's do it.'

'Yes! Okay. I'll call Mum.'

'I'll go upstairs and put on some lippy.'

Half an hour later Celia and Malcolm are ensconced in our living room with snacks, drinks and the remote control. The children – who were already tucked up – heard their grandparents' arrival, jumped out of bed and rushed down to see them. So Celia declared that normal bedtime could be abandoned, and they could choose a movie instead. Alice and Jamie are now curled up on the sofa, but I'm betting that they'll both be fast asleep within half an hour of the film starting.

Toby and I pop into the living room to kiss the kids goodbye. 'Thanks so much,' I say to my in-laws.

'It's our pleasure,' Celia replies.

'We won't be late,' I promise.

'Take your time,' Malcolm says.

'How was the town hall thing?' Toby asks his mum.

'Town hall thing?' I glance from Toby to Celia.

She shrugs. 'I went with Madeline to meet the planners earlier today. We gave them the petition for the appeal against the woodland development. It went fine, but we won't hear anything for a day or two.'

'Fingers crossed,' I say. 'They need to know how much opposition there is to it.'

'Absolutely!' Celia puts an arm around Alice, who snuggles into her grandma's side. 'Anyway, enough about that. You two go and enjoy your evening.'

'Have fun, you two,' Malcolm says, as we blow them all kisses and head out of the door with a rare feeling of celebration.

Thankfully, the rain has ceased. Instead, the air is fresh and cold, clearing my head and banishing any residual sleepiness. The pub is only a minute's walk down the road, but the narrow pavement is slippery, and I hang on to Toby's arm for support.

'I'm glad we're doing this.' Toby leans in and kisses the side of my head.

'Me too. I'm starving though. Think I'm going to have their mushroom hotpot.'

'Shepherd's pie for me. And a nice cold pint.'

As we reach the brick-built pub, I glance through the leaded windows at the cosy orange glow within. Toby opens the porch door and I follow him into the warm, noisy interior, buoyed up even more by the sound of laughter and the delicious aroma of award-winning pub grub. We wave to Mike and Lucy behind the bar. They took over the pub three years ago and managed to turn it from an okay place to one of the best eateries in town. Consequently, it's always busy. Tonight is no exception.

'Those two look like they're leaving.' Toby nods in the direction of an older couple at the far end of the room, next to the wood burner. They're vacating two chesterfield tub chairs that I know from experience are the comfiest seats in the whole place.

'Quick, quick,' I hiss, glancing left and right. 'Let's grab that table.'

We giggle like teenagers as we thank the departing couple and sink into our newly claimed seats with sighs of bliss. Toby stands up again and lays his coat over the arm of the chair. 'What do you want to drink?'

'I'll have a pint of pale ale.' I unzip my coat and hold my hands out toward the wood burner that's emitting just the right amount of heat.

'And the mushroom hotpot?'

'Yeah; and get some crisps for while we're waiting.' I giggle again, feeling giddy with our sudden escape from domesticity.

While Toby's at the bar putting in our order and chatting to Mike, I glance around to see if I can recognise anyone. There are a few semi-familiar faces, but no one I know that well. I'm finally warm enough to wriggle out of my coat. I resist the urge to look at my phone. Tonight is about relaxing. Before too long, Toby returns with our beers. We clink pint glasses and take long sips. He drops two bags of salt and vinegar crisps onto the table and I tear one of them open and take a handful.

'Well, this is nice,' I remark.

'Yeah, definitely one of my better ideas.' Toby grins. 'Are we *good*?'

I frown. '*Good?*'

'Yeah, you know, after the whole Madeline thing.'

I feel my blood pressure rising just at the mention of her name. 'Shall we not talk about that tonight?'

'Fine by me. But…' He hesitates. 'I was going to tell you about the surprise.'

'What surprise?'

'You know, the one I was talking to Madeline about that day.'

'Oh.' I've been trying to put that day out of my head. I hadn't been sure if Toby was being entirely truthful, or whether he was making up a 'surprise' to throw me off the scent of whatever else they might have been doing. Thinking about the whole incident was making my head hurt. I decided that I preferred to forget about it and give him the benefit of the doubt. After all, I really couldn't picture him and Madeline together. I couldn't imagine him betraying me, as well as his brother. It would be beyond reprehensible.

It seems that all our topics of conversation tonight are going to be minefields. Perhaps we should have stayed in and watched TV after all.

'Okay. So, what's the surprise?' I take a sip of my beer and wish there was no surprise at all, and that he'd never had to meet up with my sister-in-law.

'It's a good one,' he reassures me, sensing my distrust. 'As well as our party on the Friday night, we're going to have a posh mini-break! We're booked in to stay at the hotel for two nights, along with Madeline, Nick, and my mum and dad. And Mum's booked treatments at the spa on the Saturday afternoon for you, me, Madeline and Nick!' He pauses while he waits for me to digest the news. 'So? What do you think? Madeline helped Mum to book it all.'

'Wow.' I realise that came out sounding less than excited. Ordinarily, this would be an incredible surprise. A real treat. Right now, it feels like too much. But I can't let Toby see how I'm feeling, so I take a breath and try to act really happy. 'Toby, that's amazing! Thank you.'

'So, you like the surprise?'

'I love it.'

'Are you sure?'

'Yes, thank you so much. Just one thing – what about Alice and Jamie? We can't very well leave them on their own all weekend. I know your Aunty Vivian has said she'll miss the party and take care of the kids for the evening, but what happens after that? We can't expect her to have them for the whole weekend.'

'All sorted.'

'Really?'

'Yep. Aunty Viv has already agreed to it. Which also means we don't have to pack up a load of stuff for them.'

'That's so good of her.'

'I know.'

Viv is Celia's sister. She lives just over an hour away in Poole. She's widowed with no children of her own, but she's great with Alice and Jamie, so that's perfect. Luckily, I'd already booked Saturday off work, so it seems like everything really has been taken care of. The more it sinks in, the more I'm starting to think that this weekend break might actually be really good fun. I mean, if Madeline is coming away with us for the weekend too, then perhaps she really is fine with me, and I've blown things out of proportion.

'We should probably invite my dad to stay for the weekend, too,' I suggest. 'I doubt he'll say yes, but I'd feel bad if we left him out. Especially as your mum and dad are coming.'

Toby puts the heel of his hand on his forehead. 'I'm so stupid, of course we should invite your dad. Sorry I didn't think of it before.'

'No, it's fine. Like I said, I'm sure it's not his thing anyway.' I suddenly feel a surge of contentment wash over me. 'You're an amazing husband, Toby. Sorry I've been a moody cow lately.'

He tuts. 'Don't be silly, course you haven't.'

I raise an eyebrow.

'Okay, maybe a little bit.' He grins. 'But you've been stressed. Don't worry about it.'

'Thank you. For everything.'

'You're worth it, Zo,' he says softly. 'Happy anniversary.'

'Happy anniversary.' We lean across the small round table and kiss.

'Aww, look at you two lovebirds. Married for ten years and still snogging like teenagers.'

Toby and I break off and look up at a group of around half a dozen people grinning down at us. I recognise a few faces, but my whole body tenses when I realise who's just spoken.

Cassie Barrington is standing before me, wearing skinny jeans, biker boots and a military-style olive-green parka. The whole get-up designed to draw maximum attention to her new short hair style. Her arm is looped through a dark-haired model-type who I assume is her boyfriend and it seems she's gathered together an entourage of old school friends. Thankfully my good friend Lou isn't among them, but I spot Danny and a few other familiar faces who barely make eye contact with me. I can't help wondering what Cassie's been saying to them. Whether she's been bad-mouthing me. A sudden rush of insecurity catapults me back to my schooldays, when I remember her playing these sorts of subtle mind games. I'm too old to deal with all this shit again.

As I bristle, Toby reaches across the table to place a warning hand on my arm. I shake him off as I glare up at Cassie.

'You've got a nerve.' I pick up my pint and take a couple of slow sips.

Eyebrows raise, and a few of her clique back away and lift their hands in mock surrender.

Cassie smiles and shakes her head. 'Chill out, Zoe. It's just a silly little magazine column. No biggie. I didn't think you'd mind a bit of artistic licence.'

'Tell that to Jennifer. That's her business you were trashing. Not to mention my reputation as a hairdresser. You asked for that hairstyle and I tried to steer you away from it. What you posted was a bare-faced lie. And anyway, the haircut looks incredible and you know it.'

'Thank you.' She bobs a little curtsey.

'It wasn't meant as a compliment to you.'

'Oh, come on, Zo. Cut a girl some slack. I was nearing my magazine deadline and had a case of writer's block. You have to admit, it makes for great reading.'

'So you thought it would be okay to step on me and Jennifer to get yourself out of a hole? Nice, Cassie. Good to see you haven't changed.'

'Woah.' She raises her hands. 'I only came over to introduce you to Lyle and buy you and Toby a drink, but I see you might have had a few too many already. I'll leave you to it. No hard feelings on my part, okay?'

'Unbelievable,' I mutter.

She and her group move over to the bar, laughing and chattering – no doubt about me and how I need to lighten up. I'm so angry my hands are shaking.

'One mushroom hotpot and one shepherd's pie.' Lucy's teenage daughter has arrived with our food order and is placing it on the table. 'Can I get you any condiments with that?'

Toby shakes his head. 'No thanks.'

'Okay, enjoy.'

'What do you want to do?' Toby asks carefully. 'Shall I speak to her? Tell her that what she did was bang out of order?'

I shake my head. 'No, leave it. It won't make any difference anyway. She doesn't think she's done anything wrong.' I suddenly realise this is one hundred per cent true, and always has been. That girl thinks she can do anything she likes no matter how it affects other people. She has zero empathy.

'I'm so sorry,' he says, leaning forward and taking my hands in his. 'I was wrong to suggest coming out tonight. I've only made things worse. Do you want to go back home?'

I straighten up and look Toby in the eye. 'And let her ruin our night out? No way. Anyway, this smells bloody lovely. Let's just forget you-know-who and get back to enjoying ourselves.'

'Sure?'

'Yep. I'm so excited about our spa weekend!'

'I love you, Mrs Johnson.'

'Love you too.'

We start eating and I try to ignore Cassie and her cluster of friends at the bar. But it's not easy. Her shrill laugh keeps cutting through our conversation, setting my teeth on edge. Why the hell did she have to come back to Shaftesbury now of all times? This is supposed to be a special week for me and Toby, but now it's been tainted by her selfishness.

'You sure you're okay?' Toby's forehead creases with concern once again.

'What? Yeah,' I answer brightly. 'Absolutely fine.' But my earlier excitement at our impromptu night out has evaporated, replaced by a heavy feeling of dread. As if things are closing in on me. First Madeline, then Dina and now Cassie again. The past and the present converging. The sense that something disastrous is happening and yet I can't quite figure out what it is.

CHAPTER NINETEEN

NOW

I drop the children at school and stride into work, trying to banish the dull throbbing in my gut, telling myself that I'm being ridiculous. That there's nothing to worry about. It's probably just an anxiety hangover from Cassie's appearance at the pub last night. I wish I could just erase her from my mind. The early-morning air is freezing, the sky white with snow clouds. I hope the weather holds off or our guests might not be able to make the party tomorrow.

I finally heard back from Madeline earlier this morning via text. It wasn't exactly friendly, but it wasn't rude either. Just perfunctory, telling me she'll pick up the cake and party decorations as planned. Thank goodness for that – at least that's one weight off my mind. Toby has written his speech, which he won't let me hear before the party. I asked Dad if he might say a few words, but he said that public speaking wasn't really his thing. I'm disappointed, but I have to agree with him – his speech on our wedding day was pretty basic. Just wishing us a long and happy life together. Which was lovely, but I think our guests were expecting a bit more – perhaps an anecdote or two. Luckily, Toby has arranged for his dad to say something at the party instead.

As I approach the salon, I slow my pace, that feeling of dread resurfacing. I realise it's because I'm nervous about seeing Jennifer again after yesterday's debacle with the magazine article. Thankfully, she'd calmed down by the end of the day, but I got the feeling that I still wasn't her favourite person in the world. Which, in my opinion, was a little unfair, as Cassie shafted *me* as much as Jennifer. Anyway, I'm here now, so I may as well go in and get it over with. I arrive at the same time as Becky, who gives me a sympathetic look. But we aren't given the opportunity to dissect yesterday's disaster as Jennifer opens the door for us and ushers us in.

'You girls okay this morning?' she asks.

'Bloody freezing,' Becky replies.

'Fine,' I add, unable to gauge Jennifer's mood.

'Oh come here, you silly sausage.' My boss opens her arms and gives me a hug laced with Dior. 'I'm sorry I went off on you yesterday. Of course it wasn't your fault, babe.'

'Oh.' I put a hand to my heart. 'I'm so relieved, Jen. I really thought you blamed me.'

'No, not you. That trampy little cow Cassie Barrington. If I ever see her again, I'll…' she tails off and laughs. 'Anyway, I bought us all posh coffees and Danishes to banish the evil witch from our thoughts.' She points to the reception desk. 'Tadaaa!'

'Yum.' Becky grabs a coffee and a pastry and takes a huge bite.

'Eat them in the back please!' Jennifer gives Becky a light slap on the shoulder. 'I don't want crumbs all over the salon floor.'

'Thanks, Jen.' I help myself to a coffee but can't face a Danish just yet. Maybe later. Then again, maybe not. I watch as the staff roll in and swoop on the tray like excited starving seagulls.

The morning goes by in a blur of Christmassy cheer. I feel infinitely better now that my boss has forgiven me. I welcome in my third appointment of the day – Georgina O'Brien, a school mum who's been a client of mine for years. As she sits in the chair and I examine the ends of her wavy light-brown hair, she seems worried.

'Everything okay, Georgie? These ends could do with a couple of inches coming off.'

'I know. I'm long overdue a cut.'

'No problem, we'll soon have you looking glamorous for the party tomorrow.'

She seems to shrink a little in her seat.

'You all right? You and Niall are still coming, aren't you?'

'Uh, is it still on then?'

'What do you mean?' I let go of her hair and scratch the back of my head, that familiar sense of dread returning.

'Oh.' Her face pales.

'Has something happened?' I press.

'I thought you'd know about it.'

'Know about what? Please, whatever it is, just tell me, Georgie.'

'Okay, well I might be wrong, but Niall's brother is a waiter at the Regis and he said that the restaurant's closed because they've had a visit from the environmental health department.'

I grip the top of Georgie's chair and realise that if this is true, there's no way the party will be able to go ahead.

Georgie's face falls. 'You didn't know, did you?'

I shake my head. 'How certain are you?'

'Ninety-nine per cent. Sorry.'

My shoulders droop. 'It's not your fault. I'm just glad you told me.'

I realise Georgie has taken hold of my hand. 'Try not to worry.' She smiles at me in the mirror. 'I'm sure they'll sort out an alternative for you if their kitchen's out of action.'

'It's lovely of you to be so positive, but it's peak party season and the do is tomorrow. No. If Environmental Health are involved, then it's game over.'

'I'll keep everything crossed for you.'

We spend the next couple of minutes discussing Georgie's cut, and I do my best to concentrate and sound enthusiastic, but I'm desperate to call the hotel to find out what's going on. I can't very well abandon Georgie to make a private phone call. Not after what happened yesterday, with me running out on a client. Jennifer does seem to be happier today, but I don't want to push my luck. My emotions are see-sawing between resignation and panic. Maybe I should just forget the whole thing. I've been nothing but a giant ball of stress this week. My wedding day was a disappointment, and it looks like our ten-year anniversary is shaping up to be more of the same.

Georgie gets to her feet as Lily comes over to take her to the basins. While Lily washes Georgie's hair, I dash into the staffroom, grab my phone and call the hotel. It rings for a while and then, frustratingly, goes to voicemail. I leave a message asking them to call me back urgently. I also call Vicky, the general manager, on her mobile, but she doesn't pick up either. This isn't a good sign. I've never been unable to get through to her before. I leave another message and also tap out a quick text, feeling my heart grow heavier as I press send. Next I call Toby, but he doesn't reply either. Not that I expected him to. He's probably on site, in the middle of a job. I decide not to worry him by leaving a message. I'll wait until I hear something definite. I try all the numbers again, but no one is picking up.

I don't normally have my phone while I'm with my clients, but I know Georgie won't mind if I keep it with me just this once. I can't afford to miss a call from the hotel. She agrees to keep the news to herself for now and I promise to call her as soon as I hear anything one way or the other.

Forty-five minutes later, I wave goodbye to Georgie and her newly shining locks, and she says she'll let me know if she hears anything more. I now have an hour and twenty minute lunch break, during which I'd originally planned to pick up some groceries for Vivian and the kids to have over the weekend. But I'll have to leave that for now. It's about a ten-minute jog home to get the car and then a fifteen-minute drive to the hotel. If I leave immediately, I can make it there and back with time to spare.

I check my phone, but no one from the hotel has come back to me, so I slip off my ballet flats, tug on my boots, grab my coat and bag from the staffroom and head to the front door, catching Becky's eye on my way out. She's laughing with her client but must have noticed my anxious expression because she stops and raises an eyebrow in my direction. I mouth back that I'll tell her later.

'Zoe!' I'm tempted to pretend I don't hear Jennifer calling my name, but I can't bring myself to do it, so I turn around, trying to appear calm. 'One of Mark's clients has popped in for a fringe trim. He's out on his break so would you mind doing it before you leave for lunch?'

I mentally grit my teeth and turn to Mark's customer with a wide smile. She has a sharp blonde bob, and her fringe is almost over her eyes. 'Of course. Come and sit down.' I spend the next ten minutes trying my best to remain calm and friendly, and not hack into this woman's fringe.

Finally, it's done, and she leaves, pressing a fiver into my hand on her way out. Jennifer nods her approval and I'm able to make my escape.

Stepping outside onto the pavement, my breath hitches in my throat at the icy wind barrelling down the street, stinging my ears and making my eyes water. As I battle my way through freezing air and Christmas shoppers, I can't help looking out for my sister. Although I mustn't dawdle if I'm going to make it back in time for my next client. Why the hell did this health thing have to happen today of all days?

I jog down Gold Hill, the impact from the cobblestones juddering up my legs. Finally, I reach my car, throw my bag onto the passenger seat and drive out to the hotel, trying not to speed, as I know the police are out in force at this time of year. Normally, I'd whack on the radio and sing along to some tunes, but right now I need to get my thoughts in order, so I opt for silence. I try to work out what I'm going to do if it turns out the restaurant is closed, and the party has to be cancelled. If Madeline and I weren't going through this weird awkwardness, I'd ring to ask if she could throw some of her amazing canapés together. She'd do it, I know she would. But with the way things are between us, I doubt she'd even return my call.

Eventually, I turn off the main road and onto the hotel's long, winding driveway. I pull up outside the creeper-covered building, leave the car and jog up the front steps, worried I'm going to find the entrance doors locked. Thankfully, I'm able to push them open and I walk into the lobby, where an extravagant gold vase bursting with red-leaved stems and Christmassy flowers sits on a polished circular table. At the reception desk, an employee I don't recognise stares at a computer screen. He looks up as I approach and gives a genuine smile. That's what I love about this place – the staff are all so friendly.

'Good afternoon. Can I help you?'

'Is Vicky Trentwith in? I need to speak to her. It's urgent.'

'I'm afraid she's in a meeting. Can I help at all?'

'No. I need to speak to Vicky. I'm having my anniversary party here tomorrow evening.'

'Oh, yes, you must be Mrs Johnson.'

'Yes, I'm Zoe. Please can you let her know I need to speak to her urgently.'

'She should be out in half an hour or so. If you go through to the brasserie, I'll get someone to bring you a drink while you wait.'

'Coffee? Are you serving food as well?'

'I… uh.' His face flushes and he seems a little lost for words. This doesn't bode well.

'Mrs Johnson.' I turn at the sound of a woman's voice. 'I thought I saw you pull up outside.'

'Vicky, thank goodness. I really need to talk to you.'

Dressed in a tailored pale-grey suit, Vicky, the hotel's general manager, is about five years older than me, tall and slim, with a sleek conker-brown ponytail. She gives me a bemused look. 'Nothing wrong, I hope.'

'Well' – I decide to launch straight into it, I'm on a tight schedule here – 'I've just heard a rather worrying rumour about the environmental health department, and I need to talk to you about it.'

Her eyes widen and she ushers me past the reception desk into the back office, where a couple of staff sit at desks and glance up as we walk through. It feels a little strange to be in an area obviously not meant for customers' eyes.

'Sorry to bring you back here,' Vicky says in a low voice, 'but we all get a bit twitchy when that particular department's name is spoken aloud.'

'I'm sure. So is it true?'

'Come through to my office.' She ushers me through into another functional room with a bookshelf, a desk and a view out onto a deserted courtyard. 'Would you like a drink?'

'No, I'm here on my lunch break. I don't have long. Didn't you get my voicemails or my text?'

'Sorry, no, I've been in meetings all morning.' She smooths her jacket, sits in front of the desk, rather than behind it, and gestures to me to take a seat next to her.

'So, what's going on?' I sit, getting a bad feeling. She's definitely looking a bit shifty. I think about the nightmare of having to call everyone to cancel tomorrow's party. To explain what's happened. I suddenly feel like crying with disappointment and exhaustion.

Vicky blows air out through even white teeth. 'Look, there's nothing to worry about, Mrs Johnson.'

'So you didn't have a visit from environmental health then?'

She tilts her head from side to side. 'We-ll. We did—'

'What?!'

'But it's fine.'

'Why didn't you tell me?'

She pauses. 'Because there was no point in upsetting you for nothing.'

'What happened?'

'Nothing.'

I give her a look.

'They did a spot check yesterday evening. Found that everything was in order. And then they left.'

I hardly dare hope that that's the full extent of it. That my overactive imagination can now stop conjuring up images of salmonella-ravaged guests and scurrying rats.

'And that's it?'

'Pretty much.'

'So they just showed up out of the blue? Is that normal?'

Vicky crosses her legs. 'Can I ask where you heard about this?'

I realise that Georgie's brother-in-law could probably get in trouble for blabbing about it. 'One of my colleague's clients mentioned it.'

She frowns and purses her lips. 'Do you know their name?'

I shrug and wince at my lie. 'Sorry, no.'

Vicky squares her shoulders. 'Sorry you had to hear about it like that. But it wasn't common knowledge and I'm obviously not over the moon that people are talking about it. But please don't worry about tomorrow evening. Everything will be perfect for you and your husband.'

'I'm just relieved that you're not being shut down.'

'Quite.'

'Is it normal for the environmental health department to just show up like that?' I ask again, as she didn't answer me the last time.

'It's not normal, no. I mean, it happens. But it's not a regular event. It can sometimes happen if someone complains about something, or it could just be a random spot check.'

'So someone could have called them and reported you?'

'Well, yes, I suppose they could have. But it's unlikely.'

My body tenses up and I clasp my hands in my lap, trying not to let my imagination take over again.

'Are you okay, Mrs Johnson?'

'Uh, yes. Fine, thanks.' I make an effort to relax my shoulders. 'And please call me Zoe.'

'Of course… Zoe. Would you like to stay for a complimentary lunch while you're here?'

I check my watch. 'Thanks, but no. I'd better get back to work.'

'Okay, well, if you're sure. And, like I said, please don't worry. Tomorrow's party will be wonderful.' She gets to her feet and I do the same before following her back out into the hotel lobby where a well-groomed family are checking in, their matching luggage being wheeled in on a trolley by one of the young porters.

Vicky and I say goodbye and she hurries off. My earlier adrenaline has ebbed away, leaving me tired and hungry. I'm irritated that I've had to come on this wild goose chase for nothing, that I've wasted my precious time, and now I'm going to have to scramble even more to get everything done before the party.

I march back out to the car, wishing I'd asked Vicky for a sandwich to eat on the way back. I open my handbag and find a couple of Polo mints in their wrapper. They'll have to do. I pop one in my mouth, slide into the car and head back to work, thinking about who might have reported the hotel to the health department. Could it have been a random spot check, like Vicky thought, or might someone have had a more specific reason in mind? A rival hotel? A dissatisfied customer? Or something else entirely?

I can't believe this is a coincidence, not with all the other stuff going on. I don't want to be paranoid, but after what happened with Cassie, I wouldn't put it past her to try to sabotage my anniversary party. This has got her name written all over it. The one person I'm praying has nothing to do with this is Dina. I know we're not exactly on the best of terms, but surely she wouldn't be so malicious as to try to ruin something that means so much to me. *Not my own sister.*

CHAPTER TWENTY

THEN

With my hand on my not-quite bump, I pace the small kitchen, wondering what I should do about Dina possibly being back in the UK. Calling the police would be the sensible option, wouldn't it? But maybe that's an over-reaction.

I don't want to tell Dad my discovery. Not yet anyway. There's no point alarming him. But who am I kidding? Dad doesn't get fazed by anything. I'm more worried by the likelihood he *wouldn't* be alarmed. That he would give his usual shrug of the shoulders and say Dina will contact us when she's ready. It would seem that I'm the only one who actually gives a damn. And I'm not even sure why.

She left the UK almost ten years ago and hasn't once been back for a visit. Sure, she keeps in touch sporadically via text and the occasional email. But the sad thing is, she usually only contacts me or Dad when she needs something. I try not to dwell on that. If she really is back in England, then surely it's an opportunity for us to reconnect. To make amends for past hurts. But I know I'm kidding myself. If Dina is back and hasn't got in touch, then she's even more selfish than I thought. After the last time we spoke, I felt like I never wanted to talk to her again. But she's still my sister. I need to know one way or another, partly for Dina's sake, but mainly for my own peace of mind.

I stop pacing and sit at the table, annoyed by the tears of self-pity and anger that are threatening to fall. I sniff loudly and snatch up my phone again, this time calling the one person I trust to know what to do.

'Hi, Zo.'

'Toby, are you busy?'

'We're laying a patio over in Fontmell Magna.'

'Oh, okay, don't worry. I'll speak to you later.'

'What is it?'

I will myself to sound calm. 'Nothing. I was just seeing if you were free to come home for lunch, but—'

'Hang on a sec…'

'Toby…' But he's not listening. I hear muffled voices down the line, but I can't make out what they're saying.

'Zo?'

'Yeah, I'm still here.'

'I'll be back in twenty minutes. Can you make me a sandwich?'

'You don't have to.'

'I want to.'

'What about the patio?'

'Dad and Nick can manage for a bit. We were off to the pub for lunch anyway.'

'Okay, see you soon.'

I feel instantly better now that I know Toby's on his way back. He'll know what to do. And even if he doesn't, it will help to have someone to talk to about things. He already knows how shaky things have been in the past between me and Dina. Okay, so he doesn't know everything. But that doesn't matter.

I busy myself making us both a cheese salad sandwich until finally I hear his key in the lock.

'Hey!' he calls out.

'Hey, in here,' I reply.

Toby comes through to the kitchen, rubbing his hands together, bringing with him the fresh scents of damp earth and cold air. 'You okay? That sarnie looks amazing. I'm starving.' He gives me a lingering kiss followed by a hug.

'I'm really glad you're here, Tobes. Sit down. Do you want tea?'

'Please, that would be great. You all right? You sounded wobbly on the phone.'

'It's Dina. But it's probably nothing.'

Toby washes his hands at the kitchen sink. 'Oh yeah? What's happened?' He sits at the table, picks up half his sandwich and takes a huge bite.

'Her phone number doesn't work anymore. It says it's not in service.'

'So maybe she lost it. Or got a new one.'

'But now I have no way of getting in touch with her.'

'I'm sure she'll let you know her new number once she gets one.'

I set my husband's mug of tea in front of him and take a seat opposite.

'Are you really that worried about it?' he continues.

I pick at the corner of my sandwich, breaking off a piece of crust and squashing it between my thumb and forefinger.

'Zoe?'

'I'm just… I was over at Dad's this morning, telling him about the baby, and he didn't even seem that bothered.'

'You know what your dad's like. He's low-key. He doesn't make a song and dance about anything.'

'I know, but it's such a let-down. It makes me think about what things would have been like if Mum hadn't died.'

'Hey, hey…' Toby comes around to where I'm sitting and pulls me up into his arms, strokes my hair and kisses my forehead. 'I can't imagine what that must feel like for you, but your dad still loves you, even if he doesn't always show it. And your mum would've been incredibly proud of you.'

'I wish she'd got to meet you.'

'I know. Me too.'

'Maybe if she hadn't died, Dina and I would have had a better relationship. Or any kind of relationship. She's like a stranger to me. I mean, what kind of sister doesn't care about becoming an aunt? She doesn't want anything to do with me! I tried to take care of her after Mum died. Tried to be a mother to her, I suppose. But she just kept pushing me away. Got annoyed with me whenever I tried to look out for her. What was I supposed to do? Just leave her to get on with things herself? She was only eleven.'

'Yes, but you were just a kid too. It wasn't your responsibility. It was your dad's. Stop beating yourself up about it. Right now, she's probably just off enjoying herself and has completely forgotten that you're over here worrying about her.'

'Maybe.'

'Definitely.'

I extricate myself from his embrace and sit back down. 'Sorry for being on such a downer. It must be the pregnancy hormones. Finish your lunch.'

Toby takes his seat again.

'The thing is, I rang the hostel where she was staying, and they said that she left Thailand last year.'

'Oh?'

'Yeah, they said that she came back to the UK months ago.'

Toby takes another mouthful of sandwich. 'Well we know that's not true, because she was still in Thailand when we got married. Didn't she say that she couldn't come to the wedding because—'

'Because she was still in Thailand. Yeah, I know. But what if she was lying?'

'Why would she do that?'

'I dunno. Maybe because she didn't want to come. Because she resents me for some reason.'

'Look, Zoe, I don't know what's happened with your sister. Maybe she's lost her phone, or maybe she's gone off the radar on purpose because she's got issues. But whatever it is, it's not your fault, and there's nothing you can do about it. She's a grown woman. You can't let her selfishness ruin your happiness.'

I hear what he's saying, but Toby doesn't know the truth of what went on. And I can't tell him. 'I was thinking about calling the police to see if they're able to track her down.'

'I mean, you could try. But I'm fairly sure that it would be almost impossible for them to trace someone who's been living abroad for however many years it's been.'

'Almost ten.' I blow air out of my mouth. 'I can't believe it's been that long.'

'Give it a few days. Maybe she'll get in touch.'

'Okay. You're probably right.'

'And then, if she doesn't, we can go to the police station together and tell them what's happened.'

'Thanks, Toby.'

He gives me a smile. 'Of course. I'm sure we're worrying over nothing though.'

I hope he's right.

'Are you feeling any better about things now?'

'Kind of.'

He puts the last piece of sandwich in his mouth and washes it down with the rest of his tea. 'I better get back…'

'Yeah, sure. Sorry I dragged you all the way home.'

'What? Don't be sorry. I got to share lunch with my beautiful wife instead of staring at Nick and Dad's ugly faces.' He grins.

'Actually, Toby, I think I am going to speak to the police.'

His smile fades. 'Are you sure?'

'I'll be worrying otherwise.'

'If you wait till this evening, I can come with you.'

'No, it's okay. I'll be fine going on my own. I'll just tell them what's happened and ask if there's anything they can do. If they can, they can, and if they can't… well then I'll have to think of another way to find her.'

'I'll get Mum to come with you.'

'You don't have to do that. She doesn't need to be dragged into my family drama.'

'She won't mind. And anyway, we're all family now. I'll call her on the way back to work. Bit of moral support for you.'

'Thank you.'

'I'd do anything for you, Zo. You know that.'

He puts his arms around me, and I thank God for the day I met Toby Johnson. I can't wait until we have our own little family. I know you can't control these things, but I'm going to try my hardest to make sure that we all look out for one another, that we communicate, that our kids are as close as Toby and Nick. I want what they have in their family. That deep unshakeable bond that means they would do anything for one another. Dina and Dad and I – we're broken. We've forgotten how to be family. And it hurts every day.

CHAPTER TWENTY-ONE

NOW

It's finally here. Our anniversary weekend! And it's kicking off with the party I've been planning for so many weeks. After yesterday's environmental-health scare, and all my worrying and stressing about how the party is going to go and who's going to show, I've come to the simple realisation that this party is just one night out of my life. Whoever's here or isn't here, it doesn't matter. However the evening turns out, I should just try to enjoy it. It's supposed to be a celebration. I'm here with my husband and I intend for us to enjoy ourselves.

I'm feeling pretty good in my new dark-green satin cocktail dress with matching killer heels and a glitzy diamante wrist cuff. I've left my hair loose and straight – Becky tidied up the ends for me at work earlier today – and I bought the perfect pair of diamante drop earrings to complete my outfit. Our favourite tunes are playing over the speakers while the swing band sets up on the stage, and I sit at a table chatting to Becky and her boyfriend Sam. The ceiling is festooned with twinkling lights, streamers and balloons. Waiting staff weave between guests, carrying trays of finger food and glasses of champagne.

Toby's speech earlier was so emotional and heartfelt that he had more than half the room in tears, including me. I think it wasn't until that moment, where he thanked me for being the best wife a man could wish for, that I actually started appreciating tonight and what it means. Ten years of marriage to the love of my life, a beautiful family, and – if I'm doubly lucky – a lot more of the same to come.

I'm relieved the evening seems to be going well so far, despite not yet having plucked up the courage to talk to Madeline or Kim. Although this is my party, so they'd better not be rude or offhand. Toby's currently chatting to Nick and Madeline at another table. I know I should go over and talk to them, but I'm burying my head in the sand for now. I'll have a couple more drinks before saying hello. I already hugged Celia and Malcolm, who are now at a table with a group of family friends.

I'd have thought more people would have sought me out to say hello. I've already seen several of the school parents – Georgina, Ellen and Liz for starters – go over to speak to Toby, but they haven't greeted me yet. And perhaps I'm being paranoid, but I can't seem to even catch their eye. I tell myself to stop worrying. I think I've spent so many days stressing about everything, that I'm now unable to simply relax. I remind myself of Toby's speech. Of what this evening is about. And I resolve to put my worries aside. To stop thinking about everyone else.

'Toby told me you were staying over for the whole weekend.' Becky lifts a glass of champagne from a passing waiter.

'Yes, two nights of luxury and a spa treatment tomorrow afternoon.'

'Lucky cow. Think of me on my feet all day at work tomorrow.'

'Aren't you both off to the Caribbean over Christmas?'

'Well, yeah, but that's almost a week away. I'm not sure I can hold on until then.'

Sam rolls his eyes. 'I think you'll be okay, Becks.'

'It's all right for you, you've got a desk job.'

'Yeah, but who has to massage your feet when you get home?'

'You love it.'

'Ew.' I wrinkle my nose. 'Too much information.' I know what she means about the workload though – the salon's crazy at the moment. At least Jennifer's recovered from the magazine debacle. She's here tonight and seems to be enjoying herself. She hasn't mentioned anything about Cassie this evening, thank goodness for small mercies.

'Uh oh.' Becky lowers her gaze and then gives me a nervous glance.

'What?' I fiddle with one of my earrings.

Becky purses her lips and glances at Sam.

'*What?*' I demand.

'You'll never guess who's just walked in. Don't turn around,' she adds quickly.

My stomach swoops. 'Please, God, not Cassie.' Bang goes my resolution to relax and enjoy this evening.

'Hmm. I take it you didn't invite her?'

'We-ell…'

'Oh, Zoe! Why on earth would you send that poisonous bitch an invitation?'

'I didn't!'

'So she's gatecrashing?'

'Not exactly. It was before the whole article thing… when she was in the salon… she was dropping massive hints about wanting to come and not having seen our schoolfriends for ages. And, well, I couldn't very well not ask if she wanted to come. You know what I'm like.'

'Yeah, you're too much of a pushover.'

'Becky!' Sam tells her off.

'Thanks, Sam. I prefer to think of it as being a nice person.'

'Well there's nice and then there's masochism.'

'I honestly didn't think she'd come here, not after what she did. I mean, no normal person would do that, would they?'

'The girl has absolutely no shame.' Becky glances past me surreptitiously. 'Oh shit.'

'What?' Sam and I reply in unison.

'Jennifer's spotted her.'

It's no good, I have to see what's going on. I shift my chair around, making sure I'm still partially shielded by Becky. Peering beyond my friend's shoulder I spy Cassie at the bar where she's standing with her boyfriend, head thrown back, laughing dramatically. 'The absolute cheek of the girl. I still can't believe she's here. Actually, scrub that, I *can* believe it. Part of me even finds it quite hilarious that she's got the nerve to come to *my* party after what she did. You don't think she'll try to speak to me, do you? I really hope not.'

Becky shakes her head and turns back to gape at her. 'You've got to admit, she looks bloody stunning.'

Gallingly, she does. Wearing an almost indecently see-through white lace knee-length dress that fits in all the right places, she's also dyed her cropped hair pure white to match. 'I wonder which salon she went to, to have *that* done,' I mutter.

Jennifer is now striding across the dance floor, making a beeline for Cassie.

'I hope there isn't going to be a scene.' Becky's hand goes up to her mouth, and I'm sure I can detect a gleam in her eye. My friend isn't vindictive, but she's never been able to resist a bit of drama.

As I watch in horrified fascination, Jennifer taps Cassie on her shoulder. Cassie turns around, frowns, and then smiles at my boss. But Jennifer's face is stern, her feet planted apart and her hands clamped on her hips. As she begins to give Cassie a piece of her mind, the immediate area around them slowly clears, and I worry that things might turn violent.

Cassie's face quickly shifts into her fake-apology expression – head tilted, and eyes wide with concern.

But Jennifer's eyes still haven't lost their murderous glare. Her tirade isn't loud enough to be heard over the music, other than sharp snatches of words like 'Cow!' and 'My salon!'. More people are starting to notice, and my heart is pumping way too hard. They're both going to end up ruining my night, and I don't know what to do about it. If I go over there, I'll draw even more attention to the scene.

I notice that Toby and Nick are on their way over. Hopefully they'll be able to defuse the situation before it turns into something physical. I don't think Cassie would want it to go that far, but I wouldn't be so sure about Jennifer. She's crimson-faced and fuming. Suddenly, her arm jerks upwards really fast, and Cassie's hand flies to her face.

Becky gasps. 'Did you see that? Jen chucked her drink in Cassie's face! Go on, Jennifer!'

'Becky!' Sam and I both glare at her.

'Sorry. But you have to admit she deserved it.'

Jennifer turns on her heel and strides away. She sweeps her bag off the back of a chair and exits the room. After a decent interval, Cassie's boyfriend puts an arm around her and leads her away. Hopefully Cassie has now got the message and is going home.

Toby and Nick never made it over to them. I think they've come to the conclusion that they're no longer needed. I bet they're relieved. I notice that Nick seems to have lost quite a bit of weight. His suit is hanging off him and his cheeks are hollow. I hope he's okay. Maybe he had that bug that Madeline was talking about a few weeks ago.

Toby's gaze lands on me, and he mouths to ask if I'm all right. I nod and we both roll our eyes and shake our heads at the close call.

'I still think it would've been great if Jen had punched her,' Becky muses.

'You're such a troublemaker,' I retort.

'*I'm* not the troublemaker,' she quips.

'Well, I for one am glad there isn't going to be a fist fight at our ten-year wedding anniversary, that I've spent weeks organising, thank you very much.'

'The night's still young.' Becky laughs and Sam elbows her in the side to be quiet, although he's also trying not to laugh.

I cross my arms on the table and sink down over them. 'It's not even nine o'clock yet and my nerves are shredded.'

'Aw, babe. Don't worry about it. Looks like they've both gone now.' Becky stands and pulls me to my feet. 'Knock back your drink and let's dance. I love this song.'

I do as she suggests and the two of us totter onto the dance floor where we're instantly joined by a raucous posse of my other friends, some from the salon, others from my schooldays, as well as a group of school mums. Everyone's really made the effort to dress up, and we pull out all our cheesiest dance moves.

Toby comes up behind me, slipping his arms around my waist. I turn around and my stomach flips at how handsome he looks in his suit. 'Having fun?' he murmurs in my ear.

'I am now that Fight Club's been averted. Did you see the look on Jennifer's face?'

'I did. Nick and I were terrified. Thought we'd have to intervene. We didn't fancy our chances against either of them.'

I give him a playful push. 'Don't even joke about it.'

The smile slides off his face. 'Okay, stay calm, but I think Cassie and Whatshisface might be coming over.'

My stomach gives a flutter of dread. '*What?!* I thought they'd gone home.'

'Apparently not. Want me to head them off and ask them to leave?'

'I love that you're offering, but no. I don't want any more confrontations. Let's just get this over with.'

CHAPTER TWENTY-TWO

I turn around just as Cassie comes within shouting distance. To my surprise, I find that I'm suddenly past caring about Cassie Barrington and all her drama.

'Hi, Zoe,' she cries with far too much enthusiasm. 'Just wanted to wish you and Toby a really happy anniversary. You look stunning, by the way.'

'Thanks,' I reply coolly, resisting being my usual polite self and returning the compliment. I'm sure she knows just how beautiful she looks without me boosting her ego.

'Yeah, thanks for the invite,' her American boyfriend drawls. 'It's been an interesting evening.'

'Indeed.' I give them both a thin-lipped smile that doesn't extend to my eyes.

'Still no Dina, I see,' she says with false concern. 'Looks like you were mistaken and she's not back in town after all.'

For a moment, I'm stunned into further silence by her breathtaking insensitivity. I manage to stutter out a strangled, 'Looks that way.' I try to swallow down my emotions, to stop the biting retorts that fly to my lips like a swarm of wasps. I manage to stay silent, refusing to be drawn into whatever bitchy game she's playing.

'Cassie…' Toby's voice is icy. 'If you can't say anything nice, please just go home. You've already caused enough drama here for one day.'

'*What?* I didn't say anything wrong. I was just asking after my friend's sister. And that thing earlier was hardly my fault. Zoe's psycho boss was responsible for that.'

'Fine, but right now, your insensitivity is upsetting my wife.' Toby fixes Cassie with a stony glare.

'Like I said, I was only asking about her sister.' Cassie looks mortally offended, as if she truly didn't realise that her words would cause hurt. But she forgets how well I know her. 'If Zoe's that sensitive then that's—'

Toby holds up a hand. 'Let me just stop you there. This isn't a debate; this is our anniversary party and we'd both like you to leave.'

Her skin pales ever so slightly, and then she gives a light shrug. 'That's fine. We weren't planning on staying. It's not really our thing. Nice to see you guys though.' She turns and leaves with Whatshisface trailing in her wake.

The party comes back into focus again and I let out a breath before leaning in to hug my husband. 'Did I ever tell you how glad I am that I married you?'

His arms stay around me. 'Yes, but you can keep on telling me; I don't mind. This is *our* night, Zoe. Cassie Barrington can piss off.'

But something is still niggling me regarding what Cassie said about Dina. I slip out from Toby's embrace. 'I'll be back in a minute, okay?'

'You're not going after her?'

'No, just nipping to the loo. I'll be back in a minute.'

'Make sure you are. We haven't had that dance yet.'

I blow my husband a kiss, leave the dancefloor, and head towards the exit. I catch sight of Cassie in the lobby talking to… Lyle – that's it. She has a face like thunder as he tries to appease her.

She spots me and scowls before rearranging her face into another mask of faked nonchalance. 'Come to apologise for your husband's rude comments?'

I don't waste time with niceties. 'Cassie, if you've got something to say about my sister, why don't you just spit it out.'

She puts a hand on her boyfriend's arm. 'Lyle, would you mind waiting outside for me?'

'No way. It's freezing out there!'

'I won't be long,' she wheedles.

'I'll wait in the lounge.' He swaggers off, muttering under his breath.

'So?' I glare at my ex-best friend.

'Fine,' she huffs. 'If you must know, your dear darling sister was blackmailing me.'

I drop my defensive stance. Dina was blackmailing *Cassie*? This is not what I was expecting. Not at all. 'What are you talking about?'

'If you'd let me finish… quite soon after I became famous, she got in touch with me. I thought it was weird because although you and I were friends, I never really had a lot to do with your sister. Dina kept herself to herself. Don't think I'd ever done much more than nod in her direction.'

'How do you mean, *she got in touch*? She'd left the country by then.'

'Yeah, well, she called me. No idea how she got my mobile number. Probably through some moron friend from school.' Cassie takes a pack of cigarettes from her coat pocket and pulls one out. 'God, I'm dying for a ciggie, but it's far too cold to stand out there.'

'So? What did she want?'

'What most people want of course – money.' Cassie curls her lip.

'And what was she holding over your head?'

'Oh, it was something and nothing. The little cow was clutching at straws.'

'So you never paid her?'

Cassie puts the unlit cigarette in her mouth for a moment.

'Oh, I'm sorry, miss,' the woman on reception calls over. 'You can't smoke in here.'

'It's not lit!' Cassie waves the cigarette and rolls her eyes at the woman before turning back to me with a sigh. 'I did pay her.'

'You did? So why—?'

'Because I had this gig as a TV presenter on a kids' show and Dina was threatening to tell the papers that I used to deal drugs.'

I snap my mouth closed at Cassie's revelation, stunned at Dina's audacity. Yet at the same time, not surprised at all.

'It was all a bunch of crap.' Cassie pouts. 'I bought a bit of weed at college and sold it to some of my friends. No biggie. I think I even got you to try a spliff once, remember? Anyway, Dina said she'd bought some off me one time – I don't even remember if that's true. But she must have realised it could hurt my career. She bled a few thousand out of me over the next couple of years. I couldn't think how to get rid of her, so I had no choice; I had to keep paying her off. Until one day she just stopped asking.'

'When was this? When did she stop asking?'

'Just before your wedding, actually. That was the last demand. I remember it because she asked me to put the money into a different bank account that time – a British account.'

I try to stop myself from physically reacting to this last piece of information. To keep my face as neutral as possible. 'I'm sorry she did that to you, Cassie.'

'Yeah, well, so am I. She better not show her face around here again, that's all I'm saying.'

I nod, realising that Dina's behaviour might have something to do with the way Cassie's been treating me lately. It doesn't excuse her, but at least it sheds some light on it. 'Thanks for telling me.'

Cassie shrugs. 'It's all in the past now.'

I think of the two instances I've spotted Dina around Shaftesbury recently. Of the silent phone calls I've been receiving. If she really is back, then I have to hope she's changed, because it wasn't just Cassie that my sister treated badly; the last time she called me, she was way out of line. Almost out of control. I feel an overwhelming urge to confront my sister right now. To have it out with her. If I spot Dina again, I won't hesitate to go after her. To make her explain why she treated me the way she did. Why she was so dismissive of everything I did for her. Why she seems to hate me so much. I give myself a shake to try to dislodge these bitter emotions. 'Okay, well, I better get back to my party.'

Cassie doesn't reply. She merely nods and walks away towards the lounge, presumably to retrieve her boyfriend.

After that, the hours pass in a haze of dancing, eating, drinking, speeches and loved-up chatter. I even dance with Madeline and Kim, who seem to have returned to their usual friendly selves – whether this is a permanent state of affairs, or just an act put on for tonight, I don't actually care. Once the band gets going, Celia and Malcolm come onto the floor for a couple of dances, but otherwise they stay seated at a table with a lively group of their friends.

Dad made it to the party for a full half hour before retiring to the lounge bar at the other end of the hotel, happy enough to sit by the fire with his newspaper and a pint of real ale. Miraculously, he took me up on my offer to stay over at the hotel with us for the weekend. But it wasn't because he wanted to celebrate our anniversary – his central heating packed up yesterday and the spare part he needs for the boiler won't be back in stock until Monday. He told me this weekend away was perfect timing, as apparently the house is like an icebox and there's snow forecast for tonight. Of course, I'd rather he'd have come here for me and Toby, but my dad is my dad. He's not about to change his personality any time soon.

The party finally begins to wind down, and I find myself sitting on a bar stool chatting to my schoolfriends Lou and Danny about this week's encounters with Cassie. Apparently it isn't just me she's been annoying with her self-centred behaviour.

From the corner of my eye, I spot Madeline leaving the room. I still haven't had a chance to speak to her properly tonight. I'd like to have at least a quick chat before tomorrow. Make sure everything's good between us. I excuse myself and go after her, trying my best to stay upright in my ridiculous heels before slipping them off one by one and sighing with ecstasy as my feet are released from their torture.

'Hey, Madeline!'

She's weaving down the corridor, her blue crepe dress billowing around her calves, her blonde chignon the worse for wear with sections of hair hanging down haphazardly, and not in an elegant way. The hairdresser in me is itching to pin it back up. From her erratic movements, I'd say she's pretty drunk.

'Madeline, wait!'

She turns and squints in my direction and then raises a hand. 'I'm off to bed.'

'Hang on.' I trot after her, my shoes in my hand, but she turns and continues on her way. I soon catch up. 'Come and get a coffee with me in the bar,' I suggest, walking by her side.

'You shouldn't have coffee after four p.m.,' she chides. 'You won't be able to sleep.'

'I think you'll sleep just fine,' I say with a smile.

'Don't laugh at me.' She stops walking and wags her finger in front of my face.

'I'm not laughing, I'm just saying, you've had a bit to drink. A coffee will take the edge off, stop the room spinning later.'

'No thanks.'

'Water, then. Or a soft drink.'

She waves me away and carries on walking.

'We're good now, though, right?'

'You're Toby's wife.'

'Yes, that's right. You really are quite drunk, Madeline. Where's Nick? Do you want me to get him?'

'You're Toby's wife. But I know what you did.'

Now it's my turn to stop walking. 'Wait, what are you talking about?'

She keeps going without me. 'You shouldn't have done that. Poor Toby.' She shakes her head and repeats, 'Poor, poor Toby.'

I'm not sure if her words are the incoherent ravings of an extremely drunk person, or if there's something she wants to tell me. I call after her, 'What do you mean "Poor Toby"? What's the matter with him?'

'Don't pretend you don't know.' She stops and looks around. 'Where's the lift?' I catch up to her, but she's ignoring me, trying instead to get her bearings.

'I'll take you up to your room, if you like.'

'Yes please.' Her shoulders drop and she seems relieved. 'I'm a bit pissed actually.'

'You'll be okay,' I say, linking my arm through hers. 'Come on, let's get you upstairs. You're on the same floor as me and Toby.'

'It's a shame what you did, Zoe.' She looks at me sadly and strokes my cheek.

'What did I do?'

'You know.'

'Remind me.'

'The affair.'

I stop dead and unlink my arm from hers. 'Um, Madeline, I didn't have an affair.'

'S'okay, you don't have to lie to me. I know all about it. Nick told me.'

I speak slowly and clearly so there's no misunderstanding. 'I have no idea why Nick would tell you that, but I'm telling you now, Madeline, I absolutely did not have an affair.'

However, my sister-in-law doesn't appear to be listening. 'I'm so disappointed in you, Zoe. Toby didn't deserve that. The worst thing… the very worst thing…' She makes jabbing motions towards me with her forefinger. 'Is that I thought you were better than that. I actually looked up to you – bet you didn't know that!

Not anymore though. No. Not anymore. No more looking up to the wonderful Mrs Zoe Johnson.'

I'm utterly astonished by Madeline's accusation. Is this why she's been so off with me recently? Why Kim has also been snubbing me? In fact, several of the school mums barely spoke to me this evening. It would make sense if this was the reason. It's just another hideous lie to add to everything else that seems to be upending my life at the moment. The feeling that nothing is quite right. That my whole world is off balance. But why the hell would Nick tell Madeline such a thing in the first place? Where did he hear it, and why was he so quick to believe such a thing? I need to have a word with him. Right now.

CHAPTER TWENTY-THREE

NOW

'Madeline, listen to me. Where did Nick hear about this so-called affair?'

She presses her knuckles to her mouth. 'I shouldn't have told you. Nick said I wasn't supposed to say anything. I'm in big trouble now.' She walks unsteadily over to a flight of carpeted stairs next to the lift and sits down heavily on the second stair. 'Look at me, I'm on the naughty step.'

'Madeline, you should have spoken to me about this earlier. I could have put you straight.'

'I wanted to talk to you, Zoe, but I wasn't allowed. And now I'm in trouble. I'm in so much trouble.' She leans against the wall and closes her eyes.

'I have *never* had an affair.' But I'm not sure she's even listening to me anymore. I'm desperate to speak to Nick, to find out where he got his information from, but I can't leave my sister-in-law like this. I manoeuvre her off the stairs and into the lift and take her up to her room. After much fumbling about in her bag for the room key, we finally make it inside. She sits on the bed and slowly lies down, closing her eyes, but I sit her back up and lead her over to a plush velvet chair by the curtains. I draw them open a little and pull down the sash window to let in some fresh air. A sudden freezing blast makes me gasp, so I close it back up, leaving just a crack.

'Don't fall asleep yet, Madeline, I'm going to make us both some coffee.'

'Is it after four o'clock?'

'What's this obsession with not drinking coffee after four? No, it's not,' I lie, putting a capsule into the coffee machine, place a cup beneath the spout and switch on the machine.

'Good.' She rambles on for a while about coffee until I cut her off.

'Let's have these coffees and then I'll fetch Nick. Try to sort out this mix-up about me and my imaginary affair.'

'S'not imaginary. It's real. Nick's been quite ill about it. For weeks.'

'He can't have been ill over *me*.'

'He's been worried, Zoe. It's not fair making him keep secrets like that. Especially from me. Toby swore him to secrecy.'

'*Toby* knows about this?'

'Poor Toby is devastated. Course he is.' Madeline points at me. 'You've caused all this upset you know. Shouldn't have done it.'

'But it's not true!' I stop what I'm doing and think back to how Toby's been behaving over the past few days. There's been nothing to suggest that he thinks I'm cheating. Nothing at all. I think Madeline must have got hold of the wrong end of the stick. 'So tell me, Madeline, who am I supposed to be having this affair with? Where did the rumour even start?' My mind suddenly flies to Cassie. This reeks of her handiwork. It would make sense, as she's always had it in for me. Maybe she started the rumour to sabotage my anniversary party. Maybe she's jealous of me. Or maybe she just wanted to punish me because of what Dina did to her. She couldn't get back at my sister, so I was the next best thing. I pass Madeline her cup of coffee and put a fresh capsule into the machine for me. I'm more than a little drunk myself. This all feels so surreal.

Madeline sets her drink on the glass table with a clatter. 'You should just come clean, Zoe. Lying doesn't help anyone. There's poor Nick making himself sick with worry. And dear Toby sticking up for you, even after this type of betrayal. The man is a saint.' As Madeline sips her coffee, she's starting to sound a little more coherent. 'I tried to get Toby to talk to you about it, but he wouldn't hear of it. Said it would only make things worse.'

Something occurs to me. I take my coffee and sit on the end of the bed opposite Madeline. The cold air streams in through the tiny gap in the window and I find myself shivering. 'When exactly did you speak to Toby about this?'

She screws up her nose as she tries to remember. 'Some time last week… Friday, I think. Yes, definitely Friday, before Nick and I went away for my birthday. You ruined that too – Nick wasn't himself at all.'

'I still don't get why Nick would feel sick about me having an affair. Sure, he'd be upset on Toby's behalf, but *sick*? No. I don't believe it. It makes no sense.'

'Believe what you want, but it's true,' she slurs. 'Nick has morals. He doesn't like lies or secrets. He's got a conshus… conshuns… conscience.'

I'm beginning to wish I'd let Madeline fall asleep. She's growing more bolshy by the second. 'I saw you meet up with Toby at our house last week. Is that when you spoke about it?'

'How did you see us?' She frowns for a moment and then waves the thought away. 'Never mind. Yes, Toby asked to see me so he could explain why he wanted to keep your affair a secret. He said it was because of the children, so of course I had to agree.' She folds her arms across her chest and gives a little shiver.

'Toby told me he'd met up with you because of the surprise. He said you were helping him to plan it.'

'What surprise?' She reaches forward for her coffee and takes a couple of sips.

'This whole weekend away.' I gesture around me to the room. 'This was the surprise.'

'No.' She shakes her head vehemently. 'It was nothing to do with that.' Her eyes seem to be growing heavy again.

I take a few big gulps of my coffee before reaching into my bag for my phone and calling Nick's mobile. It rings and rings before going to voicemail, so I try Toby instead. He answers almost immediately.

'Zoe, where are you? I was just about to call you.'

'I'm upstairs with Madeline. She's had a bit too much to drink, so I'm getting her to drink some coffee.'

'Oh.' There's a pause.

'Toby, are you still there?'

'Yes, sorry. Is she okay now? With you I mean? Did she tell you what's been bugging her?'

'Actually, yes. Yes she did, and it's a bit strange. Can you come up here, please? And bring Nick. We're in his and Madeline's room.'

'I…' But he tails off.

I end the call, unsure whether to be anxious or angry at what's been going on. But until I know how the rumour originated, I guess I'll still be confused and in the dark.

Madeline's eyes are closed now, and she's slumped back in her chair, her mouth slightly open. I think about waking her up but decide against it. It'll be easier to talk to Nick and Toby without Madeline adding in her low opinion of me.

As I wait, my stomach churns and I start to feel faintly queasy. Despite the strong coffee, I'm still not fully sober. There are too many conflicting questions in my head for me to make sense of anything – I need to question Nick and Toby before I start jumping to any conclusions.

Faint rumbles of music and laughter drift up to the room, an echo of the party below. It feels like days since I was down there dancing and having fun. By the time this mix-up is all sorted out, the night will be finished. I stand and walk over to the window, which looks out across the sweeping carriageway drive. Pressing my nose against the pane, I see wide beams of light from the hotel's exterior lamps illuminating thick twirling flakes of snow that are beginning to settle on the driveway and flower beds.

I'm startled away from the view by the sound of the door opening. I turn to see Nick striding in while Toby follows behind, his face clouded with anger.

'Nick, you need to calm down.' Toby puts a hand on his brother's shoulder, but Nick shakes him off, heading for Madeline.

'Maddy, are you okay?'

'She's all right,' I reply. 'Just had a bit too much to drink and now she's sleeping it off.'

Nick whirls around to look at me. Up close, he looks even worse than I previously thought. Granted, he's obviously a bit pissed, but his eyes are bloodshot and sunken in their sockets, his skin is pallid, and the shoulders of his suit are powdered with dandruff.

'Nick!' Once again, Toby tries to pull him back.

'No, Toby, enough is enough. Zoe needs to know the truth.'

'For fuck's sake.' My husband swears under his breath and I'm starting to get really worried now. Something is very, very wrong, and I don't think it's anything to do with Madeline's crazy story about an affair.

'Is one of you going to tell me what's going on?' My voice sounds strange to my ears and I feel a little light-headed.

'It's fine.' Toby turns to me with a forced smile. 'Nick doesn't know what he's talking about.'

'That development's going ahead, Toby. And when it does it will all come out anyway.'

'Nick, shut your mouth. You're drunk.' He turns back to me. 'Zoe, why don't you go back to our room and I'll follow you there in a bit?'

'No, that's okay.' I stare from one brother to the other. 'I'd like to hear what Nick wants to tell me.'

'Good,' Nick slurs, 'cos I'm sick of having to keep this secret.'

'If this is about some imaginary affair that I'm supposed to have had, I can tell you right now, I never have and never will cheat on my husband.' I turn to Toby and will him to hear the truth in my voice. 'Did Cassie say something? Because you know you can't trust a word that comes out of her mouth.'

'Oh, we know you wouldn't cheat, Zoe,' Nick says, dismissively.

'Then why have I just spent the last twenty minutes defending myself to your wife?'

'That was what Toby told her to throw her off the scent.' Nick gives a bitter laugh.

'Why are you doing this *now*?' Toby snaps at his brother. 'You've kept quiet for so long.'

'It's this bloody party, in this bloody hotel!' Nick cries. 'And the housing development. I've been having nightmares about all of it, Toby.'

'Then you should have talked to me.'

'What good would that do? You'd only tell me what you're telling me now – to keep my mouth shut.'

'Because it's the right thing to do.'

'Well whether it's right or not, I can't do it anymore.' Nick takes a step towards me and I brace myself to hear whatever shocking secret has him so agitated. 'Zoe…'

Toby steps in between us. 'Nick, you're my brother and I love you, but you need to shut up, or I'll have to make you shut up.'

'Fine, make me. I don't care anymore.'

Toby sighs. 'Okay, just wait a minute. I'll tell Zoe, okay?'

'You promise?'

'Yes.'

'So do it *now*.'

'I will, but Nick… you need to promise not to interrupt. Let me do it my way.'

'Fine.'

I pull at my husband's arm. 'Tell me what?'

'Zoe…'

Toby turns to me and I look from his face to Nick's. As they stand there in their suits, facing me with such serious expressions, I get the strangest feeling of déjà vu. My skin prickles.

'What is it? Just tell me.' I can't seem to take my eyes off Nick. He really does look terribly ill.

'Zoe!' Toby repeats. 'Zoe, look at me.'

I manage to shift my gaze to my husband. He takes both my hands in his and I stare into his dark eyes. Whatever he has to tell me, it can't be that bad. We can surely get through it together.

'Zoe,' he says carefully. 'Dina isn't missing. I'm sorry, but she's dead. And the truth is… you killed her.'

CHAPTER TWENTY-FOUR

NOW

I stare at Toby for a moment before giving a small disbelieving laugh. 'Don't be ridiculous.'

'I'm sorry, Zo, but it's true. Ten years ago, on our wedding day, you killed your sister.'

'Toby!' Nick cries.

'Nick, shut up. You wanted me to tell Zoe, so I'm telling her.'

'But—'

Toby glares at his brother. 'I'm doing this my way.'

Nick slumps down onto the floor with his head in his hands next to where Madeline is passed out in the chair, as Toby tells me this preposterous thing.

'I think I'd know if I did something as horrendous as killing my sister.' I shift my gaze from Nick to Toby.

'I'm so sorry, Zoe, but I'm telling you the truth,' Toby says.

I shake my head as though I can dislodge his words. 'Why are you saying this? Just tell me what's really going on. Please.' I bend down to shake my brother-in-law's shoulder, trying to get him to look at me. 'Nick! Tell me the truth!'

Toby gently pries my hand away from his brother and turns me around to face him. 'I know it's a lot to take in, Zoe. But let me explain what happened.'

'Firstly, I don't believe she's dead! And second… second…'
There's a high-pitched whistling in my ears and I can't seem to
catch my breath. I stagger sideways and my knees buckle.

Toby puts an arm around me. 'Come on, Zo, come and sit on
the bed, put your head between your knees.'

'This isn't real, is it? What you said, it's some kind of sick joke.'
As I sit down, I'm frantically trying to make connections between
what he's saying and what happened in the past, but I have no
memory of what he's accusing me of. I rake my hands through
my hair, pushing it off my face and then letting it fall back down.

I sense Toby's gaze on me. He's about to say something else,
but I cut him off.

'What about the affair thing?' I latch on to that as if it's some
kind of lifeline. 'What's that all about?' I grip the end of the
king-size bed and do as Toby suggested, leaning forward with
my head between my legs, trying to breathe. The patterned rug
beneath my feet is making my head spin so I close my eyes, but
that feels even worse.

Toby sits next to me. 'Like Nick said, the affair was just something I told Madeline to throw her off the scent.'

'I can't listen to any more of this,' Nick groans from the floor.
'I just want it all to go away. Get out of here, Toby.'

'Fine,' he mutters. 'Nick. You need to pull yourself together.
Zoe and I are going to our room now. But, you and I, we'll talk
about this tomorrow when you're thinking straight and you're not
so drunk. Now go to bed and don't talk to anyone until you've
spoken to me, okay?'

He doesn't respond.

'I mean it,' Toby says through gritted teeth.

'Okay, yes, I heard you, Toby!'

'Good.'

'I think I'm going to throw up,' I tell my husband.

'Can you hold on till we get to our room?'

The short answer to that is *no*. I run to the en-suite bathroom and vomit several times into the toilet. Toby follows me.

'I'm so sorry I had to tell you like this.' Toby rubs my back while I empty the contents of my stomach. 'If Nick hadn't started losing his shit, we could have just gone on as normal.'

I rinse my mouth out and splash my face. 'How can any of this be normal?' I turn to stare at him, feeling separate from my body, like I'm talking through someone else's mouth.

'You've had a shock,' he says.

'That's an understatement. I just… I don't believe what you told me.' My teeth are chattering and I'm shivering all over. 'First, you say I'm having an affair, then you say I've killed my sister – how can I believe anything you're saying? It all sounds like you're telling me one outrageous story after another.' Toby takes off his suit jacket and drapes it over my shoulders. 'It just can't be true. I'd know if it was. And anyway, I saw Dina outside the salon. I've seen her twice now. How could I have seen her if you're telling the truth?'

'It obviously wasn't her. Come on, let's go to our room and I'll explain.'

I let him lead me out of the en suite. Nick and Madeline are exactly where we left them. Madeline's snoring lightly, but I'm worried about Nick, who's still crouched on the floor, his head in his hands. It doesn't seem right to leave him there. Toby doesn't seem too concerned as we walk past him.

We head along the corridor to our room. I'm dreading going in there. Dreading what else Toby is about to tell me.

He opens the door and switches on the light. We're in the recently revamped bridal suite – a vast room with lots of character – mullioned windows, wooden beams, an eclectic mix of traditional and contemporary. The same beautiful room we stayed in ten years ago, only now the décor has all changed. We checked in earlier, so our cases are already open, traces of our preparation for the party scattered around the room – make-up, a couple of empty glasses, a few discarded clothes draped over the ottoman at the foot of the bed. On the dining table are an enormous bouquet of flowers, an opened bottle of champagne, an exotic fruit basket and a selection of handmade chocolates – a celebration from another time, before my husband upended my world. Before this churning in my stomach and tightening in my chest. Before this nausea and tingling light-headedness.

I walk past all these redundant signs of celebration towards a pair of leaf-print armchairs arranged either side of a circular table in front of the window. I gingerly settle myself in one of the chairs, pulling Toby's jacket around me, getting wafts of his spicy cologne. It smells at once familiar and foreign. Outside, the snow is still whirling, the night sky almost as white as the settled snow beneath.

Toby follows me and closes the curtains against the outside world. He sits in the chair opposite and starts talking.

'I'm sorry I had to lie to Madeline. But it was to cover up the truth. Nick has had a hard time dealing with this recently and he told her he was keeping a secret for me. I told her you've been having an affair, because that was the first thing that jumped into my head. She must have mentioned it to her friend Kim, and maybe some of the other school mums, which is why you and Alice were being snubbed. I really am so very sorry about that. I made a bad judgement call telling her that lie.'

I take in his words, but they offer me no comfort whatsoever. If anything, they make me feel worse. A swell of anger gives me a boost of energy. 'That's great, so the whole school thinks I'm a slapper, and on top of that you're accusing me of murder. You better have a fucking good explanation for all this. Toby! I need you to tell me the God's honest truth about my sister and why you think… why you think I would ever hurt her.'

'Okay.' Toby pauses. 'Okay, I'll tell you what happened.' He takes a breath. 'So, Dina came here to the hotel on our wedding day.'

'She was *here*? She made it to our wedding? She told me she couldn't come. I thought she didn't care.'

'Zoe, can you just let me tell you what happened, without interrupting. It's… it'll be easier to get through it that way.' He shifts in his seat.

'Okay.' I twist the hem of my dress in my lap, the green satin crinkling and creasing as I wait for Toby to give me answers to all the questions tumbling around my brain.

'The thing is, I knew Dina was back in the UK. I'd got in contact with her to get her here in time for the wedding as a surprise. I knew how much it would mean to you to have her there.'

My heart swells at Toby's thoughtfulness. But then it judders when I think about the supposed outcome of her visit.

'My plan went badly wrong. I met up with your sister a few times to plan when she should arrive and how she should surprise you. She was funny and charming, and told me lots of cute stories about you both as children… I guess you could say we hit it off.' He pauses and wipes his forehead with the cuff of his shirt.

This doesn't sound like the Dina I knew. My sister was always quiet and sullen. But then I guess I hadn't seen her for years. Maybe she'd changed. 'Go on,' I prompt, wanting to know, yet dreading hearing the details.

Toby swallows. 'Like I said, things went a bit pear-shaped. Dina… she… well, she made a pass at me.'

'She what?!'

Toby holds up his hands. 'I swear I didn't lead her on. I was simply being nice to her, like anyone would towards their fiancée's sister. But she must have somehow taken it the wrong way. I tried to turn her down gently, but she just wouldn't take no for an answer. It was like she thought it was all a game. She kept saying she'd make me realise that I was with the wrong sister.'

I'm hit with another wave of nausea, but I swallow it down, forcing out words to form questions I don't want to hear the answers to. 'Did you kiss her? Sleep with her?'

'No! Of course not. I didn't touch her. I was engaged to *you*. I only had eyes for *you*. Dina and I got on well, but she's not my type romantically – too hippyish. She seemed too much of a loose cannon, if I'm honest.'

'So…' I try to make my voice calm, but I can't help imagining Dina saying those things. 'She made a pass at you. Then what happened?'

'I mean, that was it.' Toby hunches his shoulders. 'I didn't see her after those few times. Not until the day of the wedding. I messaged her that it might be best if she didn't come after all. I was worried she might make a scene. But she didn't listen.' He looks around the room. 'I'm thirsty. Do you want some water?'

I nod, realising that my mouth tastes dry and sour.

He strides over to the minibar, takes out two bottles then brings them back to the table. I take small sips of mine. He drains half of his in one go before sitting back down.

I don't think I believe Toby is telling the truth. It's all too outlandish. Too much to take in. I think I'm in shock, because my voice sounds so calm. 'So what happened when she showed up here on our wedding day?'

'She messaged me while I was getting ready in my room to say that she was going to tell you she was in love with me. Of course, I raced round to your room to try to stop her. It was the most scared I've ever been. Knowing she was going to try to ruin everything for us.'

'And you promise nothing happened between the two of you?' I ask. 'Not a kiss, or a touch? Nothing?' My heart is racing as I wait for his reply. I'm not even letting myself think about the rest of the story – about what he says happened to Dina after that.

Toby fixes me with his gaze. 'Zoe, I swear it.'

I return his gaze and he looks as sincere and distressed as I've ever seen him.

He shakes his head. 'When I got to your room she was already in there with you. She'd waited until my mum and the others had gone, and you were on your own.'

I nod slowly before getting up and walking away. 'I just don't believe this. It can't be true. It *isn't* true. It's mad. It's not happening. I'm drunk, or dreaming, that's all this is.' I chew the inside of my mouth and rub at my arms, feeling like a crazy person.

Toby follows my erratic pacing around the room. 'Zoe, I know it's a lot to take in. Why don't you come and sit down?' He gestures back to the table and chairs and tries to put an arm around me, but I shake him off and whirl around with a glare.

'If all this happened like you say it did, *why don't I remember any of it*?!'

CHAPTER TWENTY-FIVE

This woodchip wallpaper is an absolute nightmare to strip. If I'd known what a hideous job it was going to be, I might have taken Toby up on his offer to do it on his day off. But he works so hard and most of his spare time is taken up with running for town council. So I'm happy to make a start on decorating the baby's room. Annoyingly, instead of loosening the wallpaper, this handheld steamer is reducing the woodchip to a gloopy, porridgy mess that has to be painstakingly peeled from the walls with a palette knife. I'm hot and tired and bored, so when my phone rings, I welcome the distraction.

The number isn't one I recognise, but right now I'll take a cold call over woodchip removal, hands down. I turn off the steamer, wipe my hands on my dungarees and snatch up my mobile before it goes to voicemail.

'Hello?'

'Hello, is that Zoe Johnson?'

'Yes, speaking.'

'Hi, this is Police Constable Alfie Graham. We spoke a couple of months ago about your sister, Dina Williams.'

'Oh, yeah, hi.' I remember talking to him at the station. Celia and I joked afterwards about how he didn't look old enough to be a police officer, with his smooth skin, pale blond hair, and wide-eyed concern. Despite his looks, he seemed capable enough.

'We've got some follow-up news for you. Is it okay if we call round?'

'To my house?'

'Yes, if that's okay? Or you can come to the station if you prefer.'

'No, that's fine. You can come here. Have you got the address?'

'Yes.'

'Did you find Dina? Is she okay?'

'There's nothing to worry about. We're just up the road from you, so we'll be with you in a couple of minutes.'

'Okay, see you soon.'

I rush to our bedroom to inspect my appearance in the mirror, noting my bright-red face, greasy hair tied in an unflattering ponytail, and my woodchip-splattered dungarees. Oh well, I don't know why I'm even bothered. I think I'm just focusing on my appearance to stop myself worrying about what the police might have discovered. I almost wish I hadn't gone to report Dina's disappearance in the first place, because right now my heart is beating uncomfortably loud and my belly is swirling with anxiety at the thought of what news they might be bringing.

The doorbell rings, startling me out of my worry for a moment. PC Graham must have been almost outside the house when he called. I hurry down the stairs and open the front door to the same two uniformed officers I spoke to last time.

'Police Sergeant Sarah McCormack,' the officer says, holding out a hand to shake mine. 'Nice to see you again.'

I usher her and PC Graham through the hall and into the small front lounge. Thankfully, it isn't too messy. Just a few empty mugs. The curtains are still closed though, so I pull them apart, letting in a hazy cloud of afternoon sunshine. 'Please, sit down.'

They sit next to one another on the edge of the sofa while I perch on the arm of the other sofa, my hands instinctively settling on my bump.

'You're expecting?' Sergeant McCormack asks.

'I'm due in July.'

'Congratulations. My two are almost grown-up now.'

'Thank you… You said you had news about my sister.'

'Yes,' she removes her hat and smooths back a strand of loose ash-blonde hair that's escaped from her bun. 'Two pieces of news, actually, that both came back this week from the Missing Persons Unit.'

I chew my lip and wait for her to continue.

'So, first, I can confirm that Dina Williams returned to the UK from Thailand on the fifteenth of August last year.'

'August?' I know that Matt from the hostel said he thought she'd come back to the UK last year, but I wasn't convinced he was right. Because why wouldn't she have called me? She would have at least got in contact with Dad. 'Are you sure?'

'Yes. It was Dina's passport.'

Something occurs to me. 'Could she have flown out of the UK sometime after that?'

'We checked. That was the last time her passport was used. Also, her bank card was used in the UK frequently since she came back.'

I unclench my jaw. 'Have you got an address?'

'Her only registered address is your family home.'

'So where's she been living? Because Dad hasn't seen her.' I get to my feet and fold my arms across my chest.

Sergeant McCormack gives me a sympathetic look. 'The cash withdrawals have mainly been over the border in Somerset, in and around Glastonbury.'

'Glastonbury?' I try to think about who I might know there. But the only time I've ever been to Glastonbury is when we were kids. Mum and Dad took us there on a day trip. I remember it was really hot and after we'd looked around the town, we had a picnic in a field, and a farmer with a shotgun shouted at us for trespassing.

'The cash withdrawals were fairly regular until the end of last year.'

'What happened after that?' I ask.

'They stopped.'

I try to decipher the expressions on the officers' faces, but they're unreadable. 'What does that mean?'

'We wouldn't want to speculate.'

'So you're saying you don't know what's happened to her.'

'Not at this time, no. I'm sorry. I wish we could be more helpful.'

'But there are other things you can do, right? What about checking CCTV cameras or finding out where she lives or works?'

'I'm sorry, Zoe. Because she hasn't been in the country for so many years and we have no new address or place of work for her, it's almost impossible. Of course, Dina's details will stay up on the missing persons database, so if anyone comes forward with information, they'll be able to cross-reference it there. But chances are, she'll get in touch with you eventually.'

'But what if she's been hurt?'

'We did a check of hospitals and mortuaries in the area and no one of her description has been admitted.'

I realise I'm going to have to let Dad know what's been going on. I wonder what he'll make of it all. I think I'm in shock at the fact that my sister doesn't want to be found – not by us anyway. She's decided to shun her own flesh and blood. Then again, I guess she already made that decision when she left home at sixteen, but at least she kept in touch, no matter how erratically. It hurts that she's cut us out of her life so completely. Yet… I can't help admitting to myself that things are easier without her around. Whenever she does get in touch, there are always conditions attached. Either that, or she wants something.

I notice that the officers are on their feet. 'So, is that it?' I shake my head helplessly.

'Obviously, we'll let you know if we hear anything else. And if you could keep us posted if you hear anything, that would be great.'

Dina and I aren't the best of friends, but it doesn't stop the rocks in my belly from sinking a little further. What if I never see her again? I tell myself there's nothing I can do about it. I'll simply have to get on with my life without her in it. At least I have my new family now, and things will certainly be less… complicated without my unpredictable sister. But, try as I might, I can't hold onto that rationality. I'm suddenly overwhelmed by a rush of emotions. I honestly can't tell if I'm furious with my sister, worried about her, sad, or something else entirely. I need the officers to leave so I can try to process the depth of my feelings. There's something in my gut that isn't chiming right. A twisting, gnawing sensation that has me almost panicked. Like I'm free-falling and I won't know what's wrong until I crash to the ground.

CHAPTER TWENTY-SIX

NOW

I have absolutely no recollection of seeing my sister on my wedding day. Toby's story feels like fiction, not real life. I keep expecting that any second I'll wake up.

A thin sheen of sweat has appeared on my husband's forehead and upper lip. Either he's lying about Dina, or the stress of remembering is taking its toll. I want to believe Toby is telling me the truth. But I also want it to be a lie, because otherwise that means I killed my sister. I clasp my hands in front of me to stop them shaking. I don't think any of this has sunk in properly.

Toby takes a breath. 'Zoe, I'm sorry you don't remember that night, but maybe it's a good thing, considering what happened.'

I'm about to dispute this, but I need to hear the rest, so I bite my tongue and force myself to sit back down at the table. Toby follows me. 'Dina was drunk,' he continues. 'Not just tipsy, but almost paralytic. Staggering all over the place. Saying all kinds of crazy stuff like she was in love with me and she couldn't believe I was going to marry you. That we had a connection.' He darts a look at me across the table and swallows. 'You were standing there in shock. I tried to reassure you that what she was saying was all nonsense, but it didn't feel like you were even listening to me. I felt absolutely powerless. I could see our relationship slipping away. I felt like I was going to lose *everything*!'

Toby gets to his feet, agitated. He walks across the hotel room, then turns and walks back. I want to prompt him to continue talking, but again I manage to stay quiet. To wait for him to carry on. He finally sits back down and continues his account.

'Anyway, eventually you snapped out of your shock and started quizzing us both. I can't remember exactly what you said, only that you were understandably upset. It's all a bit of a blur. Dina kept insisting that I shouldn't marry you, that she and I were meant to be together. I told her that she was deluded, and that the best thing she could do was to leave, and for us all to forget this ever happened. It seemed like she was finally going to do as I asked. She started walking towards the door, but at the last minute she turned and pulled a knife out of her pocket and held it to my throat.'

'No! *A knife?* What the hell?' I bring a hand up to my mouth and hold my other hand up to stop him talking while I try to digest this. I feel like I'm seriously going to lose the plot in a second. My eyes fill with tears as I try to get my breathing under control.

'Zoe, are you okay?'

I can't even talk. This is all insane. Finally, I manage to nod, and he continues.

'It's shocking, I know. She moved so quickly, I really thought she was going to slit my throat, but you saved me. You picked up this heavy glass vase of flowers from the table, came up behind her and smashed it down on her head.'

'What?! *No!*

'She went down straightaway. There was glass and water everywhere – the floor was soaked. That's when you slipped, fell backwards and smashed your head on the edge of the desk. You knocked yourself out. But I'm afraid Dina was already dead.'

'I don't believe it.' I ball my hands into fists and shake my head. Toby's story truly sounds like something from a movie, not something that actually happened in real life. 'I know Dina was headstrong,' I admit, 'but she wasn't crazy… or deluded. To say she pulled a knife on you… that doesn't sound like anything she would do.'

'Zoe, you hadn't seen her for years. The Dina I met was… she was unpredictable.'

I think back to the last time I spoke to her on the phone; the demands she'd made of me. Deep down I know that what Toby is telling me is indeed entirely plausible, I just don't want to admit it. Especially in light of Cassie's revelation about Dina blackmailing her. If she could do that to someone she barely knew, then what else was she capable of? But I don't want to believe any of this. It's too much.

'So why can't I remember?'

'You were out cold. I think the trauma and the knock to your head must have affected your memory.'

I scrape my chair back and stand, gripping hold of the table for a moment. 'You should have called for an ambulance. Maybe they could have saved her!'

'It was too late, Zoe.'

My brain races and the room swirls while I try to make sense of what my husband is telling me. I don't think I can take it all in. He's saying that Dina died ten years ago. *Ten years ago!*

'So… she really is dead. My sister is dead.' I sit back down heavily. 'I can't believe it. How am I going to tell Dad?'

'You can't tell him.' Toby gives me a hard stare. 'You can't tell *anyone*.'

I don't see how I'll be able to keep this from my father. But I realise something else isn't adding up. 'Why is your brother freaking out about this? I mean, if all this really happened, and you've both known about it for ten years, then why is he falling apart *now*?'

'Because he helped… afterwards.'

'Helped?'

Toby grimaces. 'With your sister. We had to get rid of…' He pauses and winces. '… her body. It was our wedding night – I couldn't exactly get away – so he did most of it.'

I think about what this must have entailed and break out in a queasy sweat. 'How…? I mean where did you…?'

'She's buried in that patch of ground by the woods.'

'You mean…'

'Yes, where the new housing development is due to be built. That's why Nick's been panicking recently. He's sure they'll discover Dina's body, and they'll link her remains to the three of us. He's the one who encouraged Madeline to start up a petition against the development. But now the appeal's been rejected, they'll probably break ground soon.'

'Wait a minute, why didn't you just call the police in the first place? From what you've told me, it was self-defence, so surely they would have understood. I mean, if someone comes at you with a knife, you're within your rights to defend yourself.'

'I know, but I was pretty traumatised. We didn't know if the police would believe what had happened. Maybe in hindsight it would have been better to call them and explain, but we made a judgement call in the heat of the moment, and we've had to live with that decision. I didn't want you to go to prison for protecting me from Dina. I couldn't take the risk.' Toby's voice breaks. 'I love you so much, Zoe. I'd do anything to keep you safe.'

I stare at my husband. At the grief and concern etched across his features. And I realise that he must be telling the truth. That my sister is really dead. I let out a sob and cover my mouth. Dina is dead. She's been gone for all these years. 'I don't believe it,' I murmur. But this time it's without conviction. 'Is she really gone?'

Toby reaches across and takes my hand. 'I'm sorry, Zo. I'm so, so sorry.'

I choke back another sob as I think of my little sister lying in that patch of lonely waste ground by the woods. No funeral, no headstone, no one to mourn her passing for all these long years. While I've been enjoying a comfortable happy life of wedded bliss. How will I ever come to terms with this? How will I ever be able to forgive myself? I don't even care about her ill-judged pass at my husband-to-be. It seems childish and trivial compared with what happened to her afterwards.

If only I hadn't lost my memory back then, I could have persuaded Toby to tell the police. Saved years of secrets. Of lies. I squeeze my husband's hand. 'Let's just call the police now. Get it over with. Dina deserves a decent burial. We can give her that at least.'

Toby's face closes down, and he snatches his hand back. 'No. Can't you see? It would be a disaster for everyone who covered it up. We would all go to prison – you, me, Nick. Terrible as it was, it was an accident. It happened so long ago. What good would it do to bring it all out into the open now?' He starts pacing the room again. 'Truth doesn't always play a big part in these types of investigations. Especially not after so many years. The police will be doubly suspicious that we didn't tell them in the first place. And it would destroy our parents if we were all found guilty. Even if by some miracle we're cleared, well, mud sticks. Our careers would be ruined. We'd probably have to leave the area. And if you can't stay quiet for *us*, think of what would happen to the children.'

My mind puts together all that Toby is saying, and I realise that no matter how wrong it feels, it makes sense. I know without a shadow of a doubt that I would be willing to go to prison to pay for my crime – if I really did this thing – but could I expect everyone else to pay such a high price?

'What about the development?' I ask. 'If they find her, then I'll go to prison anyway. Surely it would be better to come clean before that happens. I could say my memory came back. I could change the story so that you and Nick aren't involved. At least that way you'll be around for the children.' My heart almost stops at the thought of doing this, but I need to take responsibility.

'No,' Toby says. 'Don't worry about her body. I'll sort it out.'

'What?!' My mind jumps ahead to what he could possibly mean, and I don't like what I'm imagining.

'You don't need to even think about it, Zo.'

'How can I *not*?' This is all too much to take in right now. Everything is crowding into my brain and filling it up until I can't make sense of anything anymore. I stare down at the table, my eyes unfocused, my mind in freefall. Until suddenly it comes to an abrupt halt. 'Why did you keep it from me, Toby? All these years you hid the truth.'

He finally stops pacing and comes to a stop in front of me. 'I was trying to protect you, Zoe. Your memory was obviously suppressing everything, so I decided there would be no benefit to bringing you so much pain. And the truth is, I was scared. I didn't know how to tell you such an awful thing.'

I stare up at my husband. 'I feel… I feel like I've ruined your life. Yours and Nick's.'

'No, you haven't.' He takes my hand and kisses it. 'I think it would have been worse if you'd remembered. How could we have got married and lived a happy life together both knowing what had happened on our wedding day? It was easier for me to try to forget about it. To bury it. And anyway, you saved my life. If you hadn't acted Dina might've slit my throat.'

'What about poor Nick?'

Toby sighs and shrugs. 'He'll be okay. Once he sobers up. I'll talk to him tomorrow.'

I lay my head on the table for a moment, needing to process everything, yet still unable to believe my little sister is dead. That I killed her. For all her faults, I would never have wished this fate on her. As I close my eyes, I cast my mind back to the hours leading up to the wedding, but all I seem to recall is that overwhelming fuzzy sensation I had throughout the day, after I 'fainted'.

And then, like an express train slamming into me, I experience a sharp fragment of memory. A snapshot of Dina screaming at Toby, wild-eyed and violent. I sit up and hold myself very still, trying to keep hold of the memory, yet at the same time, terrified to let my mind go back there.

'Zoe, what is it?'

I place my palms flat on the table. 'I think my memory might be coming back.'

'Really?' His eyes widen. 'What do you remember?'

'Nothing much, just Dina shouting at you, calling you a bastard.'

'Can you remember anything else, anything at all?' He crouches in front of me, staring so hard that I'm starting to feel uncomfortable.

'No, there's nothing else, that's it. I'm trying to remember more, but it's all so hazy.'

He finally looks away, stands and runs a hand over his head. 'Maybe now would be a good time for you to remember more. Then you'd realise how traumatic it all was. Not that I want you to suffer the trauma. I just want you to understand what it was like. To know that we acted in your best interests.'

'It's all such a shock. I still can't believe it. Maybe the rest of my memories will follow. But I think part of me is too scared to remember.'

'That's natural. It's not exactly something you want to think about.'

'That flashback, it was so vivid. Like I was there. Maybe I'll have more. Maybe it's because I'm back here in this hotel. Or maybe hearing you talk about what happened that day has triggered something in my brain.'

Toby nods thoughtfully. 'I think we should probably both try to get some sleep. Talk about it some more tomorrow.'

I close my eyes for a moment. 'My head's throbbing. Toby, I don't feel well at all.'

'I'll get you some paracetamol.'

I open my eyes and get to my feet, but I don't know what to do with myself. I put the heel of my hand to my forehead and press against the skin as though rubbing my mind clean of everything I've learned. My sister is gone. She's dead. I killed her.

'Please,' I whisper.

'What?' Toby asks. 'What do you want? I'll get you those painkillers.'

I grab his arm. 'No. Please tell me it isn't true.' I feel the weight of his revelation push against my chest and harden in my gut. 'Tell me it's all a lie. That I didn't… do it.'

Toby stares down at me with pity in his eyes. He's chewing his bottom lip. His teeth white against the pink flesh. It all looks wrong. Everything feels so weird and wrong.

'I'm sorry,' he finally says. 'I really am.'

There's a lump in my throat, and a bright, jagged pain has wrapped itself around my heart. I don't think I'll ever recover from this. It's too much. It's too awful.

'Why don't you get into bed?' Toby says softly. 'I'll get you those headache pills.'

'How can I get into bed?' I cry. 'How will I ever be able to sleep after what you told me? This is a nightmare. An absolute living nightmare.' I stare wildly around the room, hating the sight of it. Suddenly realising that this is where it happened. 'It was in here! This is where she died, wasn't it?'

'Shh, shh, Zoe. Keep your voice down. It's okay. It was a long time ago. It's over now. It's finished. It was an accident.' He gathers me into his arms as I try to hold back great wracking sobs.

'We need to leave.' I gulp out the words. 'I want to go home.'

'Tomorrow.' He strokes my hair and kisses my tear-streaked face. 'Right now, you need to get some sleep. You need to calm down before you make yourself ill. Shh, shh,' he soothes. 'It's okay. It'll be okay. Come on, let's get you into bed.' He carefully peels off my clothes and helps me get into the enormous bed, the hotel sheets crisp and cold. I shiver and lay my head on the pillows, too tired to think any more. I close my swollen, tear-filled eyes and let sleep claim me.

CHAPTER TWENTY-SEVEN

NOW

Dina's hands are snug around my neck and I claw at them, desperate to pry them free. I kick and flail at her body, but all the energy has drained from me and I can't seem to move my limbs properly. My vocal cords are being squeezed so tightly that I'm unable to even cry out. Nothing I try is having any effect. I'm too close to her face to make out her features clearly, but her eyes are narrowed, and her mouth is twisted, her breath hot on my face. My vision keeps blurring and I swing between sheer terror and utter disbelief that this is it. That I'm powerless to escape. That I'm about to die. Surely something will happen to break her grip on my flesh. Surely someone will intervene to save me.

I wake with a wordless cry, still in the grip of my nightmare, gasping for breath with my hands at my throat. My body is bathed in sweat and my head thumps like a bass drum. My heart pounds as I remember my dream – I was being murdered by my sister. For a few moments I have no idea where I am. It's dark. I'm lying in Toby's arms, the heavy curtains blocking out all but a faint thread of light from a tiny gap where they don't quite meet. And then it all comes flooding back to me. I'm at the hotel… my sister is dead… I killed her. Each realisation is a crushing blow to my chest. I clench my teeth and screw my eyes shut again.

Toby doesn't stir as I extricate myself from his embrace. I sit up, trying to get my breathing under control. What's going to happen now? I really want to get out of this hotel and go home. But the children are back at the house with Celia's sister Vivian. And anyway, how will I be able to face my beautiful Alice and Jamie knowing that I'm a murderer? That I killed my sister. How will I be able to face *anyone*? I still can't believe I did it. Why didn't I pull Dina away from Toby, rather than smashing a vase over her head? But she had a knife, maybe she would have used it on *me*. If only I could remember more than just Dina shouting at Toby. I concentrate on trying to recall anything else from that blank spot, but all I get for my trouble are shooting pains across my temple.

Toby is still sound asleep next to me. I'm glad. I could do with a few moments to myself to try to make sense of everything. I can't deal with him waking up yet. I don't want to talk to anyone. As I ease myself up, he stirs and mumbles. I freeze. But then he turns over and I'm able to make my escape, tiptoeing into the bathroom wearing just my underwear.

I catch sight of my reflection in the mirror. Last night's make-up is patchy and streaked, highlighting the dark circles beneath my eyes. My hair is plastered against one side of my head and my fake eyelashes are squashed and misshapen. I peel them off and drop them on the side of the sink, then I step out of my underwear and into the large shower cubicle.

As the hot-water jets batter my body, I wish I could switch off my thoughts, but it's impossible. Toby's story comes back to me in pieces, and with each fragment, it feels as if I'm being re-made into a different person. A person I don't recognise.

An image jumps into my brain. Of me crouched on the floor, staring down at Dina's crumpled form. I turn her face towards mine and recoil when I see that her eyes are blank, staring at nothing. With a pull on my gut, I remember the shock. The horror. And, even more shocking and unexpected, the feeling of rage I felt towards her. *Another memory.*

As the water rushes over my skin, my whole body begins to shake uncontrollably. My poor, poor sister. I know she was a troubled soul, but she didn't deserve this. She didn't deserve to die. I realise Toby was telling the truth. I hadn't quite wanted to believe that my sister was dead. But there's no disputing the sharpness of that flashback. I'm still shaking, my hands trembling and my knees soft as sponges.

What am I going to do? Is Toby right? Should we keep this a secret? I deserve to go to jail for what I did, but why should Toby and his family also be punished simply for looking out for me? And what would knowledge of my crime do to the children?

A knock on the shower door makes me jump. I turn to see Toby standing there in his boxers, his face and body blurred behind the steamed-up glass.

'Zoe, you okay?' His voice is muffled.

'I'll be out in a minute.' My voice wobbles.

'Can I jump in with you?'

'Hang on, I won't be long.' I turn away from him and hope he understands that I want to be alone. Just a few moments more to try to compose myself. A few moments more until I have to go out and face reality, more questions and answers that I'd rather not deal with. But as I stand here quivering, with hot water streaming down my body, I'm overtaken by a rush of shame. I'm behaving like a child. This was something *I* caused. It was *me*. *My* sister. *My* family who dragged Toby and Nick into this. I need to step up and take some responsibility. I can't blame Toby for simply telling me the truth. Even though he should have told me ten years ago. I can't hide from what I've done.

I'll give myself one more minute in here, and then I'll dry off, get dressed and face whatever today holds. I can't believe that I've spent the last decade thinking Dina didn't want anything to do with me. That she'd cut herself off from her family, when in reality she was gone. I choke out an unexpected, violent sob. Tears mingle with shower water and my shoulders shudder. But I have to stay in control of my emotions – at least for now. There are too many other people to consider in all this for me to fall apart.

Before I can change my mind, I turn the shower dial to cold. The effect is almost instantaneous. Freezing jets shock me out of my crying jag. Gasping, I turn them off and stand dripping and shivering, but more awake and clearer-headed than seconds earlier.

I push away the image of Dina's blank-eyed stare, step out of the cubicle, grab a thick grey bath towel from the radiator and wrap it around my goose-fleshed body. The towel is blissfully warm. I take another for my hair. My mouth is dry and sour. There's a complimentary toiletry kit by the sink. I tear open the wrapper and fish out a bamboo toothbrush and mini-toothpaste tube. I brush my teeth badly and quickly; thankful the mirror is too steamed up to show my reflection again. Steeling myself with a deep breath and a squaring of my shoulders, I leave the bathroom.

Toby is sitting by the window drinking coffee, already dressed in jeans, a shirt and V-neck jumper. He must have decided to skip his shower. He glances up as I enter the room. He doesn't quite smile but manages to give me a sympathetic look. 'Snow,' he says. The curtains are open. Through the window lies a world of white – the grounds, the sky, the branches of the trees, the ledges of the mullioned windows, all blanketed with thick snow. I briefly think of the kids, and how excited they'll be to wake up to this. My stomach heaves.

'What's the time?' I croak.

'Almost nine.'

'What am I going to do?' I wail, then bite my lip, telling myself not to lose it.

'You're not going to do anything.' He holds out his arm. 'Here, come and sit. I'll make you a coffee.'

'I don't want coffee.' That's a lie. I'd love a coffee.

'I'm going to make you one anyway.'

'Okay. I'll get dressed.'

I notice my suitcase has been placed on a bench by the wardrobe, the lid propped open. Obviously my husband's handiwork. I take out the first suitable clothes that come to hand – socks, pants, a bra, a camisole, dark blue skinny jeans and an oversized cream jumper. I quickly dry off and get dressed. Toby hands me a milky coffee and I greedily inhale the aroma, before taking a sip and burning the roof of my mouth.

'You said I shouldn't do anything. But how can I not?' I stand by the window and stare down at the drive. There are several tyre tracks and footprints. A young couple are walking outside bundled up against the cold and wearing wellies. I envy them.

I turn back to face my husband. 'While I was in the shower, I had another flashback to that day. I can remember seeing Dina… afterwards. She was…' I let out a sob. 'She was dead.' My hands start shaking again and I put my drink on the windowsill, splashing coffee down the curtains in the process.

'Hey, hey.' Toby comes and holds me, strokes my hair and kisses the top of my head. 'It's a shock, I know.'

'What am I going to do?' I gulp down more sobs.

'Right now, you're not going to do anything. We'll take it a day at a time, and we'll get through it together.'

'Maybe we should tell your mum.'

'No!' Toby tenses up, his voice ringing through the silence. He winces and relaxes his hold on me. 'Sorry for shouting, but the last thing I want to do is bring my parents into this. They wouldn't be able to handle it.'

'I disagree. Your mum is the most calm and capable person I know. She'd have good advice. Yes, it would be a shock, of course it would, but she'll know what to do for the best.'

'Absolutely not.' Toby takes a step back from me so he can look me in the eye, his expression is dark, his eyes hooded. 'Nick and I already discussed this and we both decided long ago that we'd keep this between ourselves. We can't afford to tell anyone else. And it's not fair to involve my parents.'

A sudden wave of guilt engulfs me. Toby's been protecting me all these years, living with this knowledge, and yet loving me anyway. And now I'm talking about putting his family in danger. How can he even bear to look at me? I don't deserve him. 'You're right. I'm sorry. Of course we shouldn't involve your mum and dad. I was being selfish.'

Toby's face softens. 'No, not at all. Look, I've had years to process this. To go through all the pros and cons of what to do and what not to do. You've only just found out, so it's going to take a while to come to terms with what happened.'

'But what about my dad? Surely he has a right to know about Dina. She's his daughter! What if – God forbid – what if it were Alice or Jamie? Wouldn't we have a right to know?' Although I realise that if I tell my father, I'll also have to tell him that it was my fault. I'll have to confess what I did.

Toby holds both my arms and looks into my eyes. 'Zoe, I know this is hard, but you're going to have to learn to live with this. I'd rather not have told you at all, but my brother…' He lets go of me and blows out a noisy breath. 'If I hadn't told you, Nick would have said something. He's already a loose cannon, freaking out about this bloody development. Like I said yesterday, I'm going to have to do something about her body.'

An unwelcome image comes to my mind. If she's been buried out there for ten years, then what does she look like now? My milky coffee curdles in my throat.

'I'm sorry.' Toby has the grace to look down. 'I shouldn't have brought that up again. This is all so fresh for you. Like I said, Nick and I have had years to get used to it. Well, not used to it, but…' He trails off, probably realising that there's no tactful way to talk about this.

I walk across the room, trying to shake the image, when something else pops into my head. I turn back to look at my husband. 'Something doesn't add up.'

He frowns. 'What doesn't?'

'I messaged Dina after the wedding telling her that I was pregnant. I remember because I was pissed off that her replies weren't more enthusiastic. Don't you remember?'

Toby's cheeks flush and he bites his lip as I realise…

'Did you have her phone?'

'I'm sorry.'

'So it was *you*! You replied, pretending to be her!' I sit down heavily on the edge of the unmade bed. This is all too real. All too awful and horrible and vile and whatever other bad words I can think of.

Toby comes across the room and stands in front of me, his eyes heavy with apology. 'I'm so sorry. I hated doing that. But it was all part of protecting you. And then I worried that her phone might have been somehow traceable, so I got rid of it.'

I'm startled by the sound of my own phone ringing. I reach down to pick up my bag from the floor and extract my mobile. 'It's my dad.'

'Are you going to answer it?'

'I can't. I can't lie to him. But he's here in the hotel. How am I going to avoid him? I can't do this! I can't lie! Toby, what should I do?' I see he's left a message, so I play it on speaker. He says he's in the conservatory downstairs having breakfast. He wants to know if I'm coming to join him.

'What do you want to do? We could go down just to show our faces for ten minutes, if you feel up to it. We don't have to talk much.'

'No. No way. I can't go down there. How can I face everyone – Madeline, Nick, your parents, my dad? It's impossible. No. You'll have to go down by yourself. Tell them I'm still asleep, or I that

I don't feel well. Say I've got a hangover if you like. I don't care what you say. But I'm not going down there. I can't.'

'Okay, Zo. Okay. Don't worry. Whatever you want to do is fine with me. Do you want me to call your dad back? Tell him you're not feeling well?'

'Maybe.' I let out a breath. 'I don't know. Do you think it'll be strange if I don't go down? Suspicious? I really can't face it. All I want to do is crawl under the duvet and hide.'

'Then do that. And no, it won't seem strange at all – not if I tell them you're ill. No one else apart from Nick has any inkling of what happened back then, so it's not going to look suspicious. Go back to bed if you like. I'll order room service and stay with you, okay?' He sits and puts an arm around me. Pulls me close to him and I rest my head on his shoulder, breathing in his scent.

'Thank you,' I murmur. 'I'm not hungry. But you order some breakfast for yourself.'

'You sure you don't want anything? Some toast? Orange juice?'

I shake my head, feeling close to tears again. 'No thanks. I'm just going to have another sleep, so why don't you go down on your own. Make excuses for me.'

'I don't like to leave you up here alone. Not while you're so upset.' He rubs my back soothingly.

'I'll be fine. I just need some time on my own to try to get my head around it. Go. I'll feel better knowing you're putting everyone's mind at rest. Especially my dad's.'

'Okay.' Toby stands. 'If you're sure.'

'I am.'

My husband kisses me on the lips and gives my hand a squeeze. I manage a small, unconvincing smile before he picks up his phone and the door key and leaves the room.

CHAPTER TWENTY-EIGHT

NOW

After Toby leaves me to go down to breakfast, my brain continues its frenzied pinwheeling from one panicked thought to another. I realise that I forgot to tell Toby to come up with another excuse for later, because we're all due to have lunch together and then go to the spa this afternoon. And I can say with absolute certainty that I won't be doing that. I should text him to tell him to let everyone know that I'm not up for doing anything today. But I don't have the energy even for that.

I wobble to my feet and walk over to the window, staring out at the snowy landscape. A Range Rover disappears down the driveway, which is miraculously clear of snow. They must have gritted the drive last night. I blink and try to marshal my thoughts, but they won't stop skipping around. The skin on my face feels dry and taut, my eyes scratchy, my throat constricted. I don't know how I managed to get any sleep last night. I don't think I'll ever be able to sleep again. Not with the knowledge of what I've done.

I cast my mind back. My brain starts speeding, flipping through everything that happened on my wedding day. How can my mind have locked the truth away from me for so long? Why am I only just now beginning to remember?

I feel as though my thoughts are caught in a loop – trying to recall those forgotten events and then telling myself that it's all impossible. I'm going to quickly drive myself mad if I don't stop. I need to do something to distract myself from all of this. Just for a while, to calm myself down. I pick up my phone from the table. There's only nine per cent battery life left, but I decide to call the children just to hear their voices. To have some normality.

Vivian answers the home phone and asks how last night went. I give her some vaguely positive reply in a voice that doesn't sound like my own. She says that the children have been as good as gold. I speak to Alice and Jamie in turn, hearing their excitement about the snow, letting them ramble on about each little thing they've done since we've been away. It's a blessing to hear their innocent voices. To be transported for a moment to my regular world where my sister isn't dead, and I'm not a murderer.

'I miss you so much, Mummy,' Jamie says.

'I miss Mum too!' Alice calls, not to be outdone.

I smile and tell them that I miss them more and can't wait to see them tomorrow. As I end the call, I realise I'm crying.

I wipe away my tears with the back of my hand and locate the phone charger in my suitcase. Spying a plug socket beneath my bedside table, I connect my phone and set it on the table. I'm startled by a knock at the door. Then I realise it's probably housekeeping.

'No thanks!' I call, resolving to put out the 'Do Not Disturb' sign as soon as they've gone.

There's another knock and I'm about to call out again to say I don't need them when a familiar voice comes through the door.

'Zoe! It's Dad.'

My heart begins to race. I thought Toby was going to put him off coming up here. What if Dad sees me and can tell something's wrong? What if he starts asking questions?

'Can you let me in, love? I won't stay long.'

I open my mouth to make an excuse, but I just can't do it. I've never been any good at saying no or turning people away. I check my face in the mirror and wipe away a long smudge of tears with my fingertips. Then I inhale deeply and go over to the door. My only plan is to say as little as possible and feign tiredness in the hope he leaves quickly.

I glance around the room, checking for – I don't know what. It somehow feels like the story Toby told me happened just now, not a decade ago. I'm almost expecting to see smashed glass on the floor, or blood, or Dina's crumpled body. I shudder and shake away the gruesome image in my head.

'Zoe? You in there?'

'Coming!' I call, my voice steadier than it has any right to be.

I walk quickly across the room and fiddle with the door catch, finally turning it and pulling open the door. Dad stands there, a little way down the corridor, gazing at a piece of modern art on the wall. 'What's this supposed to be?' he asks. 'Looks like a big squiggle. It's got a price. They want four hundred quid for it!'

'Hi, Dad.'

'Didn't see you at breakfast.' He finally glances up in my direction and follows me into my room.

'No, sorry, I had a bit of a lie-in. Didn't Toby tell you?'

'I didn't see him down there. Must have missed him. A lie-in, eh? Too much partying?'

'Something like that.'

My dad looks around the room. 'This is nice. Good view out the front.' He walks over to the window and stands there with his hands tucked behind his back. 'Haven't been to this place since your wedding.'

'I know. Seems like so long ago.'

'Not that long. Ten years has gone by in the blink of an eye. You all right, love?' He squints over at me. 'Looking a tad peaky if you don't mind me saying. You been crying?'

For a moment I debate whether to go against Toby's wishes and tell Dad what I found out last night. The urge to break down and confess is so strong that I almost ache with it. But I can't do or say anything rash. I need to think this through. Once I say something, I can't unsay it. And this is about my sister, his daughter. It's not something I can just blurt out, is it?

'I'm just feeling a bit rough. I think I overdid things yesterday.' It's the truth, so why does it feel like a lie? Maybe because it's a lie by omission.

'You sure that's all it is?' Dad's eyes narrow and he really looks at me.

The moment ends when a knock at the door makes us break eye contact. I'm sure it must be housekeeping this time, and I'm about to turn them away when Celia's voice rings through the closed door.

'Zoe, can I come in?'

My heart sinks at the thought of having to pretend some more. At this rate I may as well have gone down to breakfast.

'Want me to tell her to go?' Dad asks.

I briefly consider his offer, before deciding against it. Celia could well be a breath of fresh air. A no-nonsense antidote to the dread and despair into which I find myself sinking. 'It's okay, I don't mind if she comes in.'

Dad gives a brief nod. 'Well, okay, I'm going for a walk. I've got my phone with me. Call if you need anything.'

I'm a little stunned. Dad has never asked if I needed anything. Not since I left home, and even before that he wasn't the most forthcoming of parents. Maybe he's sensed my fear and worry. Maybe it's activated some recessive parenting gene.

'Okay, Zoe?' He shakes me out of my musing.

'Yeah, okay, thanks. Wrap up warm. I'll see you later.'

He nods, leaves the room and lets Celia in on his way out. They mumble a brief greeting to one another as they pass.

'Sorry…' Celia steps hesitantly into the room. 'Guy's not leaving on my account, is he?'

'No, he's going for a walk.'

'Good. I hope I'm not intruding. I was just a little worried when you didn't come down to breakfast. Toby said you weren't feeling too well. I've brought you up some paracetamol and some pastries from the buffet. I know you can order room service, but you might not be bothered to do that if you're feeling peaky.'

'That's so kind. Come and sit down, if you like.' I wonder if she'd be quite so kind if she knew what I'd done.

'Do you want a cup of tea?' She opens up her capacious handbag and pulls out a couple of napkins which are now shedding flakes of pastry over the floor. 'Oh dear, I'm making such a mess.' She places the napkins on the table by the window. 'You sit there, and I'll get the kettle on, unless you want coffee?'

'Tea's great. I already had a coffee.' I do as she suggests and sit at the table as though I'm acting a part.

'That was a lovely evening, wasn't it?' She bustles about at the large dresser and I let her get on with it. 'Did you enjoy yourself? I thought our finger-food selections were spot on. Everyone at our table was raving about the arancini balls. You looked like you were having a good time anyway.'

'I did have a good time, thanks, Celia.' *Until I wasn't anymore.*

'You left quite early though,' she says pointedly.

'Yes, I know, sorry. I was just telling Dad that I think I overdid things. I was looking after Madeline – she had a bit too much to drink – and then I suddenly came over all tired.'

'You do look a little washed-out this morning, if you don't mind me saying.' Celia brings over our cups of tea and settles herself opposite me. She's dressed casually in a blue floral jumper, dark-grey jeans and navy ankle boots. Her make-up is light, with just a touch of blush and a smear of pale-pink lipstick. 'I knocked on Madeline's door too, but I think she must still be asleep.'

Just like my urge to unburden myself to Dad, I really want to tell Celia what I learned about my wedding day. It's like an itch I need to scratch.

'Have one of these.' Celia unfolds the napkins to reveal some squashed mini pastries. 'The maple and pecan are delicious.'

I'm not hungry, but I make a pretence of tearing off a corner and popping it in my mouth. I can tell Celia's not fooled; she raises her eyebrows and her nostrils flare delicately.

I leave the pastry and reach for my tea instead, sipping at the scalding liquid. 'Being back here at the hotel has really brought back memories of our wedding day.'

'I'm sure it has.' Celia takes a sip of her tea. 'Such a magical ceremony.'

I hesitate. 'Do you remember what happened when I... passed out?'

Celia pauses mid-sip. 'Oh, gosh, yes, that's right, you fainted, didn't you?'

'But how did it actually happen?'

'Well, of course I didn't see it. I was downstairs with your bridesmaids getting my make-up done. That girl really overdid my eye make-up. I had to wipe most of it off. But that's beside the point. Nick called to tell me what had happened. Asked me to come straight up and check you were okay. He was worried sick, poor soul. You gave us all a real fright.'

'It's just weird that I can't remember it at all. One minute I was getting ready with you, Lou and Becky, and the next I was waking up on the floor.'

'Well we found out later that you were pregnant with Alice, so that explained the fainting episode. I used to get very dizzy when I was expecting Toby. I fainted on a bus once. It was quite embarrassing.'

'It's weird, because since I've been back here, I think it's triggered something in my brain. I'm starting to get flashbacks of that day. Only I can't make proper sense of them.' I need to shut up now. Celia has always been my go-to person to confide in. But I know she's the last person I should be saying anything to. Toby would be so upset if he thought I was going to burden his mum with any of this. It wouldn't be fair. 'I just wondered if, as a nurse, whether you think my memories might return properly. Have you come across this type of thing before?'

'Memory is a very unreliable thing,' Celia replies. 'Especially in your situation, where you have a blank spot. It's entirely possible that your brain could create false memories that might trick you into believing they're real.' She picks up a custard crown and takes a bite. 'Mm, this is heavenly. I've already been such a greedy Gertie this morning, but I can't resist a good hotel breakfast. Sorry, as I was saying, memories are tricky little beasts. I know mine's getting worse as I get older!'

'You're right,' I reply. 'I should probably stop driving myself mad trying to remember what happened. It's just a bit disconcerting, you know?'

'Well, yes and no.' Celia gives me a smile and reaches across to pat my hand. 'Maybe it's your body's way of blocking out an unpleasant thing. I mean, who really wants to remember fainting and hitting your head on a desk?'

If only that were all I was blocking out. 'You're right, as usual.'

'It's nice to be right occasionally. Now, tell me, why aren't you eating anything?' As Celia takes another bite of her pastry, flakes drop onto her jumper. She brushes them off.

'Well, aside from the flashback thing, I think I'm a bit hungover.'

'Aah, that explains why you're looking so green. You should have some more tea, get back into bed and catch up on your sleep. Hopefully you'll have recovered by lunchtime.'

'I'd feel so lazy doing that.'

'Nonsense.' She wipes her fingers on the corner of one of the napkins. 'This is your anniversary weekend. You need to get better so you can enjoy the rest of it. Sleep will help.'

'You sure you don't mind?'

'Why should I mind?' She takes a sip of tea.

'What about the others? Won't they be expecting me to show my face? What are they going to do today?'

'Let me see…' She counts off the others on her fingers. 'Malcolm's playing snooker in the bar with another of the guests; Madeline's like you – in her room, a little worse for wear; I sent Nick and Toby for a walk. And you said your dad's gone for a walk too.'

'Yes.'

'Well, there you go! I'm going to find a quiet spot by the fire in one of the lounges and settle down with my novel.' She reaches into her bag and takes out a small enamel pot. 'Now, have a couple of these headache tabs and climb into bed. We can meet later when you're feeling better.'

I take the tablets from my mother-in-law and wash them down with the rest of my tea. Celia draws the curtains, but I find I'm too distracted to even take off my clothes and get into my pyjamas. I had hoped that talking to my mother-in-law would have helped to set my mind at rest. But as I lie on top of the covers, I can't help scratching at my hazy memories, trying to sharpen them into something clearer. I remember seeing my sister's lifeless body. I remember a smashed vase, water everywhere, winter roses. And Dina shouting something. *What was she shouting?*

After closing the curtains, Celia walks away across the darkened room. 'Get some sleep,' she says softly, opening the door. A shaft of light from the corridor illuminates her, and washes into the room, casting strange shadows.

I'm too enmeshed in my thoughts to say a proper goodbye. Instead, I mumble something vague and exhale with relief as Celia closes the door behind her, plunging the room into darkness once more and leaving me alone. For a moment, I wonder what the hell I'm still doing here. In this room. In this hotel. Where it happened. Where I…

I sit bolt upright, my eyes wide, my body frozen as an avalanche of memories cascades into my brain like a pack of playing cards being dealt too fast. My whole body shudders as though I have the flu, my skin going alternately hot and then ice cold.

I can remember.

I can remember *everything*.

CHAPTER TWENTY-NINE

THE DAY OF THE WEDDING

I turn one way and then the other, gazing at my reflection in the full-length mirror. It doesn't even look like me. My hair normally hangs in a dark curtain down my back. Today it's been softly curled and held back off my face by the pearl comb and veil which my mother wore at her wedding. My ivory lace dress is fitted, flaring out slightly at the hem, its tiny seed pearls catching the winter light that streams through the huge sash windows. I'll wait until Celia comes back before attempting to attach the billowing tulle train. There's still over an hour to go before the ceremony starts and I don't want to be tripping over it.

The door opens with a click. 'Wow, Zoe, look at you!'

I turn at the sound of a familiar voice, not daring to believe she actually made it. 'Dina!' Standing before me is my sister, windswept and red-cheeked. Her hair is longer than I've ever seen it before, cascading over her shoulders – a rich brown mane with reddish highlights – either dyed, or maybe lightened by years of sunshine. 'You came! I thought you were in Thailand. You said you couldn't get away… It's been so long I hardly recognise you!'

The door closes behind her and she stares at me, her eyes glittering, her mouth slightly open. I shouldn't be this happy to see her – not after the last conversation we had. But the fact that she's here must mean she wants to patch things up.

'I know we left things on a weird note, but I'm so glad you changed your mind. It just didn't feel right, getting married without my little sister here.' I find that I really mean it. Despite what's gone on between us, I'm desperate to move on and forgive the past. I take a step towards her to give her a hug, but my sister recoils, stopping me in my tracks.

'Save it, Zoe,' she sneers. 'I know you don't want me here any more than I want to be here.' Her words hit me in the gut. She's not here to make amends after all.

I shake my head. 'Why are you being like this, Dee? Is it because of the money?' If she still has a problem with me, why did she have to choose today of all days to come back into my life? Maybe she planned it on purpose to ruin my big day. Well, she's succeeding… unless I can shrug her off and not rise to the bait. 'How did you even get into my room?'

'Told them I was your sister. They gave me a key.'

'Well they shouldn't have. You could have been lying for all they know.'

'It was Mandy on reception. You know, with the big boobs and glasses. I was in her year at school.'

'She still shouldn't have given you the—'

'Are we really going to stand here talking about what Mandy should or shouldn't have done?' There's a slight drawl to her voice which I first take as heavy sarcasm, but she might be slurring her words.

'Have you been drinking?'

She snorts out a laugh. 'You could say that.'

'Look, I realise we've got lots to discuss, but as you can see it's my wedding day. Surely this can wait for another time. Why don't we sit down, have a quick catch-up?' I gesture to the seating area. 'We haven't seen one another for almost ten years. Not since you were sixteen. The least we could do is—'

'I'm not here to catch up,' she snaps. 'I'm not even here to see you.'

'Okay. Well, Dad's downstairs in the bar getting a coffee with Cassie and her family. We can surprise him.'

'Not here to see Dad either.'

'So why exactly are you here?' I throw my hands up in despair and disappointment.

'Where's Toby?'

'Dina, no! You can't tell him!' My hands have started shaking uncontrollably.

Her smile is mean and my heart sinks as I realise the reason she's come. For some kind of twisted revenge, even though I already helped her out once before. My mind races and I try to think of a way out of this. 'Look, I'm sorry I couldn't give you all the money, but I needed it.'

On our twenty-first birthdays we each received a lump sum from our mum's trust. It wasn't a huge amount, but I've since put my share towards buying a house with Toby. It made me feel good that I could chip in fifty per cent of the deposit.

Dina burned through her inheritance within a few months of receiving it, and then called to ask if I could lend her some of mine, as she had an opportunity to invest in a beach bar. I'd told her I was saving my share, but she kept on and on, saying I was standing in the way of her future.

Eventually she seemed to accept my decision, but I should have realised that was wishful thinking on my part. She asked me if Toby knew about my drug habit. I said that trying a spliff one time didn't exactly count as a drug habit. And anyway, I'd been pressured into it by friends – or one particular friend actually. But while I bluffed to Dina that Toby wouldn't care, I knew very well that he wouldn't have been happy with the news. He likes the fact I'm a goody-two-shoes.

Dina went on to say that, the way she remembered it, back when we were teenagers, is that I was an addict and a dealer. I laughed aloud at that, until I realised she was deadly serious. The penny dropped.

She was actually attempting to blackmail me. Given Toby's ambition to run for town council, having a fiancée who had dealt drugs wouldn't have gone down too well with him or his family – even though it was a complete fabrication. I worried he might even have gone so far as to break off our engagement. So I ended up giving Dina some of the money. But I lied and said I'd spent the rest. That seemed to satisfy her at the time. But now here she is, back again. This time on my wedding day, wanting to speak to Toby!

'Dina, you swore you wouldn't say anything about all that. Why would you lie about me? What good will it do? If you need some more cash, I'm sure I can scrape some together…'

But she turns her back and leaves the room. I trail after her, pleading for her to reconsider, knowing that this kind of revelation could ruin everything. I'd like to think that once I explain to Toby that my sister is lying, he'll eventually understand, but it will take time and it will mean that today won't be the magical day I was dreaming of. In fact, it's already tainted. I'm trembling with anger and shock, terrified about what my husband-to-be will do when he hears Dina's exaggerated version of my past. And what about Celia and Malcolm? They'll be horrified.

'Dina, come back! You're drunk! Please… you don't know what you're saying. Why are you doing this?'

She knocks on the door next to mine and then moves on to the next. 'Toby, are you in there?' She glances back at me, a vindictive expression on her face.

Last night, Toby stayed in a room next to his parents', just along the corridor from me. Dina is almost outside his door now. Thankfully, no one else has answered Dina's knocks – I'm hoping those rooms are unoccupied and I'm praying that by some miracle Toby doesn't answer.

'He's on the next floor up,' I bluff, hoping she buys it.

'Why would you tell me that?' she scoffs, now knocking on Toby's door.

I pray for Toby to be anywhere but in his room, but a moment later, he opens the door, his mouth falling open at the sight of my dishevelled, drunken sister. He's already in his suit, the top button of his shirt open, his black tie hanging loose around his neck. My husband-to-be – unless my sister ruins everything. 'Dina? Uh…' And then he spies me behind her and his face blanches. 'Zoe, what's going on? You shouldn't be here. I'm not supposed to see you until later.'

Dina pushes past him into his room. 'Hello, Toby.'

Toby makes to close the door before I can follow her inside. 'You go back to your room, Zoe. I'll pretend I didn't see you. Isn't it bad luck to see the bride before we're married?'

'My sister's drunk.' I force my way past him, into his room, closing the door behind me. We're all standing in the centre of the room now, equidistant from one another.

Toby glances from me to Dina. He looks panicked and I don't blame him. But even faced with my deranged sister, he's still looking out for me. 'Honestly, go back to your room. I'll sort this out.'

But I can't leave my sister alone with Toby. I'm terrified she's going to lie to him and try to ruin our wedding. 'Toby, I'm so sorry I couldn't stop her coming to see you. She's had too much to drink and she's talking absolute rubbish. Let me call my dad. Can I use your phone?'

'I can't believe you're actually marrying her!' Dina spits at Toby. 'How could you go through with it? How could you think I would let you!'

And now it's my turn to glance from one to the other. Dina is angry at him, and Toby appears to be terrified. But what is he terrified of? I'm suddenly very hot and my dress feels too tight. Something's going on here, and I don't think it's anything to do with my schooldays.

'Shall I tell her, or will you?' Dina asks my fiancé, who is currently several shades whiter than his shirt.

'Tell me what?' My voice is little more than a whisper. The room has fallen silent. All I can hear is my heart beating.

'Zoe… I'm…' Toby's voice trails off.

'Toby?' I suddenly realise that Dina's visit is nothing to do with blackmailing me. It's to do with Toby. *Her* and Toby.

I grit my teeth and feel something akin to anger building, but it's not like any anger I've experienced before. It boils up from the depths of my core. A dark realisation that I've been made an absolute fool of by the two people I'm closest to in the world. The horror that my life as I thought it would be, is over. That nothing will ever be the same again. The love of my life is a fraud. A cheater. A bastard. But I can't lose it yet. First, I need to hear him say it.

'Zoe,' he says more firmly this time. 'You have to believe that I love you. It meant nothing.'

'Nothing?' Dina snarls. 'You prick!' She turns to me. 'We've been seeing each other for months. He loves me.' She takes a step closer to him.

'But you were in Thailand,' I say stupidly. 'You told me you couldn't get home for the wedding.'

Her lip curls. 'I lied.' She marches right up to Toby now and shoves at his chest. 'You said you wouldn't go through with the wedding! You promised me.'

'I didn't. That was when we first met, and I was stupidly seduced by you. But I made it clear that it was over. A mistake. I'm in love with Zoe. I always have been. We should never have—'

'You bastard!' Dina starts beating him with her fists. Slowly and ineffectually at first. But then she warms up, pulling at his hair, his clothes, kicking him, yelling and screaming all kinds of profanities.

'Get off me, Dina! You're insane!' He pulls away and takes several steps back towards the desk in front of the bay window.

'Zoe, do something! Call someone!'

'I hope she kills you,' I mutter, shaking and feeling utterly ridiculous and humiliated in my wedding dress. Suddenly, I'm desperate to get out of it. To rip it to shreds and stuff the pieces down my cheating fiancé's throat.

'I'm a mistake, am I?' Dina snatches up an empty coffee cup and lobs it at Toby. He ducks and it misses him, shattering against the window, but she follows it up with the saucer which glances off his chin. She's searching around for something else to throw and grabs a large heavy-looking glass vase filled with white winter roses.

'Don't!' Toby strides over to where she's standing in the centre of the room and tries to wrench the vase out of her grip before she can do any serious damage with it. They struggle and I wonder what the hell I'm even doing here. I should leave them to it. Let them kill each other. Today is wrecked. The life I thought I was going to have is over. My world is in tatters. Toby is a cheat. They both betrayed me.

Dina hugs the vase to her chest, refusing to let it go. Toby now has her by the throat. She manages to choke out a few choice swear words before eventually dropping the vase. It shatters on the wooden floor, water pooling around their feet. Winter roses mingling with shards of cut glass. Dina's face is scarlet, her eyes wide.

I suddenly realise that my wish might be about to come true. He might actually kill her. And no matter how screwed up our relationship is, I don't actually want my sister to die!

'Toby, let go.'

His face is contorted with rage, his hands still fixed around her neck.

'Toby!' I stumble over to where they stand tussling in the centre of the room, a grim tableaux. 'Stop it!' I yell, my shoes crunching over broken glass as I yank at his arm, trying to get him to release his hold on her. He pays me no attention. 'STOP! You're going to kill her!' I can't break his grip. I need to get help…

CHAPTER THIRTY

NOW

The hotel room is endlessly dark. I'm sitting up in bed, a cold sweat dampening my hair, my head pounding, my heart racing with a deep terror that leaves me gasping and gulping for air. Shaking and crying as though I'm still there in Toby's hotel room ten years ago. As though it was only seconds ago that I was screaming at him to stop what he was doing. Crunching over broken glass. Trying to break his grip from around Dina's neck.

Toby strangled my sister! I realise my hands are around my own throat and I can barely swallow. I let go and crawl forward on the bed onto my hands and knees, still gasping in shock and disbelief. It was *Toby*! Not me. I'm not a murderer. It was my husband. He slept with her and then he strangled her. And then I... I married this man. Raised two children with him.

'No, no, no, no, no.' I bury my face in the bedclothes and let out a moan. Am I dreaming? Am I in the throes of a nightmare? This surely can't be real. But it is. I remember it as clearly as if I were there. Everything has been a lie. My wedding day... my husband... my marriage... my sister. All a big fat lie.

Toby. My husband. The man I thought was the love of my life. Who has been by my side through thick and thin. In sickness and in health. He lied to me. Betrayed me. I squeeze my eyes shut. Try to gulp down some air and shut it all out. But this is too huge to ignore. Too devastating. I can hardly take it all in. The memories replay themselves – my sister's sneering expression and drunken slurs. Toby's panicked face and then his cold, cruel grip on Dina's neck. *All those lies.*

And he's still lying. Yesterday he told me that I was a killer. Blamed me for my sister's death and made out that he'd been standing by me all these years, that he'd never been even remotely interested in my sister like that. He made out that it was all her fault. Said he'd been protecting me from the truth, like he was being noble, forgiving me for what I'd done.

I push myself up into a kneeling position on the bed. He must have thanked his lucky stars when he discovered I'd lost my memory. How could he go on to make me believe such a despicable thing about myself? How *could* he? How *dare* he! Pretending that he was prepared to stand by my side through all of this. That he's been such a good and faithful husband. Looking out for me. When all along he's just been covering his own arse. He had an affair and then he killed her! Is this the man I married?

How can my husband be so far removed from the perfect man I thought he was? I clench my fists, suddenly fuelled with rage. But almost as soon as the anger hits, it ebbs away. My brain is becoming foggy. I need to open the curtains, to open the window and breathe in fresh air. Clear my head. Call the police and tell them what happened. They need to know that my sister was murdered. That my husband is a cold-blooded killer.

But what's going to happen to me? To my children?

My marriage is over.

With trembling fingers, I fumble on the bedside table for my phone, but I can't seem to locate it, so I give up, instead finding a bottle of water. I unscrew the cap, bring the bottle to my lips and drain the remaining few sips. But they do little to quench my thirst or clear my head. My mouth is so dry, but there's no time to waste getting a fresh bottle from the minibar. I need to find my phone.

I try to stand, but my legs are leaden, and my head is so heavy. Is it a hangover, or shock? Am I coming down with something? I don't understand why I'm feeling so strange and woozy. I lie back on the bed. I'll stay here for a moment until I feel strong enough to get up. Then I'll call the police. I just need a few minutes to collect myself, that's all…

I crack open an eyelid, and then another, allowing my eyes some time to adjust to the darkness. There's no hint of daylight through the curtains. I must have fallen asleep or passed out. Surely I haven't slept all day! My head throbs, and my eyelids are heavy. I don't feel as though I've slept at all. I'm tempted to simply close my eyes and give in to sleep once more. It's the only option that feels acceptable right now.

'You're awake.'

I give a start and raise my head at the sound of my mother-in-law's voice.

'Celia?' My voice is croaky. 'You made me jump. I didn't realise you were here.' Although, now I think of it, the scent of her White Linen perfume is all around me, catching in the back of my throat.

The light from Celia's phone blinks on, illuminating her face, making it appear distorted in the otherwise darkened room. She's sitting near the end of my bed tapping something into her mobile.

I take a breath and try to summon the energy to sit up. I'm still wearing my clothes and the top of my jeans is digging into my stomach, my jumper itches and I feel sweaty and gross. I could really do with a long drink of water and a cool shower. Now that I've eased myself upright, I can't seem to catch my breath. My whole body is tingling and I'm light-headed and dizzy.

'Is there any water? Where's Toby?' My tongue feels thick in my mouth. As if it's bigger than normal.

'The boys and Madeline have gone to the spa. Toby said you were so sound asleep he couldn't wake you, so I persuaded the three of them to have their treatments and a swim. I said you'd feel doubly bad if you thought they'd missed out.'

I can't imagine them all relaxing in the spa – swimming and enjoying themselves. It doesn't feel right. Not when Dina is dead.

Dina!

Toby killed her! They were having an affair. I let out a low moan.

'What wrong?' Celia asks. 'Are you okay, Zoe?'

I don't know what to say to her. I need her to leave. She's the last person I want to talk to about this. About her son. 'Celia…'

She holds a finger up, bidding me to wait a moment while she finishes doing whatever she's doing on the phone.

'Celia, I don't feel well.'

'Just breathe, Zoe.'

'I… I just need to be on my own for a while. Catch up on my sleep if that's okay…'

She finally puts her phone down and looks up. 'Your breathing sounds a bit strange.'

'I'm fine, just a bit dizzy.' But I can hear and feel my breaths coming in laboured bursts.

'Hmm, it sounds like you might be having a panic attack.'

'No, I'm okay, honestly.' But actually, I'm having real difficulty breathing and my fingers and toes are tingling. I pull at the neck of my jumper and try to take a deep breath, but nothing seems to be going into my lungs.

'Believe me, it's a panic attack,' Celia says sagely. 'I've seen enough of them in my time. It's nothing to worry about.' *That's easy for her to say.* She uses the light on her phone to guide her as she walks the short distance to my bedside table, where she switches on the side light. I wince against the sudden brightness. 'There, that's better. I can get a proper look at you now.'

The rate of my breathing accelerates, but each inhalation feels shallow and useless.

She gazes down at me critically. 'Are you able to stand up?'

'I… I don't know. I'd rather stay here. I feel too shaky to move.' Why am I so exhausted? 'Honestly, Celia, I'll be fine. You should join the others.'

'Nonsense. Come on,' she says brightly, 'up you get.' She takes hold of my legs and swings them around so they're off the bed. Then she sits and puts an arm around me, heaving me up. But my legs are unsteady, and my bones feel too soft to support my weight. 'Let's get you into that armchair.'

I glance over to see that one of the leaf-print armchairs that was previously by the window has been placed nearer to the bed. 'Why can't I just stay in bed?'

'You've had enough sleep for today, Zoe. It's making you even more drowsy. You need to sit up for a bit.'

I don't quite understand her logic, but she is a nurse, so I guess she's the expert. All I know is that I feel absolutely dreadful – nauseous, dizzy, exhausted and shaky. I let her support me and we make the half dozen shuffling steps over to the chair. Celia is sturdy and capable, and I feel reassured that she won't let me fall. Finally, I sink gratefully into the armchair. But within seconds, I start to feel awful again. I'm still having real trouble breathing. And there's a heaviness in my brain. Maybe it's the weight of my memory. The fact that my marriage is over, and my sister is dead.

'Where's my phone?' I need to call the police. But how can I do that with Celia here? I have to somehow get rid of her. But there's something really wrong with me. I don't feel well at all. 'I feel like I'm going to die.'

'Shh, you're fine, Zoe. Just try to calm down. Inhale for five seconds, and exhale for eight.'

I do as she says. Feeling the air come in through my nostrils, but I can't seem to suck it in any deeper. I try again, and this time it feels a little easier. Once I can get my breathing under control, hopefully I'll start to feel better and Celia will agree to leave me alone. Then I can make that call.

Celia takes my hand, but I can barely feel her touch – my fingers seem to have gone completely numb. 'In through the nose.' She breathes with me. 'And out through the mouth.' She guides me through this mantra a few times until my breathing finally slows a little. 'Much better. Okay, keep up the deep breathing and I'll be back in a minute. I just need to wash my hands.'

While Celia disappears into the bathroom, I keep up the breathing and, while I still feel as though someone's sitting on my chest, at least I'm no longer gasping like a landed fish. I wonder why she needs to wash her hands, unless she thinks I've got some contagious bug.

Celia returns to the room and retrieves her bag from the foot of the bed.

'Why are you wearing those gloves?' I croak. I'm sure she wasn't wearing them a minute ago.

'Oh, I always wear surgical gloves when I give injections. It's part of procedure. Hygiene, dear.'

'*Injection?*' I pant. 'What injection?'

'No need to look so worried.' She smiles. 'It's just a fast-acting sedative to help calm you down. It works far better intravenously than a pill. I often give it to patients who are suffering from panic attacks and anxiety. You'll feel calmer in no time.'

'No,' I protest. 'I'll be fine, I'll try the breathing thing again.' But the panicky feeling only worsens. My head flops back against the chair and I'm scared that I'm about to black out.

'Nonsense.' Celia brushes aside my concern. 'You'll feel so much better.'

I shake my head and tap my chest, trying to will air into my lungs. But nothing's working. I want to tell her that I'm feeling a little better now. That I don't need an injection. That I don't *want* an injection. But I daren't pause my slow-breathing exercises in case that awful, black dizzy feeling returns.

Celia rolls up the sleeve of my jumper. I'm breathing more deeply now, thankful that the dizziness is gradually receding. I'm actually beginning to feel slightly better. I open my mouth to tell her in no uncertain terms that I do not want her sedative, but it's too late. I'm dimly aware of her administering the injection – a sharp cold sensation on my skin.

'There. All done!' Celia declares with a smile. 'We'll have you sorted in no time.'

I try to turn my head at a knock at the door, but I feel suddenly and strangely too relaxed to move. Must be the sedative kicking in. That was quick.

'Right on time,' Celia says brightly. 'That'll be Malcolm. I'll get the door. You stay there, Zoe.' That phrase seems to have amused her, and she shakes her head with a smile. 'Don't mind me. It's an inside joke.'

Celia disappears from my line of sight, and I realise that I genuinely cannot move. It's very disconcerting. I wonder how I'm going to be able to get back into bed. I knew Celia should have left me where I was rather that shifting me into this chair. Maybe Malcolm will help her move me back.

He comes into the room carrying, of all things, a backpack. Celia closes the door behind him.

I want to greet Malcolm, but I can't seem to move my mouth. And strangely, he doesn't even acknowledge me, other than a brief glance in my direction. The two of them sit huddled together on the edge of the bed as Malcolm opens up the backpack. They're discussing something intensely in low voices, but I can't make out what they're saying.

Celia suddenly remembers I'm still here. 'Are you okay, Zoe?' She glances up and stares at me. But she doesn't look like herself. She's lost her soft, gentle demeanour. Her eyes are hard, assessing, critical.

I still can't open my mouth. In fact, I can't seem to move a muscle. I need to tell Celia that her sedative is making me feel extremely strange. That, actually, I'm quite scared. Surely she should be checking up on me, making sure I'm okay. She's a nurse. I'm her daughter-in-law. But she seems more concerned with Malcolm and his backpack.

Maybe I'm having an allergic reaction to the sedative. Or perhaps I'm simply frozen in shock after finding out about Dina. But this feels like something far worse than that. I can't move a muscle. I can't open my mouth. I can barely breathe.

This bridal suite must be jinxed. The last time I stayed here, my sister was murdered. And now something very strange is going on with Celia and Malcolm. What are they doing here? Why are they ignoring me?

Another strange sensation of déjà vu comes over me. Of Celia taking control of another situation. Only she wasn't with Malcolm that time. I try to catch hold of the memory that's sitting just out of reach on the edge of my consciousness. And then, just like the last time, it hits me in the solar plexus like a freight train.

CHAPTER THIRTY-ONE

THE DAY OF THE WEDDING

It's hopeless. Toby isn't listening to me. His hands are still locked around my sister's neck, choking her. Killing her. I'm screaming for help, so caught up in this nightmare that I barely register someone banging on the door.

When I finally hear it, it feels as if I'm moving in slow motion as I turn and run to the door, almost losing my footing on the wet floorboards. But I manage to fling it wide open, and Celia and Nick tumble into the room.

'Stop him!' I cry. 'My sister! He's hurting her!'

'Close the door!' Celia snaps at her eldest son.

He does as she asks. 'What's going on? We heard yelling.' Nick's gaze lands on his brother. On Dina as she sinks to the floor, limp as a ragdoll. 'Toby! Who's that? What are you…?'

My fiancé stands above Dina, panting, his eyes glazed.

I look at him, but he doesn't return my gaze, just stares down at Dina's crumpled form. 'What have you done?' I hurry to my sister's side, crouch down and turn her face to mine. Her eyes are staring, unseeing. My whole body begins to shake uncontrollably. 'Celia! Celia, I need you to help my sister. Can you save her?' But even as I say the words, I know it's useless. It's too late. Dina is dead.

My mother-in-law comes over and crouches by my side, but she shakes her head.

'Take her pulse!' I demand. 'Give her mouth to mouth! Do something!'

Celia takes Dina's limp wrist and feels for the pulse she already knows will be absent. 'I'm sorry, Zoe. She's gone.' She looks up at her son. 'What happened? Who is this?'

'They've been having an affair!' I blurt out. 'My sister and my fiancé. Your son! They've been seeing each other behind my back. And now he's killed her! We need to call the police.' I glance around and spy the hotel phone on the desk by the bay window. I walk towards it, scared about what will happen once I've made the call.

'Zoe, wait.' Celia comes after me.

'For what?' I snap. 'My sister is dead, there's nothing left to wait for. Toby is a murderer. An adulterous murderer. He needs to pay for what he's done.' I pick up the phone and dial 999. Celia tries to whip the phone out of my grasp, but I duck out of the way, moving further from the window.

'Let's just talk about this calmly.' She advances on me again.

'I know he's your son, but you can't protect him from this. That's my sister!'

'Just give me the phone, Zoe.' Celia's voice is steely, her eyes like two chips of flint. This is a side of her I've never seen before.

Nick is questioning Toby, who's standing in the middle of the room, his head in his hands. I think he's crying.

Before my call has a chance to connect, Celia snatches the phone from me and hangs up.

'Give me that back!' I try to pry her fingers off the phone, but she has too tight a hold. In a moment of desperation, I bite down on her bony knuckles.

'Hey, stop it!' Nick cries. But he doesn't try to intervene, just takes a step uselessly towards us.

'Zoe, what do you think you're doing?' Celia shoots me a venomous glare, wrenches her hands away from my mouth and gives me a vicious shove. My dress is so tight and my heels so high that I can't keep my balance. I can feel myself toppling backwards. My hands flail out to the side to try to grab hold of anything to steady my fall. But they find nothing but air.

CHAPTER THIRTY-TWO

The absolute shock of remembering makes me briefly forget my current situation. I stare at Celia in horror. She pushed me! She knocked me out cold on my wedding day.

I feel sick to my stomach.

If all of that is true, then what happens now? I literally cannot move, and Celia and Malcolm keep darting glances over towards me. I think whatever it was that Celia injected me with is not a mild sedative. It's something far worse. My insides turn to water as I realise that Celia is not in fact my friend. She's not the wonderful mother-in-law I made her out to be. She's not on my side at all and never has been. I think she's been keeping me close all these years so she could keep an eye on me after what happened with Toby and Dina. I can't stop thinking about the look she gave me when she tried to stop me calling the police all those years ago. When she shoved me backwards. It was vicious and triumphant.

Does Toby know his mother is here? Has he given her his blessing for whatever is going on right now? Oh, dear Lord, what if Celia plans to do away with me? What if I never see Alice and Jamie again and they're left to be raised by their murdering father and psychopathic grandparents? I have to get out of this. I have to save my children.

A knock at the door brings me back to my present surroundings. Please let it be someone good. Someone I can trust to help me.

'Zoe! You in there?'

Thank goodness! It's my dad! He goes quiet for a moment, no doubt waiting for my reply. I pray for him not to leave, to somehow open the door and rescue me. If only I could call out to him. I'm sending messages from my brain to my vocal cords, but nothing's happening. I can't so much as force out a whisper.

Celia looks at Malcolm and puts a finger to her lips. He nods. Their actions confirm that I'm in terrible danger.

Dad calls out once more, and I cling on to the sound of his voice. 'I tried to find the others but they're not in their rooms. I'm worried about you, love. If you can hear me, open the door!' He knocks harder this time and tries the handle. I hear it clicking up and down. But of course the door is locked. No one is going to be able to open it.

If only he'd come by earlier, before Celia had injected me with whatever it was. *Please find a way to open the door. Kick it down. Yell! Call for help. Please.*

'Zoe?' Silence. 'Ah, all right. You sleep well. I'll see you tomorrow.'

No, please, no. Come back!

Celia and Malcolm remain still and quiet until Dad's footsteps have receded. They're hunched together on the bed with Malcolm's rucksack between them, like a couple of huge spiders crouched over their prey.

After a while, Celia takes a breath. She looks at me and purses her lips. 'You've probably realised by now that what I gave you wasn't simply a sedative.'

I try to glare at her, but I can't even do that. My eyes remain open, but I can't move them at all – not to close them, or even blink. They're dry and uncomfortable, unlike my mouth, which is now filling with saliva that's dribbling down my chin.

'It's a shame it's come to this, Zoe, but if you really are starting to get your memory back, then you haven't left us with much of a choice.' Celia tilts her head as though commiserating with me.

Malcolm is removing a pack of blue silicone gloves from his bag, similar to the pair that Celia is wearing. He opens the plastic packaging and pulls them on one finger at a time. The sight of them makes me want to cry with fear.

'I've enjoyed having you as a daughter-in-law,' she continues, 'and you've given us two beautiful grandchildren. So for that, we're grateful. But right now, I have to consider the safety and wellbeing of my sons.'

Celia gets to her feet.

'I gave you some sleeping tablets earlier to keep you in your room, which is why you've been feeling so woozy. And I think they might have brought on a bit of a panic attack. I've also injected you with a neuromuscular blocking agent,' she explains impassively. 'Right now, it's in the process of paralysing your limbs and vocal cords. Unfortunately I'm not an anaesthetist so I may not have got the dosage exactly right. Naturally, I did my research, but it's not the same as having done it on a live patient. Ordinarily, you'd have been intubated with oxygen to help you breathe, in case you have a reaction to it, but obviously that's impossible here, so I've just had to make do and hope for the best. Sorry about that.' She pauses. 'Just be aware, there's a chance you may stop breathing.'

If I could sob or beg for mercy, I'd be doing it right now. I'd be pleading and crying. Appealing to her conscience, even though I now realise she hasn't got one.

While Celia's talking, Malcolm extracts a blue nylon rope from his bag. I wonder if they're going to use it to tie me to the chair. Although I don't know why they would need to do that after Celia has already incapacitated me.

'In any case,' Celia continues, 'I hope you don't stop breathing before we've finished here, because it would rather spoil our plans. We've come up with a good solution to the problem of what to do with you.' She pauses. 'We're going to have you commit suicide… because you couldn't live with the guilt of having killed your sister.'

It takes me a moment to process her words. *Suicide.* I guessed they were planning something horrific, but to hear her spell it out so baldly turns my skin to ice. All the while, as she's telling me these terrifying plans, the memories of what happened ten years ago keep hitting me like pieces of jagged shrapnel. Tearing chunks out of my heart.

Celia stands and takes the rope from Malcolm while he manoeuvres a dining chair into position next to me. She holds the rope in two hands, running her thumb back and forth along its surface, stroking it as she continues talking.

'We're using a blocking agent because if I'd simply tied you up, you'd have got rope burns and the authorities might have suspected foul play. But this way, unless they do a specific test during the post-mortem – which is highly unlikely – they'll simply believe that it was a tragic suicide. The downside, of course, is that it probably doesn't feel very pleasant for you, sitting there paralysed while all this is going on. But it won't be for too much longer.'

Malcolm steps up onto the chair with a grunt, and I notice that he's wearing clear plastic bags over his shoes. Celia hands him the rope and it's then that I see it has a loop at one end – *a noose.*

The sight of it makes me feel faint, and I will myself to pass out so that I don't have to live through the horror of them doing this to me. But although I'm light-headed, I remain stubbornly conscious. And it's terrifying.

How has my world managed to change so much in the course of a day? Yesterday, I thought my sister was back in Shaftesbury, I was celebrating ten years of marriage to the man I loved, and I believed my in-laws were the wonderful family I had always longed for. Today,

I'm processing the fact that my sister was murdered by my husband and has been dead for a decade, and the people I love the most are the ones who betrayed me, lied to me and are now about to kill me.

I'm unable to look up, so all I can see are Malcolm's legs as he balances on the dining chair. I'm guessing he's fixing the rope to one of the heavy wooden beams that run across the ceiling.

'We'd better hope Guy doesn't come back to check on her,' he mutters.

'You heard him before,' Celia replies. 'He said he'd see her tomorrow. Anyway, the man is so emotionally retarded he's probably gone back to the bar to get drunk.'

'But what if he *does* come back?' Malcolm presses.

'Then we'd better hurry up and get this done,' Celia snaps. 'We have to do this quickly anyway; the blocker only works for around six minutes and I really don't want to have to give her another dose.' She turns back to me. 'Toby and the others think Malcolm and I have gone to our room for the evening. While I came here to keep an eye on you, Malcolm waited in for room service and rented a movie on demand, so everyone will think we're spending the evening in our room. Which is where we'll be heading right after we've finished up here.'

'There we go.' Malcolm sounds pleased with himself. 'I think that's the right height.'

Celia looks up. 'I think you need to make it a bit longer. Zoe's shorter than you. Otherwise it's going to be tricky to get her up there.' She scratches the side of her mouth with a gloved forefinger.

'Hm, I think you're right,' he replies. 'Maybe another couple of inches.'

Although my body is paralysed and my vocal cords are silent, inside I'm screaming. How can they discuss this so calmly, as though they're talking about some innocuous DIY project? Neither of them seems remotely distressed by the fact they're about to commit a murder. *My* murder.

Celia bends down a little to look me in the eye. She wipes some of the drool from my chin with the finger of her glove. 'There was no need for Toby and Nick to know what we're doing here. I'm not certain they'd approve. Toby does still love you and he'll be quite upset that you decided to end things. But I'm sure you must realise that, as a parent, you'll do anything to protect your children.'

'Okay,' Malcolm says. 'I think that should do it.'

Celia gazes up at the ceiling critically. 'Yes. Good.' Malcolm huffs his way down off the chair as his wife resumes talking to me. I don't know why she's bothering. She's about to kill me, so why take the time to explain all this? Maybe she finds it cathartic. Or maybe she's proud of her plan and wants to show it off. Or perhaps she's simply a sadistic bitch who wants to terrify me.

Regardless of her reasons, Celia's monologue continues, ignorant of my silent, raging curses. 'It was such a shame that Nick couldn't handle the pressure – he's always been less robust than his brother. The whole thing was making him physically ill. Nick was about to tell you the truth, so Toby had to do some quick thinking. But unfortunately Toby was silly enough to bring up the past, telling you an altered version of events – yes, Toby came and told me everything that happened last night. Poor boy was in quite a state. He could have told you any number of lies, but instead he had to mention Dina showing up. That's probably what triggered your memories.' She puts her hands on her hips and shakes her head. 'Never mind. What's done is done. Such a pity that my lovely Toby is going to become a widower. He'll be quite devastated.' She pauses. 'Don't worry, I'll make sure he's okay and that my grandchildren are well looked after, of course. In time, I'll help him find a new mother for our angels.'

Icy anger is gradually replacing the wrenching terror in my gut. I'm hit by a raw animal need to attack this woman who's decided to end my life to save her son's skin. To ruin my children's lives by taking away their mother. I don't want Alice and Jamie to go through what I did. To experience that pain of losing a parent so young. If only I could move or speak right now. If only I could claw the smug smile from Celia's face.

A phone starts to ring, shrill and loud. It doesn't sound like a mobile. I think it must be the hotel phone. Both Malcolm and Celia freeze where they stand. After a moment, Celia's shoulders relax. 'Don't worry, Malcolm. They'll soon ring off if we don't answer.'

I pray she's wrong. But I count only nine rings before a hollow silence descends on the room once more. She turns back to me to continue her explanation. Part of me doesn't want to hear it. Each sentence she utters is painful to hear. Yet, as she speaks, I find myself greedily taking in all the details of this newly revealed past that's been hidden from me for so many years, even though each word wounds me.

'I think Toby already told you your troublesome sister is buried by the woods at the back of the hotel. She's in the same piece of land that's being developed, which is unfortunate. We found out yesterday that we lost our appeal, and so of course we can't take the chance that Dina's remains could be exposed and an investigation opened up. So this way we can pin the murder on you. It actually works out perfectly.'

Malcolm takes an envelope out of his rucksack and brings it over to where I'm slumped in the armchair. 'Fingerprints,' he grunts without looking me in the eye. He takes my hand and presses my fingers down on the envelope in several places before trudging back and placing it on the end of the bed.

'That's your suicide note,' Celia explains. 'It's all typed out, very simple and to the point, saying how you can't live with the guilt any longer and that you never meant to kill your sister, it was an accident etcetera. I've had this plan in place since the redevelopment was announced, but I hoped we'd never have to carry it out. Unfortunately, with the building going ahead and your memories returning, here we are.' She holds her hands out apologetically.

'I got you to sign a blank piece of paper a while ago when I asked for your signature for the petition. Thankfully you were busy at work and you weren't paying much attention. I used that sheet of paper for your suicide note. It's already got your fingerprints on it, and I was wearing gloves that day.'

A wave of nausea sweeps over my whole body and my stomach begins to cramp.

'Oh dear,' Celia says, squinting down at me. 'Your facial muscles are really twitching now. I imagine you must feel quite wretched. There are a few side effects to that blocker. Don't worry, we're almost done here. Not too much longer until it's all over.'

The fury I felt moments ago is quickly replaced by the darkest fear I've ever experienced. My mind rebels and judders in terror as Celia and Malcolm position themselves on dining chairs either side of me and together begin to manhandle me up onto the chair… towards the rope.

CHAPTER THIRTY-THREE

THE DAY OF THE WEDDING

I feel like I'm falling into an infinite black space. Down, down, down into the darkness. Until… *BAM!* I open my eyes and find myself staring into my fiancé's worried face.

'Toby,' I croak.

He crouches and takes my hand and I realise he's trembling. 'Are… are you okay? You really gave us a scare.' His face is chalk white, his neck red and mottled. 'We were so worried.'

'Where…?' I try to sit up, but my brain feels as though it's floating loose in my skull, so I give up and sink back down. It's then that I realise I'm lying on the floor, my head on a cushion. 'What happened?'

'Don't you remember?' he asks.

I try to think, but my mind is fuzzy. 'What's going on? Why do I feel weird?'

'You fainted, love.' Toby's mum Celia kneels by my side, one hand on my forehead, the other on my wrist. She looks different somehow. Maybe it's her hair – she's had it cut or styled or something. It looks straighter than usual, and browner. She must have had the grey coloured. 'Looks like you came down a real cropper.'

I now see that as well as Celia, Toby's dad Malcolm and his elder brother Nick are also here in the room, staring down at me, deep worry etched across their brows. I notice they're both wearing grey suits, which seems strange. And Toby's suit seems to have wet patches down the lapels.

'You feel a little clammy, but your pulse is steady.' Celia is a nurse, so if she says I'm okay, I guess I must be okay.

'I can't remember what happened.'

Celia looks up at her eldest son. 'Nick, can you get Zoe a glass of water?'

'Uh, sure.'

I notice Toby's right leg is quivering, and his hands are trembling. He's not the sort to get anxious, so his concern for me makes me love him even more. 'Toby, you're shaking!'

'I was so worried.' He swallows and leans in to kiss my forehead. 'If anything happened to you I don't know what I'd do.'

'I'm fine, silly. Just a bit dizzy, that's all. Tell him I'm okay, Celia.'

Toby glances at his mother and she gives him a comforting smile. 'Relax, Toby. Zoe's going to be just fine.' Celia sits back on her haunches. 'Well, this is an unusual wedding day.' She raises an eyebrow and squeezes my hand.

'Wedding day?' Only now do I notice I'm wearing my ivory lace dress. That's why everyone looks so smart. 'Oh no! It's today! Did I wreck it? Is it too late?' This time I manage to sit up despite my woozy head. 'I can't believe I—'

'It's okay,' Toby interrupts. 'We've still got time. The ceremony isn't due to start for another forty minutes.'

'What happened? You said I fainted, but I don't remember that at all. It's all so hazy… I was getting ready and then…'

'Like Mum said, you hit the deck.' Toby shakes his head.

I have a vague memory of rushing out of the room with someone. But I can't quite put my finger on it.

'Are you sure you can't remember anything about it?' Toby glances at his mum before turning back to me. 'That's quite worrying, Zo.'

I frown and try to recall what happened, but my brain hurts. 'Last thing I remember, I was getting ready. Celia, you were here with Lou and Becky, helping me get into my dress. That's it. That's the very last thing I remember.'

Nick returns and hands me a glass of water.

'Small sips,' Celia instructs. She tells me something about make-up and Nick borrowing a phone charger. 'Looks like you hit the back of your head on the desk on your way down. Do you feel nauseous at all?'

'A little. Not too much. I've got an evil headache though.'

My mother-in-law to be rummages in her handbag and pulls out a packet of paracetamol. 'Take a couple of these.'

I put the pills in my mouth one at a time, knocking each one back with a slug of water.

'Maybe we should get you checked out?' Malcolm runs a hand through his sparse grey hair. He turns to Toby. 'She looks decidedly peaky, son.'

'I know, but Mum said she'll be okay,' Toby replies, and I back him up.

'Well, okay. But perhaps I should let Guy know. You might be unsteady on your feet as he walks you down the aisle.' Malcolm turns to leave.

Toby stands and puts a hand on his father's shoulder. 'Wait…'

'Toby's right. Don't tell my dad. He'll only worry.' I stagger to my feet and find to my dismay that I have to lean on a chair to steady myself. My legs are so shaky. What if I'm not strong enough to stand and say my vows? I think of all the people in the little chapel next to the hotel who've come to see us get married. All the weeks of planning. My utter joy and excitement at the thought of becoming Mrs Zoe Johnson. I can't not get married, no matter how shaky I feel. I let go of the chair and square my shoulders. 'Do you know what? Celia's right, I'm absolutely fine.

Honestly, I already feel so much better. I think it must have been nerves that made me faint. Or maybe hunger. Thinking about it, I did skip breakfast.'

'Well, that'll be it,' Celia declares. She straightens the phone and picks up the receiver before ordering some cake for me and my two bridesmaids, but I ask her to stay too.

'I hope I haven't jinxed things.' I turn to Toby. 'It's supposed to be bad luck for us to see one another before the wedding.'

'You don't really believe that.' He smiles.

'No, but I wanted to do things the right way. I didn't want any drama. And I wanted to wait until I reached the chapel to see you. Now I've ruined it.'

'You haven't ruined anything.' He puts his arms around me, and I lean into him. 'I know you wanted everything to be just so. It's what I love about you, Zoe. You love family. You love tradition.'

'Even though I fainted and now have a giant egg-shaped lump on my head?' I give him a wry look. 'That's not exactly traditional.'

'Zoe, it's all going to be perfect. You're perfect.'

My heart lifts at his words and for a moment my head clears, and the pain disappears. 'I'm not perfect,' I murmur. 'No one is.'

'Okay, well you're perfect for me.'

I inhale deeply and attempt to push out all thoughts of the past. I have this strange feeling that I've forgotten something important. It's right there on the edge of my consciousness, but, try as I might, I can't quite grasp it. I give myself a little shake and tell myself to focus on the day ahead. To ignore the tiny bead of worry in my chest. Today is a day for fairy tales and happy ever afters. All that matters is that I'm about to become the person I've always wanted to be, with the man I love. Nothing will change that.

CHAPTER THIRTY-FOUR

NOW

So this is it. This is the end of my life.

I feel like I might be crying, although I can't be too sure. I trawl my mind to come up with anything good that might distract me from the horror of what's going on. I don't want the last thought I have to be about Celia and Malcolm's cold, efficient hands on my body, hoisting me up onto the chair as though I'm some inanimate thing with no thoughts or feelings or emotions. Just an inconvenience who might serve a purpose for them in death.

The noose slips over my head, brushing my eyelashes and nose on its descent towards my shoulders. I feel its weight as it lands, like a soft tickle on my neck. Maybe the paralysing drug that Celia injected me with is a blessing – it's stopping me from squirming and struggling, from begging and pleading. From losing my dignity.

Once again, I try to direct my thoughts to something distracting, something nice. But it's hard to ignore the tightening noose, and the nod that passes from Celia to Malcolm – their agreement that all is finally ready. I clutch at a handful of memories, each one shuttling through my mind too fast – a tranquil lake in summertime, the view from my mum's bench over the Blackmore Vale, my children's laughter, my dad's gruff voice, his Welsh lilt like a comforting lullaby…

And then I realise with a jolt that I really *am* hearing my dad's voice! I blink. And then I blink again. The drug must finally be wearing off. Celia said it would only last a few minutes.

Unless I'm hallucinating, I can hear my father issuing someone with instructions. 'Call the police!' he cries. 'And get an ambulance here too!'

To my frustration, I can't move anything else, just my eyelids. Celia and Malcolm are still holding me in place on the chair but are now staring in horror at the opening door. The overhead lights come on, bathing the room in brightness. The noose is taut around my neck. The cramps in my stomach are unbearable and my breathing is so shallow, I'm afraid my lungs are going to give out at any second.

A man stands in the doorway – he's wearing the hotel uniform and his face is a mask of shock.

'The police, man!' Dad yells at him. 'Call the police! Don't just stand there!'

'Yes, yes, of course!' The man blinks and disappears.

Dad rushes over and all I can see is the top of his head as he yanks Malcolm off the dining chair, then holds him upright by his shirt and punches him square in the face. Malcolm doubles over, clutching his nose, blood spilling down onto his trousers. I would cheer if I could.

Next, Dad clambers up onto the armchair with me and loosens the rope around my neck. He then wraps one arm around me, supporting my body, and throws off the noose with the other. I crumple against him.

Celia appears to be frozen by my side, her hands still seeming to hold me up, although Dad is bearing my full weight now. She finally gathers her senses and lets go of me, gingerly stepping down off the dining chair and crouching down next to her husband.

'Zoe! Zoe, love!' Dad stares into my eyes and I'm desperate to explain what's going on. But all I can do is gaze at him helplessly.

'Talk to me! Are you okay?' I blink at him. He shifts position slightly, scoops me up into his arms and carefully steps down off the armchair onto the floor with me.

Celia has begun gathering her paraphernalia from the bed and stuffing it into the rucksack. 'We found her like that, up on the chair,' she lies. 'Why on earth did you hit Malcolm? We were trying to help her, you silly man!'

'Fine,' Dad replies. 'You can tell that to the police when they get here. I'm sure they'll be interested in why you're both wearing gloves, and why Malcolm has plastic bags tied over his shoes.' Even in my incapacitated state, I'm marvelling at how calm yet scathing my dad is managing to be.

'The police?' Celia scoffs. 'That's not necessary.'

'Necessary or not,' Dad replies, 'they're calling them now.'

Celia bends to help up her husband.

'I think he broke my nose,' Malcolm mutters as he staggers to his feet.

Celia whips something up off the floor, clumsily trying to shove it into Malcolm's bag.

Dad grunts and lays me down on the bed, propping my back up against the headboard. He turns to Celia. 'What's wrong with Zoe? Why's she drooling and twitching like that? Why isn't she talking?'

'Probably shock. Looks like she was trying to kill herself. There's a note on the bed.'

'What's that you're putting in your bag?' Dad rips the rucksack from her and pulls it open, peering inside. 'A syringe? And what's in this box?' He reads from it, stumbling over the pronunciation: 'Suxamethonium… What's that?' He pauses and then reads more from the label. 'A depolarising neuromuscular blocker.' He takes hold of Celia's arm. 'Did you inject this shit into my daughter?'

'What? No, of course not. I told you, we came in and found her up on the chair like that.'

'Oh yeah, and how did you get into her room? Got a key, have you?'

Celia edges towards the door. 'Malcolm and I had better fetch Toby from the spa. He's her husband; he needs to know what's happening here.'

'Oh no you don't.' Dad strides over and blocks their exit. 'You two are staying right where I can see you until the police arrive.'

Celia's mouth drops open and then snaps shut like a trap.

My head swims and my eyes close. Their voices fade and everything goes quiet and dark.

CHAPTER THIRTY-FIVE

NINE MONTHS LATER

Dad and Madeline sit at my new kitchen table unwrapping crockery from a cardboard box, setting each piece down while I work out which cupboards to put them in. I'm renting a little three-bedroom converted ground-floor flat just round the corner from Dad until I find a place to buy. There's no hurry though; the flat is on a six-month rolling lease, so maybe we'll stay here indefinitely. It's a tiny little place with poky rooms and a square patch of garden, but it's characterful, with an open fire in the lounge and a fruit-bearing apple tree in the garden. I think Dad's nose was put out of joint when I told him we were moving, though.

'I don't know why you're throwing your money away on rent when I'm rattling around in my place,' Dad says, reading my mind; we've been very much on the same wavelength recently. 'You should all just move in with me permanently. Tell her, Madeline.'

'Don't drag me into it,' Madeline replies, unwrapping my blue china teapot.

Dad smooths out a sheet of newspaper and places it into an empty box on the floor. 'We can get the kids to make firelighters with this newspaper later,' he adds.

Madeline's and my children are currently out in our shoebox garden playing Jenga, but I'm not sure how long that will keep them occupied.

'We'd drive you mad if we lived with you full-time, Dad.' More like we'd drive each other mad, but I think he knows that.

'Hmph,' he replies.

Our cottage at the bottom of Gold Hill sold the very same day it went on the market. After all my years of resistance to selling up, it turned out I couldn't wait to be shot of the place. A young couple bought it fully furnished. They're expecting their first baby next month and were thrilled to have found the house of their dreams for a bargain price. I didn't stay for the viewing and I never met the couple – I couldn't face seeing their hopeful optimism. It would have reminded me too much of how excited Toby and I were back when we first bought the place. I try to turn my mind away from all that.

'Are you really moving away, Madeline?' I stack some dinner plates in a high cupboard. They were a wedding gift from Celia's sister, and I resist the urge to put them back in the box and take them to the charity shop. I can't afford to give away all the items I own, just because of the memories they evoke.

'I can't stay in Shaftesbury anymore,' Madeline replies. 'I tried, but it's too difficult. I need a fresh start. So do the kids.'

'I think you're really brave, starting over. But we're going to miss you so much.' I turn to her, but she's focused on unwrapping the next item.

'It's only Salisbury – not too far at all. We'll still see each other.'

My heart lurches once more at the thought of her leaving. She and Dad have been my rocks over the past nine months.

My children don't know all the details about what happened. But I couldn't shield them from everything – especially not Alice. Ten-year-old girls are pretty sharp when it comes to working out the truth. She knows her dad is in prison for killing her aunt. And she knows that her uncle Nick and her grandparents are also in prison for helping him cover it up (I've managed to keep from them that their grandparents were also sentenced for my attempted murder as well, but I'm sure they'll find out in the end). I've also tried not to bad-mouth their father within their earshot. But I can't change the facts of what he did. I just have to hope that it doesn't scar them too much. It's too late for me – I have scars on top of scars.

Perhaps Madeline has the right idea, moving away to get a fresh start. Goodness knows I've thought about it. But this is my home. It's where I was born and raised. It's where I work at the job I love. Where my friends live. I don't want to leave my support network behind because of Toby. It would feel as if he drove me away. Besides, how can I leave my dad? Especially after what he did for me. I look across at him and he catches my eye and winks.

Dad was my hero that day. He saved my life. Before he came into the room, he had no idea that Celia and Malcolm were in there with me. He was worried because he'd tried phoning, texting and knocking on the door throughout the day but hadn't had a response. He had the sense that I might have fallen ill and be in need of help. He'd tried looking for Toby or one of the others to get an update but hadn't been able to find anyone.

In the end, he spoke to the assistant manager and asked him to unlock my room. He said it was an emergency. The assistant manager tried calling my room first, but when there was no reply he did as Dad insisted and opened my door. Dad took in the situation and ordered the assistant manager to call the police, fetch a doctor and summon more staff to help out. My father was calm, cool and efficient. If he'd arrived a minute later, I would probably already have been dead.

I was hospitalised, but thankfully the blocker was already wearing off. I could move and speak once again, despite my whole body aching and cramping from its after-effects. Celia and Malcolm were taken into custody at the scene, thanks to Dad ensuring they didn't do a runner. But it wasn't until my testimony some hours later that the police also came for Toby and Nick.

The weeks and months following were a hellish blur of visits from police officers, lawyers, social services and journalists. The worst part was trying to protect my children from the fallout. The second worst part was the one and only conversation I had with Toby afterwards.

I went to visit him after he was sentenced. He looked about as bad as I was expecting him to look – pale and gaunt with bloodshot eyes – but I didn't remark on his appearance. I didn't even greet him. Just sat down and waited to hear what he had to say. I wouldn't have gone at all, only I'd been told that it might help me with the healing process. It didn't.

I had to sit there and listen to him tell me that his fling with Dina meant nothing. That it was simply a last-minute act of madness before the wedding day. He insisted that Dina's death was an accident. Self-defence when she attacked him. He seemed to forget that I was there. That my memories of that day had returned intact. And his actions had definitely not been self-defence.

He said that the only reason he had covered it all up was because his mum had told him to. Apparently it was Celia's idea to sweep it all under the carpet. Toby had wanted to come clean, but she had forbidden it. He said he was scared of her. That while she was his mum and of course he loved her, she wasn't a person to argue with. He, Nick and his father all knew that you didn't cross Celia unless you wanted a whole load of grief. How did I not know that about her?

I told Toby he was a grown man and should have made his own decisions. He should have stood by his wife. Should never have cheated on me in the first place. If he'd kept it in his pants then none of this would have happened.

Toby didn't reply to that. Instead, he said he loved me. That he'd spent the past ten years of our marriage trying to make it up to me. That a day hadn't gone by when he wished he hadn't done what he had. But I didn't believe a word. After all, when he thought that Nick was about to spill the beans to me, he had lied again, this time telling me that *I* had killed my sister. No. The only comfort that prison visit gave me was that I was lucky to be rid of him.

But it didn't stop me mourning the loss of the husband I'd thought he was.

Back then, I didn't have time to process what had happened to me. To mourn my sister. To grieve the death of my sham marriage. To accept that Toby had cheated on me with my own sister. To realise that a woman I thought of as a second mother had tried to kill me. It was all too much, so I buried it. Instead, I attempted to get on with regular things such as work and raising a family while dealing with the aftermath. At least I had Madeline and my father as support.

Madeline found herself in a similar position to me. Although she didn't have a cheating husband and a dead sister, she did have a husband who had helped to cover up a murder and was facing a long prison sentence. It was more than enough to destroy their marriage and leave her on her own with two children. Consequently, we sought one another out.

Strangely – after our initial distress and anger – whenever we got together socially we avoided talking about our husbands and their parents. Instead, we concentrated on practicalities, such as divorce, house sales and children. Right now, Madeline feels like more of a sister to me than my own ever was.

We held a small private funeral for Dina with just Dad and I in attendance. It was a sad and depressing affair. I didn't cry, but I noticed Dad wiping away a few tears. Neither of us comforted the other. In fact, we barely spoke. There wasn't anything to say that didn't involve a world of painful memories. And neither of us were ready to confront those. Dina had betrayed me, but she had paid the ultimate price. I didn't want to spend the funeral thinking about our corrosive relationship, so instead I tried to focus on the times before Mum died. Back when we were proper sisters who played together and laughed and shared silly secrets. Before it all crumbled away.

And yet… despite Dina's and my broken relationship, I can't help thinking about those two instances in town where I saw my sister days before the party. First wearing that beautiful red coat, walking along the road with a man. And second when she locked eyes with me through the salon window. Both times, I had been so certain it was her. Even now, months later, I can recall each incident clear as day. I know it's silly, but I almost believe it *was* her. Warning me somehow that nothing was as it seemed. That she had been the victim of foul play. A last attempt to somehow make amends, or at least connect with me in a meaningful way. I shiver and force my thoughts back to the present.

Madeline places the final empty packing box on the floor. 'All done,' she says, getting to her feet.

I put down the stack of bowls I'm holding. 'You don't have to leave right away, do you? Stay for tea, if you like.'

She yawns. 'I better go. I've got food to prep for a client's dinner party tomorrow.'

'Okay. Thanks for today.'

'That's all right. You can return the favour when I move into my new place.' She grins.

'We'll be there,' Dad says. 'As long as you unpack the kettle first.'

'Of course. And I'll even throw in some homemade cookies.' She hugs us both and we spend the next ten minutes prying her daughters away from their cousins.

Once she's gone, a wave of tiredness washes over me. The children disappear off to their rooms to amuse themselves, and I start preparing an omelette for our tea. Dad's still sitting at the kitchen table. Now that the boxes are unpacked, he's already made a start on the firelighters, rolling each sheet into a tube, flattening it, then bending it diagonally in the centre, folding one side and then the other until he's made a little concertina-like creation. I remember him showing us how to make them when we were kids. While Mum was still alive.

'You okay, love?' It's a question he now asks me at least twenty times a day.

'Yeah, I'm fine. Feels good to have got that lot unpacked and put away.'

'I'll make you up a box of these lighters, and then you can get the kids to add to it. It's going to be a cold winter and you'll be glad of these to get the fire going quickly on a chilly evening. I'll order you some logs from the fella I use.'

'Great. Thanks.'

After I was discharged from hospital, Dad took the kids and I back to his place. I have to hand it to him, he was incredible. All those parenting skills he'd been lacking after Mum died came out in full force as he cared for his grandchildren. While I attempted not to fall to pieces, he cooked for them, played with them, chatted with them and comforted them, all in his own understated way. I tried not to feel bitter that he'd never done any of this for me and Dina while we were growing up. He was doing it now, and that's what mattered.

After several months of living with him, I could tell that Dad was finding the noise and disruption wearing. Although he never complained, bless him.

I take the pan off the heat and slide it under the grill to melt the cheese on top of the omelette.

'I am sorry, you know,' Dad says, dropping another firelighter into the box.

'Sorry?' I ask. 'For what?' I turn the grill down and sit opposite him.

He sighs and scratches the stubble on his chin. 'I wasn't a very good dad to you and Dee, was I?'

It's true. He wasn't the greatest father. But I'm surprised to discover that I don't feel resentful any more.

'I don't want to make excuses,' he continues. 'But after I lost your mum…' He frowns and stares down at his hands, picks at his fingernails.

'It's okay, Dad, you don't have to explain.'

'But… I do. I want to.'

'You were grieving for Mum, I get it.'

He nods. His eyes bright with unshed tears. 'Even so… I shouldn't have neglected you both. Maybe if I'd spent more time with Dina instead of leaving you to do it all… you were only a kid yourself. She was such a little 'un when your mum died. And now, now it's all too late…'

'Dad, stop. You did the best you could at the time. Look at me, after all this stuff with Dina and Toby. I was a mess – still am – but at least I had your help. After Mum died, you didn't have anyone to help with me and Dina. You were on your own. I think you did a pretty good job, considering.'

Dad takes in everything I'm saying, then he clears his throat. 'Thanks, love. You're a good girl, you are.' He pats my hand and gets to his feet. 'Okay, well, that omelette smells like it's almost done. Want me to call the kids down?'

'Yes please.'

As he walks towards the door, I feel a settling of something inside me. Despite the chaos and uncertainty of everything else, I realise a large piece of my life has been resolved.

My father hesitates at the door, squaring his shoulders. 'I love you, Zo,' he says, without turning around.

'Love you too, Dad.'

EPILOGUE

I close my eyes and try to get comfortable beneath the thin sheet and blanket, turning this way and that before finally giving up like I always do. Instead, I lie on my back with my eyes open, staring into the semi-darkness, accepting that sleep isn't coming any closer. That it never arrives until it's almost time to wake up again. In this place, the nights are endless and the days roll into one another. Time works differently here.

I thought time would help to calm my anger. But it hasn't abated at all. If anything, it's grown stronger. Each cell in my body, quivering with outrage and fury at what's happened. At the travesty of justice that's occurred. I'm a mother. My job is to protect my children. To keep them safe from danger. From predators.

That girl. That bloody girl. She and her family were never good enough for my Toby. I should have trusted my instincts and steered my youngest boy away from her and her deadbeat trollop of a sister. Instead, I trusted him to make his own decisions. So stupid of me. Toby wasn't prepared for Zoe Williams and her conniving ways. I'm sure she got pregnant on purpose. Trapped him into marrying her. The dates prove she was pregnant on their wedding day. All right, so I realise she wasn't that far gone, but however she did it, she cast a spell on my beautiful boy and now our whole family is paying the price. I should have made sure she never woke up on her wedding day. That's the biggest regret of my life.

At least Malcolm and Toby are serving their time together. Toby was given fourteen years and Malcolm was given twelve. Toby will look out for his father. But Nick… the poor boy is on his own in a different prison. He does have a shorter sentence though – only two years for his part in covering up Dina's death – so I pray he'll be able to bear it. But he's not strong like Toby. He gets anxious. They'll eat him alive in there. I can't think about it. I gave him a pep talk beforehand. Told him to be strong. To act tough even if he doesn't feel like it. My worst fear is that someone will hurt him. Or that he'll grow ill with nerves. But maybe he'll surprise me, and this will be the making of him.

I'm still not used to the night-time noises here – the snoring, moaning and coughing – so much coughing. No wonder I can't sleep. But I'm not intimidated by these women. They're all just doing what they need to do to get through it. Like me. And at least I have something to focus on.

I was given the longest sentence of all – sixteen years! Just because of the medications and the fact that my actions were premeditated. But, despite what my solicitor says, I'm hoping that with good behaviour my sentence might be reduced. I intend to be the model inmate. I will do everything it takes to show that I'm remorseful. That I've changed. That I understand what I did was wrong. I've told the boys to do the same. I'm attending counselling sessions, and meeting with the prison chaplain as often as I'm able. Showing everyone that I'm a reformed woman, so that I might get out of here early.

And then I will make that little bitch pay.

Zoe and her father had better enjoy what little time they have left. She may think she's got one over on me, but she has no idea what I'm capable of. And this time I'll be more prepared. Once it's over and we've finally served our time, I'll gather my family back up and we'll be stronger than ever. Nick can win Madeline and the girls back and Toby will have his darling Alice and Jamie in his life once more. And then we can put this whole unfortunate episode behind us.

I let out a contented yawn, my eyes finally growing heavy. My mind soothed by the plans I'm making. Perhaps I will finally have a good night's sleep after all.

A LETTER FROM SHALINI

Dear Reader,

Thank you for reading *The Wife*. I hope you enjoyed it.

If you'd like to keep up to date with my latest releases, just sign up here and I'll let you know when my next novel comes out. Your email address will never be shared and you can unsubscribe at any time.

www.bookouture.com/shalini-boland

I'm always thrilled to get feedback about my books, so if you loved it, I'd be hugely grateful if you'd post a review online or tell your friends. Your opinion makes a huge difference helping people to discover my books for the first time.

I enjoy chatting online about my novels and other books, so please do feel free to get in touch via my Facebook page, Twitter, Instagram, Goodreads or my blog.

Thanks again,
Shalini Boland x

ShaliniBolandAuthor

@ShaliniBoland

shaliniboland

shaliniboland.co.uk

ACKNOWLEDGEMENTS

As always, thank you to the incredible team at Bookouture. I'm especially grateful to my amazing editors Ruth Tross and Natasha Harding for their patience, insight, and encouragement, and for always knowing just how to bring out the best in my work.

Thank you to the Three Musketeers – Kim Nash, Noelle Holten and Sarah Hardy for your tireless promotion and support.

Massive thanks to Pete Boland for giving honest feedback, suggestions and cups of tea along the way.

Once again, I'm very grateful to Samantha Smith, an officer with the Thames Valley Police. Thank you for letting me pick your brains. Any errors in police procedure are purely my own.

Thank you to my lovely beta readers Julie Carey and Terry Harden, whose feedback and typo-spotting is invaluable. Thank you to Fraser Crichton for your superb copyedits. And to Lauren Finger for being a proofreading ninja.

Thanks to everyone in the Bookouture Authors' Lounge – a safe space where we can rant and support and have a laugh. I'd also like to mention the support of several author and reader groups I belong to: The Book Club, Book Connectors, The Fiction Café Book Club and UK Crime Book Club, who always support authors and help spread the word. Their members are wonderful people who I feel privileged to have met. Thank you, guys!

Thanks to my wonderful kids Dan and Billie. You make me so proud it hurts.

And to all my readers and reviewers, to all the bloggers and tweeters, recommenders and online sharers, love and thanks always.

Lightning Source UK Ltd.
Milton Keynes UK
UKHW012208041220
374627UK00003B/216